Colters' Lady

Look for these titles by
Maya Banks

Now Available

Free Download:

Colters' Lady

A sequel to Colters' Woman

Maya Banks

SAMHAIN
PUBLISHING

Samhain Publishing, Ltd.
577 Mulberry Street, Suite 1520
Macon, GA 31201
www.samhainpublishing.com

Colters' Lady
Copyright © 2011 by Maya Banks
Print ISBN: 978-1-60928-088-8
Digital ISBN: 978-1-60928-024-6

Editing by Jennifer Miller

First Samhain Publishing, Ltd. electronic publication: June 2010
First Samhain Publishing, Ltd. print publication: May 2011

Dedication

This book is dedicated with all my love to Jennifer, my editor and friend. You're going to kick cancer on its ass, and then we're going to have one hell of a drink to celebrate.

Chapter One

Seth Colter walked into the soup kitchen and was greeted by a chorus of hellos from several police officers from his precinct.

"Hey man, I didn't think you were going to make it," Craig Sumner called.

Seth cracked a smile, surprised at how glad he was to see the guys he'd worked with for the past few years. "I said I would be here."

"How are you feeling?" Rob Morgan asked as he slapped Seth on the back.

"Better," Seth acknowledged, and for the first time in weeks, he realized it was the truth. He *did* feel better. He'd been sleeping easier lately, and his dreams weren't so littered with the images of a faceless gunman and the exploding pain of a bullet tearing through his shoulder.

"Hey, that's great. You'll be back before you know it," Craig said.

Seth nodded. Yeah, he'd be back. He hated being away from the job. He hated being away from the camaraderie of his fellow cops. For the first while, he'd sequestered himself in his house, refusing visitors. He hadn't wanted their pity. He'd resented the hell out of the fact that they were still on the job and he was stuck in his house popping pain pills and hoping he regained the use of his arm.

"What do you want me to do?" Seth asked.

Craig threw him an apron. "Get behind the serving line. We open for lunch in fifteen minutes. And hurry. Margie runs a tight ship."

"I heard that."

Seth turned to see a small, gray-haired lady standing behind him, her green eyes bathed in warmth.

"Hello, Seth." She stepped forward and pulled him into a hug. "It's so good to see you again. Are you taking care of yourself?"

She patted him on the cheek for good measure, and he smiled as he returned her embrace.

"I'm good, Margie. How about yourself?"

"Oh, I'm the same as ever. Busy. Just how I like it. Now you better get to your station before I open the doors. Looks like we have a lot of folks lined up to eat today."

"Yes, ma'am," he said with a grin.

"See?" Craig said. "She's a complete slave driver."

Feeling lighter than he had in a while, Seth tied on the white chef's apron and walked behind the buffet to stand in front of the baked chicken.

"Smells good, Margie. Who did you harangue into catering for you this time?" Seth asked.

She grinned. "I called in a favor. Or two."

He laughed. Margie Walker was simply good people. She was a surrogate mother to many, but beneath the good-as-gold exterior lay a hard-driving woman who didn't think twice about leaning on people to help her causes. Her pet project was Margie's Place. Simply named, but it was appropriate. Every day, rain or shine, she opened her doors to the homeless, and she always had enough food to feed as many as filtered through her doors. No one was entirely sure how she managed it, but she always did.

His precinct routinely volunteered and they worked in shifts. Seth and five others came in once a month to serve, although for him it had been three months since he'd last been in.

"Okay guys, I'm opening up," Margie called as she walked over to the doors.

For the next two hours, a steady stream of people came through the line. Workers from the kitchen brought out more food as soon as the trays emptied, and the guys dished it up.

The flow had dwindled when Seth looked up to see the most startling pair of blue eyes he'd ever seen in his life. In the process of extending the pair of tongs with a piece of chicken, he stared in shock at the woman standing in front of him, small hands gripped tightly around the lunch tray.

There was something infinitely fragile about her and equally arresting. His gut tightened, and for a moment he forgot to breathe. Or maybe he was unable to.

Dressed in a shabby, worn sweater and a pair of jeans so faded they were nearly white, the woman stared back at him, wispy midnight curls escaping the knit cap she wore.

She was beautiful. And haunting. Her gaze looked wounded and faint smudges rimmed her eyes. A fierce surge of protectiveness welled up inside him, baffling him.

Her fingers tightened around the tray, and she started to move forward without the chicken he still held in the air like an idiot. He thrust it forward onto her plate.

Then she smiled, and it took what little breath he had left and squeezed it painfully from his lungs.

"Thank you," she said sweetly.

She moved down the line as a man moved into the spot where she'd stood and looked expectantly at Seth. Still staring after the woman, Seth slapped the next piece of chicken on the man's tray and wondered what the hell had just happened here.

He watched as she sat away from the others, finding a corner where there were only two chairs at a tiny table that looked out a window.

"Hey, snap out of it."

Seth turned to see Craig standing beside him, his apron in hand.

"Margie's ordering us to stand down and eat. Grab a plate and join us. She has one of the kitchen workers taking over the line in case we have any stragglers."

Feeling anything but hungry, Seth fixed a plate and followed his friends to a table on the far side of the room. There wasn't a lot of talking going on. Most of the people ate in silence, though there were a few conversations from some of the regulars who knew each other or hung out together on the streets.

He positioned himself so he could see the woman and tuned out the rest of the goings-on so he could watch her and take in every detail he could.

She ate daintily and never looked up or made eye contact with any of the others. When she wasn't looking down at her food she fixed her gaze out the window, watching the people pass on the busy street. There was something wistful about her stare, and again, that protective surge came roaring to the surface.

"Who is she?" he blurted out.

"Who is who?" Craig asked.

Rob looked up and followed Seth's gaze. "You mean her?"

"Yeah, I haven't seen her before but it's been a few months. When did she start coming in?"

Craig shrugged. "I haven't seen her before. She wasn't here last month. Maybe she's new. Margie would know. She keeps up with everyone."

Seth frowned, not liking the tired look on the woman's face. She was young, early twenties, far too young to be out on the streets. Spring in Denver was often harsh with copious amounts of snow. She was so slight, and all she had was that sweater and a cap. She'd freeze to death.

"What's bugging you, man?" Rob asked.

Seth shook his head. "Nothing."

Seth forced himself to eat but watched the woman as the other people finished their meals and began to filter out. She remained, even after she'd finished eating. She pushed her plate to the side, and he frowned at the fact there was still a good portion of her food left. She rested her chin on top of her fist as she continued to gaze out the window.

He cursed when one of the kitchen workers came over to collect her plate, because even though the worker didn't say anything to the woman, the action prompted her to rise. She looked guiltily around as if she thought she'd overstayed her welcome, and then she hurried toward the door without a backward glance.

Before he realized it, he was on his feet and hurrying after her. It wasn't something he could even explain. He had to go after her. He had to know where she was going, if she was safe.

Ignoring Rob's and Craig's startled exclamations, he strode out onto the street and looked left and right to see the direction she'd gone. Seeing her retreating figure to the right, he set off after her.

He kept his distance, not wanting to spook her. He felt like a damned stalker, and maybe that's what he was. There was no reasonable explanation for his pursuit of her. It certainly had nothing to do with his cop's instincts. He'd reacted to her as a man, and something about her called to a part of him that hadn't ever awoken before.

For six blocks he followed her. His hands were clenched at his sides. She had no sense of self-preservation. She never looked up, never looked back to make sure she wasn't followed. She blended seamlessly with the busy downtown crowd, and he quickened his step so he wouldn't lose her.

He slowed when she turned into an alleyway. His approach was cautious. The last thing he wanted was to walk into a damn trap. He turned the corner and peered down to see her hunker down between two cardboard boxes. She disappeared from view, and he stood there a moment, battling between anger and...he wasn't sure.

He hadn't wanted her to be homeless. He'd hoped that she was down on her luck and needed the free meal, but that she had a place to live, protection from the cold. Refuge from the streets that took lives every single day.

What about this woman fired such a response in him? In his job, he saw all manner of people. The hungry, the homeless, the abused. There were plenty of young women in need, but none had infused a soul-stirring desire to help and protect.

It was presumptuous of him. She might not need him. She might be just fine on her own, but something in her eyes told him that wasn't so. She needed someone, and he wanted to be that person.

Crazy talk. He wondered now if that bullet had hit him in the head. But that didn't stop him from walking with determined steps toward the boxes at the end of the alley.

When he was close enough to see over the edge of one of the boxes, he saw that she was sitting cross-legged on what looked to be old towels, and she was absorbed in a tattered paperback book. After every page, she moved one of her hands from the book and held it to her mouth while she blew to warm it, and then she returned to the book to turn another page.

His chest clenched, and he moved a step closer. His foot glanced off a discarded Styrofoam cup, and her head jerked up. Alarm flashed in her eyes when she saw him, and she scrambled to her feet like a doe poised for flight.

In a lightning-fast move, he snagged her wrist just when she would have bolted. He was careful not to hurt her, only prevent her from fleeing.

A small cry of fright escaped her lips, and her eyes widened as she stared up at him.

"I'm sorry. Don't be afraid. I won't hurt you, I swear it. Do you remember me from Margie's Place? I just served you an hour ago."

Though she didn't relax, she nodded, her eyes still solidly trained on his face as if judging the validity of his vow not to hurt her.

"If I let you go, will you promise not to run?"

She looked at him like he was crazy.

He held up his other hand in surrender. "Let me amend that. Do you promise not to run as long as I don't do anything to further scare you?"

For a moment she studied him, and then slowly she nodded again. He relaxed his grip, carefully easing his fingers away, studying her body language for any sign that she meant to flee. He couldn't blame her for not trusting him, but suddenly it was the most important thing in the world for her to do just that.

"What do you want?" she asked with quiet defiance.

The shock of her voice floated over him. It was pleasing. An electrical sensation that nipped at his neck and snaked through his body like a river current. He wanted her to talk again. To say his name.

"I..." What did he want? And how to say it? He laughed

softly and shook his head. "You're going to think I'm nuts."

She smiled then, and it made her so lovely that he ached.

"I might already think you're crazy. You stared at me so funny in the line. I worried I'd somehow made you angry."

"No. No, of course not," he rushed out. "Look, will you go somewhere with me?" At her look of surprise he hurried to amend his statement. "There's a diner down the street. It's warm and we can sit and talk there."

She gave him a confused look. "But I just ate. So did you."

He frowned because she hadn't eaten much at all. "Do you like coffee? Hot chocolate?"

"I love hot chocolate," she said wistfully.

He latched on to that like a dying man struggling for one more breath. "Then walk with me to the diner. We can have hot chocolate and you can talk to me. What do you say?"

Puzzlement still shone in her blue eyes. She nibbled at her bottom lip as she clearly couldn't decide whether to accept or decline.

"I'm a police officer," he said. He rummaged in his pocket for his badge. "You're completely safe with me."

She stared at the shield, and he could swear tears flashed for a single moment before she quickly gathered herself.

"What's your name?" he asked. "My name is Seth. Seth Colter."

"Lily," she said in a soft voice. "Just Lily."

Lily. It suited her. Delicate and beautiful.

"Well, Just Lily. Will you walk down and have a cup of hot chocolate with me?"

She took a deep breath. "Okay."

Relief coursed through his veins until he thought he was going to crawl out of his skin. He held his hand out to her, unsure of the gesture and how she'd take it. He only knew he had to touch her.

With a curious look in his direction, she slid her small fingers trustingly into his. He gripped her hand, infusing his warmth into her cold fingers, and then he tugged her back down the alley to the street.

Chapter Two

Lily walked beside Seth until they reached the diner at the corner of the next street. Even then he didn't let go of her hand. It felt strong and comforting around hers. Hard and lean like Seth himself.

She studied his profile as discreetly as she could without being caught staring. He had the look of a cop—or one she associated with police officers. His stare was alert and always moving to take in his surroundings.

He was tall and solidly built. Not overly muscled in a body-builder fashion, but he was physically fit, and he carried his strength in his features. Hard jaw, intense blue eyes, and yet there was also a quietness and gentleness to him that called to her. Maybe it was why she was inexplicably following him into a diner.

He escorted her to a booth by the window and briefly let go of her hand so he could slide in across the table from her. Immediately he reached over and retook possession of her hand.

A funny flutter began in her stomach as his thumb stroked over the curve of her hand and her knuckles. She was puzzled by this man and why he'd followed her from the soup kitchen. What did he want, and why did he insist on touching her at every turn?

A waitress came over, and Seth ordered two cups of hot chocolate. Excitement and longing curled in Lily's stomach at the idea of the rich, sweet brew. It was her favorite thing in the world, and it had been too long since she'd last been able to enjoy it.

When the waitress left, Lily glanced up at Seth and asked, "Why did you follow me?"

His lips twisted into a rueful grimace. "I don't even know how to answer that, Lily. Have you ever been so affected by someone but not known why? Have you ever been compelled to see them again without knowing anything about them?

After careful consideration she shook her head. Was he saying that was how he felt after seeing her in the line? That didn't even make sense. He was a police officer and she was nobody. Nameless and faceless. People rushed by her every single day without ever seeing her. Why would *Seth* see her?

"I can't stand the thought of you being out on the streets," he admitted. "I followed you because I hoped you had somewhere to go. Shelter. Anything but a place between cardboard boxes in a deserted alley."

Sorrow tightened her throat, and long-held grief and shame bubbled up. She looked down so he wouldn't see how affected she was by his pity.

He squeezed her hand. "I'm not judging you, Lily. I was worried. Big difference. I didn't want you to be out on the streets because I work the streets. I see what's out there each and every day. I don't want you there."

His tone surprised her. For someone who'd just met her, he displayed a bewildering amount of concern.

She offered a casual shrug, not at all indifferent to the warmth in his gaze or the sincerity in his eyes. "Not everyone has a choice."

But you did and you chose to walk away. The thought took hold and reminded her of the consequences of her decisions.

He didn't look happy with her answer, and in fact, it looked like he wanted argue, but the waitress returned with their hot chocolate.

She reached eagerly for the mug and blew gently over the surface, inhaling all the while as the rich scent of chocolate filled her nostrils. Closing her eyes, she sipped, savoring the first delicious taste as it hit her tongue.

Sighing, she lowered the mug and looked up to see Seth watching her intently.

"Will you come back to my house, Lily? I'll make you all the hot chocolate you want."

She was so startled by the blunt question, she nearly let the mug slip from her fingers. She set it down with a jarring thud, and some of the liquid sloshed over the rim and onto the table.

Before she could respond, he closed his eyes and blew out his breath. "That sounded bad. Really bad. I didn't mean it the way it came out."

"How did you mean it then?"

"I want you safe. You have no reason to trust me. You don't know me, but damn it, I feel like I know you. When I saw you in the line, there was something there and I can't put a name on it. I only know that I need to know you're safe."

Flustered by the vehemence in his voice, she sat back, mug in her hands like a protective barrier. "I don't know what to say. I mean, what does anyone say to that? Of course I can't go."

"Why not?" he countered. "Lily, let's be honest here. You're living in a cardboard box. I'm offering you a warm bed, a hot shower, hot food and all the hot chocolate you could possibly want."

Her hands began to shake. It was insane that she even considered saying yes for half a second. But it had been so long since she'd had any of those things. It hurt to think about the life she'd left behind, the life that had left *her* behind. She didn't want to remember. It hurt too much, the wound was still too fresh.

"What are you thinking about?" he asked gently.

She shook her head, refusing to go back even for a moment.

"Stay for one night," he said. "At least give me that. Let me take care of you tonight. We'll talk about tomorrow when it comes."

One night. How could she say yes? How could she say no? Seth stirred emotions she hadn't allowed herself to feel in a long time. She wasn't entirely sure she wanted to give him the opportunity to unthaw her frozen heart. And he could. She recognized that.

"Why?" she asked helplessly. "You don't know me. I'm nobody to you."

"You aren't nobody, Lily," he said in a gentle voice. "I don't know who's convinced you that you're no one, or if it's you yourself that has perpetuated that lie, but that's what it is. A lie."

She took another long swallow of the hot chocolate and imagined sitting in his house, drinking more, allowing herself for one night to forget the past. To forget her present.

"All right," she said before she could talk herself out of it. "I think I must be crazy. This just isn't done. I know you feel sorry for me, but you shouldn't. You don't know—"

He held up his hand. "I know all I need to know. That's enough for now. When you trust me, you can tell me the rest."

She shook her head, but he reached across the table and caught one of her hands, bringing it down so he could hold it once more.

"You will trust me, Lily. I know it the same way I know you. We're going to be something to each other."

Again she shook her head, helplessness gripping her. But he simply rose and tugged her to her feet.

"My truck is parked at Margie's Place. We should head back now before it starts to get dark."

Seth opened the door to his house and held it as he waited for Lily to walk in ahead of him. She was nervous and on edge, and he didn't know what to do to make her feel more at ease. It would take time—time he was willing to invest—to make her understand that he had no intention of doing her harm.

She hung back, clearly uncomfortable with walking into his space. He swept by her, allowing her to position herself between him and the door. He wanted her to feel safe and unpressured.

"The guest room is down the hall," he said. "And the bathroom is right next door. I thought you could settle in and get comfortable. I'll cook us a good dinner and afterward we can kick back and watch a movie. You didn't eat much at lunch. You have to be hungry."

She smiled, and the shadows lifted and fled from her eyes.

"And of course there'll be plenty of hot chocolate," he added with a grin.

"I can't wait," she said huskily.

He motioned for her to follow him down the hallway toward his bedroom. "There's something I want to show you in the master bath. I know I pointed you to the guest bedroom and bathroom, but I thought you might want to take a soak in the garden tub in my bathroom."

When he flipped on the lights, he saw her gaze fasten longingly on the large tub in the corner. It was honestly not something he used or needed. He hadn't even drawn water in it once. He always used the shower. But he could see Lily in it, up to her nose in hot water.

His heart beat a little harder and his groin tightened because he suddenly saw her naked in the tub. He shook his head, feeling like a bastard for the turn of his thoughts.

"Are you sure you don't mind?" she asked anxiously.

But Seth could see how much she wanted that tub. He smiled and touched her gently on the cheek. "Why don't you hop in now and I'll get a start on supper."

He left her to run her water, and he headed into the kitchen to see what he could rummage up for dinner. It was lucky for him he'd gone to the market the day before so he had all the ingredients on hand for a decent meal.

His dads had taught him to cook—taught all his brothers to cook—because A) his mother was hopeless in the kitchen and B) his dads lived by one truth: Women should be cherished and protected, and there wasn't a woman more loved or cherished than Holly Colter.

Maybe that's where the overwhelming protective urge he felt when he first saw Lily came from.

He shook his head. No, he felt a certain obligation to any woman in need, but it was different with Lily. She was his. He couldn't explain it—in truth he was utterly baffled by it—but he didn't fight it. It felt...right.

After browning the boneless pork chops in the pan, he put together the casserole and then popped it into the oven. It wasn't exactly cordon bleu, but pork chop casserole was great comfort food, and Lily looked like she needed comfort most of all.

He set the timer and then his cell phone rang. The ringtone signaled it was someone from the Colter household. Probably his mom. With a smile, he dug his phone out and said hello.

"Hi sweetie."

His mom's voice, filled with warmth and love, came over the line. He relaxed. It was a natural reaction around her. He didn't know of anyone who didn't do the same when she spoke to them.

"Hi, Mom. How are you?"

"I'm good. I'm more interested in hearing how you are. You haven't called in a while."

There was gentle reproach in her voice that he didn't miss. Guilt made him cringe.

"Sorry," he mumbled. "Haven't had much to say."

"Are you feeling all right? Are you still hurting?" she asked anxiously.

"I'm fine, Mom. I swear. My shoulder hardly bothers me anymore. I have a psych evaluation next week, and as long as I don't froth at the mouth I should be cleared for work."

"You should come visit before you go back to work, Seth. We don't see enough of you anymore. After you go back to work, you'll never make it over."

"I'll see what I can do. Promise. How are the dads?" he asked.

She sighed but allowed him to change the subject. "They're as good as ever. Ethan is in town helping your brother do some repairs on the pub. They had trouble last night."

Seth frowned. "What kind of trouble? Is Dillon all right?"

"Oh, he's fine. Just a bunch of drunk college kids. Broke out a window. Lacey locked them up and they spent the night in jail."

Seth smiled. Life in Clyde. It never changed.

"Adam and Ryan are here. Did you want to speak to them?"

Though it was voiced as a seemingly innocent question, it was anything but. It was a command, and one he didn't dare ignore. His mom was about the sweetest woman on earth, but she was also a tyrant when it came to her family.

"Sure, put one of them on."

Seth sighed and waited.

"Son, how are you doing?"

Adam Colters' voice, as gruff as ever, came over the line, and Seth smiled. Damn but it was good to hear their voices. His mom was right. He didn't call often enough.

"I'm good, Dad. How are things there? Is Mom doing okay?"

Adam sighed. "It's not your mother you need to be worried about."

Seth laughed. "What's she on your asses about now?"

"You," Adam said bluntly. "You know, if you'd just come see her, our lives might go back to being peaceful."

"Is it my fault you married a tyrant?"

"Don't sass me, boy," Adam growled. "I can still whip your ass."

Seth laughed again and felt the tightness in his chest ease. A tightness he hadn't realized he'd carried around so much lately.

"How is everyone else? How is Michael's practice doing?"

"Good. Real good. He's busier than a one-armed paper hanger. Your mother stays after him about sleeping enough. Ryan and Ethan and I keep telling her that the only way the boy is going to make a success of his practice is if he gets out there where the animals are. You know your mother, though. She's only concerned that he's eating and resting."

"Yeah, I hear you on that," Seth said in amusement. "Mom said that Dillon had some trouble at his place?"

There was silence for a moment and Seth tensed.

"Dillon wasn't there when it happened. Your sister was. Your mother doesn't know that part of it, so you don't need to mention it."

"What? Callie's back? When did this happen and why did no one tell me?"

"She didn't stop in at your place when she flew in to Denver?"

Seth frowned. "No, this is the first I've heard of it. I thought she was still in Europe. I got an email from her a couple weeks ago and nothing since."

"Your mother's convinced something happened to her. Callie's tightlipped, though, and isn't talking. She just showed up a few days ago and asked Dillon if she could work behind the bar at his place."

"Damn," Seth murmured. He and Callie were close. All his siblings were, but he'd always shared a closer relationship with his little sister than his two brothers. And she hadn't said a word to him about coming back.

She *always* crashed at his place when she flew in or out of Denver. She'd been the one to stay after he'd been released from the hospital, only leaving for Europe when he'd sworn he was fine and didn't need her coddling anymore.

The fact that she hadn't stopped on her way home could only mean she had something to hide.

"So you said Callie was working last night and Dillon wasn't around. What happened? Was she hurt?"

Adam chuckled. "Oh hell, no. Not our girl. When the idiots tried to start some shit with her, she tossed one of them through the window."

There was a note of intense pride in his dad's voice that made Seth smile. That was one thing Seth could say about Callie. Growing up with three dads and three older brothers? She'd learned early how to kick ass and take names. She didn't take shit off anyone.

"Lacey is thinking about retiring," Adam said abruptly.

Seth rolled his eyes. "Dad, she's been thinking about retiring for the last ten years. It'll never happen. They'll pry her stiff carcass out of the sheriff's office at ninety."

Lacey England was the long-time sheriff of Clyde and also Seth's godmother. She doted on all the Colter children, but from the time he was old enough, Seth had followed her around, always interested in who she was arresting.

She'd been pleased beyond mention when he'd entered the police academy and taken a job as a police officer in Denver. None of her children had followed her into public service, and she laughingly told everyone that Seth was the child of her heart.

"No, she really means it this time," Adam said with a sigh. "Dan's health isn't good, Seth. They think it's cancer. They're thinking of moving so he can be closer to good hospitals."

"Oh damn," Seth murmured. "That's too bad."

"She wants you to consider moving to Clyde so you can be appointed to serve out her term. There's still two years left. You'd be a shoe-in come election time."

"Oh Christ, Dad. You know I don't want her job."

"Maybe you should think about it. You'd be close to home and family. It's a good job. Everyone knows you here. You're a damn good cop."

Seth held back the groan. Once an idea was planted in his mom's and dads' heads, it was impossible to sway them. They'd nag and cajole until he begged for mercy.

"It's a good time for a change. Fresh start after the shooting. Sure, things would be calmer here, but it would be your town."

"I'll think about it, Dad, okay?"

Adam gave a disbelieving grunt.

A noise in the kitchen had Seth turning around to see Lily sitting at the small breakfast bar. He hadn't even heard her come in. She looked tentative, as if she worried she was intruding.

He smiled at her then held up a finger to signal he'd only be a minute more.

"Look Dad, I need to go. I'll call you tomorrow to check up on things. Tell Mom I'll get up to see her before I go back to work."

"If I tell her that, you're going to come if I have to go down to Denver and haul you back myself," Adam warned.

His father wasn't kidding and Seth knew it well. "I know. I'll come."

"Okay, son. I'll talk to you later. I love you."

"Love you too, Dad. Give Mom a kiss for me and tell the other dads I'll see them soon."

Adam chuckled and hung up.

Seth put the phone back into his pocket and turned his attention to Lily.

Her nose wrinkled in confusion. "You have more than one dad?"

"Uh, yeah. Three."

"Stepdads? It must be nice to have a close relationship with them."

There was a wistful note in her voice that told Seth she thought having a close familial relationship in any context was nice.

"Not exactly. I have an unusual family."

She cocked her head to the side for a moment as if she'd say more, but then she blushed.

He chuckled. "You can ask. I love my family dearly. Wouldn't change a single thing about them, but my upbringing was definitely not typical."

"How so?"

"I have three fathers and one mother. My mother is in a relationship with all three men."

Lily's mouth rounded in shock. She seemed to want to say something but fell silent. Then she glanced up at him again. "How is that possible?"

Seth shrugged. "They all three love her more than life and she loves them. She married the oldest of three brothers but she's committed to all of them. They had four children. I'm the oldest. I have two younger brothers and my sister is the baby."

"Wow. I mean...wow. And you don't know who your biological father is?"

He smiled. "Nope. Doesn't matter to them. Doesn't matter to me. Although lots of teasing goes on now that we're adults. Mom swears I'm Ethan's child. What she means, though, is that I'm laid back and not a freak like my younger two brothers. Michael is more Adam's personality though maybe not as intense. And we all swear that Dillon was hatched because no one will claim responsibility for him."

Lily laughed. "That's so neat. You must have grown up with so much love."

Again the wistful note crept into her voice. He ached at the loneliness he heard in her words.

"I did. One thing was for certain, though. Me and my

siblings got away with nothing growing up. It was impossible with four parents in the picture."

She laughed again, and he felt the sound all the way to his soul.

"You sound very proud of them."

"I am. Wouldn't trade them for anything."

"What do your brothers and your sister do?"

"Tell you what. Why don't I fix us a cup of hot chocolate? Dinner won't be ready for another hour. We can go into the living room, get comfortable, and I'll tell you whatever you want to know."

She gifted him with a beatific smile. It was all he could do not to reach over and touch her. He wanted to pull her into his arms and assure her that nothing bad would ever happen to her again. And then he wanted to taste that mouth that had tempted him from the moment he laid eyes on her at Margie's Place.

He watched as she retreated to the living room. She curled onto the couch, tucking her bare feet beneath her. When she reached for the blanket that lay over the back, he cursed himself for not having built a fire while she was in the bath.

A few minutes later, he carried two steaming mugs of hot chocolate into the living room and set his on the coffee table. She reached for her mug with both hands, cupping them around the warm surface as if capturing and holding the heat as close to her as possible.

Without a word, he went over to the stone hearth and tossed a few logs from the wood rack into the fireplace. A few moments later, the first flicker of flame licked over the dry wood.

He returned to the couch where he took a seat on the opposite end of her. "Better?"

She smiled. "Perfect." Then she shook her head. "I'm still baffled by this whole thing, Seth. I shouldn't be here. This is...crazy."

Her fingers fluttered against her mug, and she had such a bewildered look on her face that he scooted forward on the couch until his knee rested against hers.

He touched her cheek, letting his fingers graze over her cheekbone and then down to her jaw. She closed her eyes and nuzzled into his palm as if she'd long been denied the pleasures of another's touch.

"I'm having my own set of what-the-hell-is-going-on thoughts," he said honestly. "But I'm not going to fight it, whatever it is between us. From the moment I saw you, I knew you were going to be a part of me. A big part of me. I don't understand it, but I'm not going to fight it. I don't *want* to fight it."

"I don't either," she whispered.

Triumph blazed through him with savage intensity. It was primitive and dark, and he wasn't entirely comfortable with it, but it wasn't something he could control.

"I'm going to kiss you, Lily," he murmured.

Her lips parted in a breathless gasp just a moment before he nudged forward and pressed his mouth to hers in the lightest of touches.

He savored that first brush and the electric sensation that slid over him, pricking each nerve ending on the way to his groin. He cupped her jaw and deepened the kiss, plunging his tongue inside to taste the sweet chocolate on hers.

She was his. That fact beat a steady rhythm through his body. His blood pulsed through his veins, whispering to him to take her, to fill the gap that he hadn't known existed inside him. One that she could fill.

Mine. It was all he could do not to say it. Only the thought of frightening her kept the word from pouring from his throat.

He didn't want to end the kiss. He wanted to make it endless. He wanted to carry her to bed where he'd kiss her and taste her for the rest of the night.

It's too soon.

The thought echoed in his mind as surely as if he'd said it aloud.

With a groan, he pulled away. She blinked and stared back at him with hazy, confused eyes. Her lips trembled and were wet from his tongue. She raised a shaking hand to her mouth, and he knew she felt what he did. His lips tingled and felt alive, like he'd die if he didn't kiss her again.

"Seth, what's happening here?" she asked.

He touched her face again, sweeping his hand down in tender strokes. "I don't know, Lily. But I'm sure as hell going to keep finding out."

Chapter Three

Michael Colter pulled up to his brother Seth's house and cut the engine on his Jeep Cherokee. It was barely past dawn, but Seth wasn't one to sleep in. He was probably already up with a cup of coffee.

He stepped out into the chilly morning air and stifled a yawn. Leaving Clyde at three in the morning hadn't been conducive to a good night's sleep, but he was up and not likely to fall asleep so he hadn't waited to make the trip to Denver.

He ambled to the front door, knocked once and then let himself in. It always cracked him up that Seth was a cop and he never locked his door. Too many years of living on a mountain with the Colter clan. Not many people in their right minds would try to break in there.

"Seth?" he called as he shut the door behind him.

As he walked into the living room, Seth left the kitchen, predictably with a cup in his hand. But it didn't smell like coffee. Michael sniffed the air. Chocolate?

"Giving up the good stuff?" Michael asked with a grin.

"Michael? What the hell are you doing here?" Seth demanded.

Michael arched an eyebrow as he made his way over to where his brother stood. "It's good to see you too."

Seth put his cup down and then grasped Michael's arm and pulled him into a hug. "You know I'm glad to see you, dumbass. I just wasn't expecting you. I just spoke to Mom and Dad last night. Neither said anything about you coming."

"That's because I didn't tell them," Michael said dryly. "You aren't the only one who doesn't report in to Mom and the dads on a regular basis."

Seth laughed but then grew serious. "What's up? And don't tell me nothing. You wouldn't have dragged in here at this hour without calling if something wasn't wrong."

Michael sighed. "You'll just call me a drama queen."

"I haven't called you a drama queen since you were in the fifth grade," Seth refuted. "Spill."

"Can I have some coffee or have you changed your poison? By the smell, I'm wondering if that bullet wound didn't turn you into a pussy."

A peculiar look crossed Seth's face, but before Michael could press him, Seth turned back into the kitchen.

"Come on, I'll make you a cup and then you need to make it quick. I've got things to do."

Michael blinked in surprise. Seth wasn't usually so abrupt. What the hell was up his ass this morning?

"Sit down and talk while the coffee's brewing," Seth said, pointing to the table.

"Anyone ever tell you that your hospitality sucks ass?" Michael grumbled.

Seth shot him a look and Michael held up his hands. "Okay, okay. It's Callie."

At the mention of Callie, Seth frowned as he poured the water through the coffee maker.

"Dad said she was back and that something was up."

"Yeah," Michael replied. "Something."

"What's the deal?"

"I don't know. I wish I did. It's why I came. I was hoping you'd go home for a few days. Maybe she'll talk to you. I'm...I'm worried about her. Everyone's worried about her."

Seth blew out his breath and dragged a hand through his hair. When he turned to Michael, concern had darkened his eyes.

"She not talking to anyone? Not even Dillon?"

Michael shook his head. "Nope. She's more tightlipped than Ryan."

"I'm telling you, man, Callie has to be his biological

daughter. There is no way she can be so much like him and be Ethan or Adam's daughter."

Michael laughed. "Ryan likes to think so. He's pretty damn smug about it. She looks and acts just like him."

"Scary," Seth muttered. "So she's not talking to him either?"

Again Michael shook his head. "She's not talking to anyone, Seth. It's driving Mom and the dads crazy. She came home looking like a wounded animal. For several days she holed up at Mom and Dads' and wouldn't leave the mountain. Then she came down and asked Dillon for a job. She's been working behind the bar every night since."

"And what's this about a problem the other night?" Seth asked.

"Well, that's just it. You know Callie doesn't take shit off anyone but she's usually so easygoing. Laughs about everything. The kids were being typical college buttheads. They'd had too much to drink. From what Lacey said, one of the witnesses swears all the kid did was pop off at Callie. Harmless. She put him through the window."

Seth whistled. "Sounds like our girl has some unresolved anger."

"What was your first clue?" Michael asked dryly.

Michael's gaze was drawn to the kitchen entrance where he was astonished to see a woman standing in the doorway. She was dressed in what looked like a pair of Callie's old pajamas. Her eyes were wide with...fear? She looked anxious, and she stared at Michael like she was afraid he was going to jump up and pounce.

An eerie sensation niggled his nape and snaked down his spine, spreading like wildfire. What the hell? He couldn't take his eyes off her. She had the most stunning blue eyes he'd ever seen on a woman. Her hair fell over her ears and to her chin in soft curls. She looked...enchanting, like some delicate fairy come to life.

And what the fuck was he doing sitting here mooning on about goddamn fairies? Jesus on an eggshell but he was losing his ever-loving mind.

He was starting to think stupid things, like he'd do

31

anything at all to remove the fear from her gaze. He wanted to protect her.

And she was coming out of his brother's bedroom. Or at least from that general vicinity.

"S-Seth?" she asked in a wavery voice. But before Seth could respond, she said, "I should go. I need to go."

Her voice was whisper soft, and before he could catch himself, Michael was on his feet—to do what? Keep her from going?

He forced himself to stand there while Seth hurried toward the woman.

"Lily, no," Seth said in a soft, urgent voice as he took her shoulders in his hands.

So Lily was her name. Michael watched as Lily skittered away from Seth's grasp, her eyes darting toward Michael as she did.

"Honey, it's only Michael. My brother Michael. Remember, I told you all about him last night?"

"The vet," she said in a husky voice.

"Yes, that's right. He just started his practice back home."

"I should go," she said again, and Michael saw her edge toward the hallway that led to the bedroom.

"Stay and eat breakfast. I made you a cup of hot chocolate. It's probably cold by now, but I can pop it into the microwave for you."

She hesitated, her gaze going between the two brothers.

"I need to get dressed," she said faintly.

"Okay. I'll be here in the kitchen. I'll make breakfast so you can eat when you get out."

She was gone before Seth could say another word. When he turned back to Michael, there was something decidedly desperate in his older brother's eyes. A desperation that for some reason, Michael felt in equal measure.

"Who is she?" Michael rasped out. Hell, he couldn't even talk right. He had a knot in his throat the size of a boulder.

Seth cut an impatient glance at his brother. "Lily," he bit out. "Just Lily."

"Who is she to *you*?"

Seth swung around, his eyes blazing. "Why the hell do you want to know that?"

"I want to know," Michael said. "I need to know, because damn it, I just had the most powerful reaction to a woman I've had in my entire life, and I damn well need to know if I'm poaching on my brother's territory."

Seth's mouth gaped open. "You stay the hell away from her."

"So it's like that," Michael said grimly. "You've staked a claim."

"Are you out of your mind? You just met the woman. What are you planning to do, haul her off over your shoulder?"

"Maybe," Michael said calmly. "Probably."

"Over my dead body."

"When did you meet her?" Michael asked. Seth hadn't mentioned a woman. Not to anyone. He would have known. The dads wouldn't have kept something like that quiet. They would have been too busy giving him hell.

"Yesterday," Seth said in a gruff, pissed-off voice.

"Yesterday? *Yesterday?* And you're going off on me for having just met her?" Michael laughed. "You fucking hypocrite."

And then the thought came. Stuck in his head like someone had hit him with a hammer. He'd walked into his brother's house and met a woman he instantly and absolutely had to have. It wasn't just sexual. No, his reaction to her hadn't even been sexual. It was *emotional.* On a level he couldn't even explain.

The same woman his brother was having some psychotic caveman episode over.

"Oh no," he whispered. "Oh *hell* no."

"What are you talking about?" Seth demanded.

"Goddamn it, I thought it was bullshit. I thought it was some hokey bullshit that the dads made up to make Mom feel all soft and mushy."

Seth got into his face, breathing fire he was so pissed off. "What. The. Fuck. Are. You. Talking. About."

Michael closed his eyes and let out a helpless laugh. "It's some fucked-up Colter gene. It has to be. There's no other explanation."

Seth threw up his hands. "I swear to God if you don't start making some fucking sense, I'm going to knock the shit out of you."

"Think about it, Seth. How many times have we heard the story over the years? The dads met Mom and they knew immediately and with absolute certainty that she was the one. *The one.* They said it was instant and so powerful they didn't have a prayer of fighting. They wanted to love and protect her, wrap her in cotton and lock her away for about a hundred years. Now you tell me. Is that what you're feeling when you look at Lily? Because I sure as hell am, and it's worse for me because I don't even know the goddamn woman."

Seth looked like someone hit him square between the eyes with a bat. For a moment, Michael thought Seth was going to hit *him.*

"That's crazy," Seth finally said. "She's a beautiful woman. Of course you'd have a strong reaction to her. You probably haven't been laid in a year."

"No need to get insulting," Michael drawled. "I've probably gotten lucky at least twice since the last time you shed the monk robes. And sure, she's beautiful, but step back a moment, Seth. Really look at her objectively. She's not the most gorgeous woman you or I have ever seen."

Seth's lip turned up into a snarl and Michael held up his hand. "Let me finish. We've seen any number of women who were heart-stoppingly gorgeous, but tell me this. Were you tripping over yourself like this with them? You look at her and you see something beyond beauty. I know because I saw the same damn thing."

Seth shook his head. "I'm not listening to this. This is insane. Our dads may have fallen for the same woman, but you can't tell me we'll do the same."

"You're forgetting the granddads. Explain that one, Seth. If there isn't some hinkey shit going on in the gene pool then why are you and I about to go to fist city because we're both determined to get close to Lily?"

Seth's eyes looked haunted as it all sank in. "Damn it, Michael, this isn't what I wanted. It can't be possible. It has to be some stupid coincidence."

"Yeah, well, believe me, sharing a woman with my two bonehead brothers doesn't exactly appeal to me either, but unless one of us suffers a fast change of heart, we're either going to have to do some serious compromising or one of us is going to go home to Mom in a pine box."

"I'm not having this conversation with you right now," Seth bit out. "There are things you don't know about Lily. I can't even convince her to let her guard down around me. She walked in here, saw you and now she's ready to bolt."

"What the hell's going on?" Michael asked, now dead serious.

Seth glanced down at the mug of hot chocolate, swore and then stuck it in the microwave. Then, as if realizing how much time had passed since Lily had gone to get dressed, he glanced at his watch and frowned.

"She's been gone too long," he muttered.

Michael watched as Seth stomped off down the hall. A few seconds later he heard "Son of a bitch!" And then the unmistakable sound of a fist hitting the wall.

Michael surged to his feet, adrenaline spiking sharp through his veins. Seth came barreling out of the hallway and then ducked into the dining room. He came back out, face set in stone.

"What the hell is wrong?" Michael demanded.

"While you and I were out here discussing Lily, she took off."

Michael's eyebrow went up at the urgency in Seth's voice. "Won't she be back?"

"No, goddamn it. She's homeless, Michael. She doesn't have a place to stay. I found her between two cardboard boxes on the fucking street. She's scared and alone, and she has no place to go. It took me forever to convince her to come here, and now she's run scared."

Michael's stomach bottomed out with a thud. "Homeless? What the *fuck*?"

Seth whirled around like he couldn't figure out what he needed to do first. He grabbed up his keys and then shoved his feet into his shoes.

"Yeah, homeless. I served her in the soup kitchen yesterday. I volunteer there once a month. She came in and bam. I mean I still don't know what happened. When she left I followed her because I couldn't stand the thought of her having no place to go. I found her in an alley, cold and alone."

"Son of a bitch," Michael muttered.

Seth pointed a finger at him. "Right now I don't give a damn about what you feel for her or think you feel. I don't give a shit about some fucking Colter gene that you think we got from the dads. All I care about is getting her back. Here. Where she belongs. Get your ass out to your Jeep so you can help me look. Everything else is just going to have to goddamn wait."

Chapter Four

Seth punched in Michael's cell number as he backed out of the drive. Michael picked up on the first ring.

"She can't have gone far, Michael. We'll skirt the perimeter of the house and make our way downtown. She's probably heading back to the only place she knows."

"I'll keep my eyes peeled."

Seth hung up and focused his attention on the streets. At each intersection, he crawled forward, glancing each way for any sign of her.

For an hour he traversed the streets around his neighborhood, gradually falling away to the cityscape of downtown Denver. She could have caught a bus. She could have walked the entire way. Or she could be at any point in between. Cold. Alone.

Gentle rain began to fall, almost certainly a precursor to sleet and later snow. Seth cursed as he turned his wipers on. Not only would it make it nearly impossible to see her, but now she would be cold and wet with no protection from the elements.

"Where are you, Lily?" he murmured as he turned down a narrow street just a few blocks from the café where he and Lily had hot chocolate. "Why did you run? What are you running from?"

At the end of the street, he slammed on the brakes as he was confronted by a sea of flashing blue lights. Patrol cars were everywhere. Two SWAT vans were blocking traffic on two streets. Several unmarked cars were mixed in with the ambulances and fire trucks. It looked like the entire world had gone to hell around him.

Recognizing his lieutenant, Seth jammed the gear into park and then bolted from the truck, dodging through the rain as it slid down his neck.

"L.T.!" he called as he ran up.

Lieutenant Monday turned, his expression startled as he saw Seth. Then he scowled. "What the hell are you doing here, Colter?"

"What's going on?" Seth demanded.

Monday rubbed an irritated hand through his hair. "Fucking drug dealers went to war over turf. I wish the fuckers would just kill each other and be done with it, but they insist on taking down innocent civilians with them. I've got bodies over eight blocks. Most of them the assholes in question, but I've got at least three bystanders in body bags and two more en route to the hospital."

Seth's stomach tightened into a knot. "Shit."

His lieutenant looked up. "Why are you down here?"

"I'm looking for someone. Her name is Lily. Short. Maybe five-one. Short, curly black hair. Vivid blue eyes. If you saw her, you'd remember."

Monday frowned. "Don't recall, but then I've seen a damn lot of faces today. Check with Houston over there. He has a list of the people we've ID'd."

"Thanks, L.T."

Seth hurried over to where Carl Houston stood barking orders into his radio.

"Hey man," Seth said as Carl turned around. "L.T. said you have a list of casualties."

"Looking for someone?"

"Yeah. Young woman named Lily. No last name."

Carl picked up a clipboard and flipped through the pages. "We have two women accounted for so far. One is a Jane Doe. Older. Bag lady found dead in an alley. Caught in crossfire. Other is a hooker named Star."

Relief crushed him. "Okay, thanks, Carl."

Seth turned to walk away, and Carl called out to him. "Hey,

what are you doing out here anyway?"

Seth ignored him and kept on going. He flashed his badge at the group of officers who had cordoned off the street and then ducked under the tape to get back into his truck.

He punched Michael's number and hoped to hell his brother was having better luck than he was.

Michael ignored the angry horns as he slowed to a stop to look down the intersection. Sirens in the distance told him something big was going down. Probably a downtown pile-up. He shuddered as he accelerated toward the next block. He hated the city. Hated traffic. Hated people. Most people anyway. Animals were much better company.

He found a place to park curbside and got out, pulling his jacket up around his ears. He'd never see anything from the truck in this weather, and he could get into the nooks and crannies on foot.

His phone rang, and he pulled it out of his pocket.

"Any luck?" Seth demanded.

"No. I just got out to search on foot. Rain makes it hard to see shit."

"Be careful. Fucking drug dealers had a turf war. It's going to make finding Lily even harder with everything in chaos."

"I'll holler if I find her," Michael said before punching the end button.

He frowned as he turned down another side street and shivered as rain slid down his neck. It was crazy that he was turning downtown Denver over looking for a woman he'd spent all of a few minutes with. Even more insane that his heart was about to pound out of his chest over the thought of not finding her.

After an hour, he was clenching his teeth in frustration. He strode through an alley that cut between two of the main streets and almost missed her.

He caught movement from the corner of his eye and stopped in midstride, his gaze drawn to the small woman huddled against the side of a dumpster, her head down to her knees.

Adrenaline spiked in his veins. The hairs prickled at his nape in sudden awareness. It was her. It had to be her. She wore a threadbare knit cap but her rain-slicked hair peeked from the edges.

She'd made herself into the smallest ball she could manage, and it had almost worked. He would have walked right by her, and many others probably already had, never seeing her and if they did, they didn't care.

"Lily?"

She reacted violently to her name. Her head came up, and wide, frightened eyes met his. Automatically she surged up as if to flee.

"Lily, it's me, Michael. Seth's brother. Remember? I'm not going to hurt you. I'm here to help you."

Slowly she slid back down the wall, one hand going to the cracked pavement. The other arm she held tight against her chest in a gesture that screamed self-protection.

"Why are you here?"

He crouched down so he could look her in the eye. "I want you to come back with me, Lily. Seth is worried. *I'm* worried. You don't need to be out here. It's cold and raining. You're going to make yourself sick."

She stared at him, her eyes cloudy with confusion. "I'm used to it."

"But you don't have to be."

"It was only for one night," she whispered.

"It doesn't have to be."

She cocked her head, unease sliding across her face. He ran his fingers gently over her cheekbone. Whether she meant to or not, she nuzzled into his palm and closed her eyes.

The gesture told him a lot. He also knew the moment she realized her slip. She stiffened and drew away, but not before he saw the longing in her gaze.

In a lot of ways she reminded him of the animals he loved so much. Wary. But starved for love and affection. Both needed an extremely gentle hand.

He tried a different tack. "Lily, honey, it's cold and wet out here. Seth is running all over downtown freezing his ass off, and he's worried sick about you. Come with me so we can all get out of the weather. I'll make some hot chocolate and we'll get you into some dry clothes. My hot chocolate is better than Seth's anyway."

She frowned and shifted slightly then grimaced. His brow furrowed as he stared at her in question.

"Are you all right? Are you hurt?"

She shook her head. "No. No, I'm fine."

He held out his hand to her, hoping she'd take it, that she'd agree to come with him. He hadn't exaggerated the fact that it was damn cold.

Instead of slipping her hand into his, she pushed herself upward with the hand on the ground but kept the other arm tight against her chest. Her posture was awkward, and his frown deepened as she staggered to her feet.

For a moment she stood, hand resting against the wall of the alleyway, and she leaned, head bowed as if catching her breath.

He waited, not wanting to press her, but he held his breath as he watched to see if she'd agree to come with him.

She took a step away from the wall and nearly fell.

Michael lunged forward and caught her before her knees completely gave out. She felt light and infinitely fragile against his chest. She shuddered and quaked, and her breaths came in rapid bursts.

For a long moment he simply held her, enjoying the sensation of her curled into his arms. And he wanted her to feel safe, so he made no sudden movements. Just let her grow accustomed to having him so close.

"I'm okay," she whispered. "You can let me go."

Reluctantly he drew away, but he was careful to keep his hands on her shoulders. Her clothing was damp through, and he was more determined than ever to take her back to Seth's so they could get her into dry clothes and warmed up. After that? Who the hell knew? What was he going to do? Move in on a woman his brother had clearly staked a claim on?

His lips drawn into a grim line, he drew her protectively

into his side so he could shield her from as much of the weather as possible. They walked down the alley, and at the end, she stared apprehensively down the street.

"I'm not far," Michael murmured. "Let's get you inside where it's warm and I'll call Seth. He's looking for you."

She shivered and frowned as he ushered her forward. "He shouldn't have."

Michael turned in surprise. "Shouldn't have looked for you? Shouldn't have cared?"

"Either."

He wanted to argue but didn't. Seth could fight his own battles. Michael had to figure out how the hell to get past Lily's defenses himself.

When his Cherokee came into view, Michael quickened his pace and all but dragged Lily with him. The interior was still warm when he opened the passenger door. He helped her in, shut the door behind her and hurried around to his side.

He got in, started the engine and turned the heat on full blast before pulling out his cell phone. Lily listed a little in the seat and leaned away from him so that her right shoulder rested against the window.

Her expression was wary, but now she seemed more tired than anything. And worried.

"Seth, I found her. We're heading back to your house."

"Thank God," Seth breathed. "I'll meet you there."

Michael put the Jeep into gear and drove off, frowning as his wipers just made a bigger mess of his windshield. He had the girl. But now what did he do with her?

He glanced sideways when he stopped at a red light and studied her delicate features. Then he shook his head. Fucked-up Colter gene. There was no other explanation. He needed to dump her back at Seth's and run like hell. But he knew he wouldn't. That he was well and truly stuck in this bizarre situation and that he was going to ride it out.

Seth could just unstake his claim.

Halfway to Seth's house, Lily's eyes closed. They rumbled over a pothole in the road, and she never stirred. She looked exhausted.

When they pulled into Seth's driveway, Seth hadn't arrived yet. Michael parked and leaned over to gently shake Lily awake.

"Lily," he said in a low voice. "Wake up, honey. We're at Seth's."

He slid his hand higher up her arm and curled his fingers into the damp material as he shook just a little harder.

A flash of red caught his attention as his hand moved upward. He turned his palm outward and stared in bewilderment at the coating of red, sticky blood on his skin.

His gaze jerked back to her face, and her pallor took on a more ominous meaning. He touched her sweater again, and pulled at the material. The red was well disguised against the black material, but once again, his fingers came away glistening with fresh blood.

His pulse ratcheted up and his chest squeezed until each breath stuttered painfully across his lips. This wasn't good. Not good at all.

"Ah, Lily," he whispered. "What the hell happened to you out there?"

Chapter Five

Lily stirred, and for a moment she had no awareness of her surroundings. Where was she? She blinked and then heard a low voice to her left accompanied by a hand on her shoulder.

She tried to turn, but pain splintered down her arm.

"Easy, don't move too fast."

Michael. Seth's brother. He'd come for her. She was in his truck. She looked through the windshield to see they were parked in front of Seth's house.

Once again she tried to shift, but Michael prevented her with a gentle hand. When he pulled it away, she was stunned to see his palm red with blood. She stared in bewilderment at the concern in his eyes and then looked down at her arm.

"What happened?"

"I was hoping you could tell me," Michael said in a grim voice.

She shook her head. "I don't know. I didn't realize... It was all such a blur."

"I need to get you inside so I can take a look at your arm and see what's going on, okay? We may need to take you to the hospital."

Instant nausea rolled in her stomach. The smell of the hospital was vibrant in her nose. The sights. The sounds. She couldn't go back there. She could never go back there.

Distant weeping. Shouted denials. Shock. Her world crashing around her.

She shuddered and purposely blanked her mind, refusing to go back to that place.

"No hospital."

The words sounded harsh on her lips. Michael's eyes flared in surprise, and he studied her thoughtfully.

"We may not have a choice, Lily."

She shook her head again, ignoring the pain the vehement action caused her.

Michael sighed and opened his door. He walked around to her side and opened her door. For a moment he stood there as if studying the best way to handle her. She was struck by the differences between him and Seth. Even though Seth was the cop, Michael... He seemed more intense. Subtle power emanated from him in waves. There was confidence to his movements, and his attitude suggested he was used to taking charge and used to people following his directions.

His hair was longer. It clipped the tops of his shoulders but was shoved behind both ears as if he impatiently tucked it there often. The only resemblance she could find to Seth was the color of his hair and eyes. They both had beautiful blue eyes, though Seth's were lighter. And their hair was a darker shade of brown.

"Tell you what," he finally said as if coming to a decision. "For now, let's go inside so I can take a look. Until I know what we're dealing with, it's senseless to have this argument."

He reached for her, to help her, but she pushed at his hand.

"I can walk. I'm okay."

His mouth turned down into an expression of disapproval, but he didn't press. He simply took a step back and waited for her to get out.

She swung her legs out and tried to get down too fast. Her feet hit the ground, and a moan escaped as the action jarred her upper body. Michael cursed, and before she could protest, he pulled her into his side, supporting her weight as they started for the house.

Once inside, the heat washed over her, thawing some of the numbness in her limbs. What should have felt like heaven quickly became hell as more feeling washed into her arm.

Michael sat her on the couch and knelt in front of her, his

intense gaze finding hers. "I'm going out to my truck to get my bag. I don't want you to move."

She tried to smile but her lips quivered with the effort. "I thought you were a vet."

His eyes lightened and he smiled. "I am. But people...animals...what's the difference?"

She laughed at his joke but promptly shut up when the movement proved too much.

He got up and hurried out and once again she found herself staring around Seth's house, taking in the smells and atmosphere of a home.

It lacked a woman's touch, but then she'd seen no evidence that Seth was involved with someone. He'd kissed her. Acted like he cared, though she couldn't wrap her brain around that. She hadn't done anything to encourage his attention—she wouldn't have. She'd spent too much time trying to make herself invisible.

Life was for others to live. It was for her to survive.

Michael returned a moment later carrying a large duffel bag that he set on the floor in front of the couch. He knelt back down in front of her and took her hand in his, his fingers moving carefully over hers in a soothing manner.

"We need to get your sweater off, but I don't want to pull it over your head so I'm going to cut it away from your arm so I can see where the bleeding is coming from."

She glanced between her arm and him and then nodded. He seemed relieved by her acceptance and opened his bag to take out scissors.

He started at her wrist where the tattered cuff of her sweater all but swallowed her hand. He worked methodically upward until the sleeve fell apart in two distinct pieces. She sucked in her breath when she saw the blood seeping down the inside of her arm.

"Do you have anything on underneath the sweater?" he asked gently.

"A T-shirt," she said huskily.

"Okay, good. I'm going to cut away the sweater. It's not salvageable anyway."

Michael paused as he placed a bandage over her wound. "Did my showing up frighten you?"

Frighten? That was probably the wrong word. Unsettled. His appearance had effectively popped the fantasy bubble that she'd existed in for the previous night.

"No, not frightened," she said.

"I don't want you back on the streets, Lily," Seth said fiercely.

She cocked her head and stared up at him. "Where do you want me then?"

His blue eyes focused intently on her. There was no guard, no hesitation, no hint that he was speaking from anywhere but the heart. He brushed his fingers over her face, gentle and perhaps a bit shaky.

"Here. With me."

Chapter Six

Despite her resolve not to allow herself the luxury of the fantasy Seth offered, she couldn't stop the yearning, the desire for human contact. Affection. Casual conversation. She'd sentenced herself to a life alone, but she didn't *want* to be alone. She wasn't meant to be alone.

Her brain knew that it was time to stop punishing herself, that it was time to forgive herself and move on, but her heart was utterly broken. And how did she repair something like that? How could she ever break free of something so terrible—something she could have prevented?

It was stupid and melodramatic at its core. She knew this. But it didn't stop the flood of grief, sometimes so strong that she wondered if living wasn't the worst punishment of all.

She waited—every day she waited for the pain to stop. Everyone said that time soothed all hurts—forgave all sins.

"Lily?" Michael asked in a soft voice.

She blinked and looked down. He was finished bandaging her arm. The gauze was thick and bulky and prevented her arm from lying fully against her side. It ached fiercely but she welcomed it. Somehow it was better than the numbness that seemed to take over more with each passing day.

"I'll need to make you a sling. I'd rather you not move that arm around much until the wound heals."

"How long will I have to wear it?"

"A few days. Not too long."

He turned to Seth. "Do you have any ibuprofen?"

"She needs something stronger than that," Seth growled.

"I'm fine," she said quickly. "Really."

Seth shot her a disbelieving look but left to get the medicine.

"He's right, you know," Michael said after Seth was gone. "You don't need to be out on the streets. Not before. Not now. Not ever."

She looked away, discomfited by the intensity in his gaze. "I don't have anyplace else to go."

"Look at me, Lily."

Reluctantly, she turned to face him again.

"You do have a place. We're offering you one."

"We?"

Michael's lips tightened for a moment. "Yes, we. I don't know what's happening here, Lily. I can't explain it, but we'll work it out."

Her lips parted as her mouth fell open. Seth returned then and took her hand. He dropped the tiny pills into her palm and then held out a glass of water. She swallowed them down and then leaned back on the couch and closed her eyes.

Firm lips pressed against her brow, and she opened her eyes to see Seth bending over, his kiss warm and sweet on her skin.

"Do you want to be down here or in the bed you slept in last night?"

The thought of having to move was excruciating. "Here."

Seth straightened. "I'll get a blanket and some pillows so you'll be comfortable."

As she watched him walk away, it seemed to her that she hadn't even considered leaving. Not yet. The idea of going back to her world scared her to death. She could stay here. Just for a little while.

Seth glanced over at Lily who had fallen into a fitful sleep. She stirred frequently, a frown marring the delicate lines of her face. Then he looked over at his brother who watched Lily with absolute fascination.

This was crazy. He didn't even know how to broach the

subject. And what would he say anyway? Back the fuck off? She's mine? Or, how do you feel about sharing?

As if sensing his turmoil, Michael turned and caught Seth's gaze.

"I think we should bring her home."

Seth frowned and motioned for Michael to follow him into the kitchen. "Home?" he asked after they were out of earshot. "I live *here.*"

"It isn't home," Michael argued. "We should take her to the mountain. She's uneasy here, and you'd have to worry at every turn that she was going to take off again. There...there she could rest. Eat good food and have a roof over her head."

"Are you suggesting we take her to Mom's?" Seth asked incredulously.

Michael hesitated. "No. My place."

Seth's eyes narrowed. "You're serious about her. You're not going to let this go."

"Would you?" Michael asked.

"Hell no."

"She needs us. She needs a home, a place she feels safe. You're needed at home, Seth. Callie needs you. Mom and the dads want you there. It just makes sense that we take Lily back to Clyde."

Seth ran a hand through his hair. He'd forgotten all about Callie. Forgotten everything once Lily had disappeared.

"What are we doing here, Michael? Are we really considering the kind of relationship the dads have with Mom?"

"I don't see we have a choice," Michael said quietly.

"Christ. What about Dillon? Are we going to have to go throw Lily in front of him to see if he loses his mind too?"

Michael smiled faintly. "Are you asking me if I think it's possible he'll react as we have?"

Seth nodded.

Michael sighed. "Yeah, I'm thinking it's possible. Am I going to go shove Lily under his nose and say, 'Hey do you like her'? Uh, no. But you can be damn certain I'm going to be watching to see how he reacts when he meets her."

"Jesus, this is weird. Beyond weird. I've witnessed this sort of thing all my life, but I never thought for a minute that I'd share a woman with my brothers."

"You aren't the only one struggling, Seth. This isn't exactly how I envisioned my life either."

"Yeah, I get it." He glanced in the direction of the living room again. "So how are we going to convince her to go home with us?"

"We could always kidnap her," Michael said with a shrug.

Seth looked at him like he was deranged. Maybe he was.

"I'm a cop, remember?"

"I'm merely suggesting that we bundle her up and go for a ride. A long ride. And if we end up in Clyde, all the better. If she truly freaks out, we can always drive her back, but I don't believe for a minute that either of us is going to idly stand by and watch her walk back onto those streets."

"Hell no."

"So we take her to Clyde—to my house. I don't want to overwhelm her with Mom and the dads right away or she'll feel ambushed. I think we should ease her into things there— namely our family."

"You assume a lot, Michael. What if she doesn't want anything to do with us? She's running from something or somebody. She could be in a lot of trouble."

"To quote one of the dads, when they laid eyes on Mom, her walking away simply wasn't an option. They were willing to do whatever they had to in order to make her stay. As I recall, there was a lot of cooking, pampering and worshiping."

Seth rolled his eyes. "Depends on who you ask. Of course Mom is going to spout that nonsense."

Michael shook his head. "No, that came straight from Ryan's mouth. Hell, Seth, you see the way they still are around her over thirty years later."

"That's the way it should be," Seth murmured.

"But will it be that way for us?"

"I don't know," Seth said in frustration. "Do you realize how stupid this conversation is? We can't make her return our attraction."

"No, but we can damn sure show her our caring—and

eventually our love."

"Yeah, you're right. Okay, so we pull off the kidnapping. Christ, I can't even believe I'm going along with this."

Michael chuckled. "It's not like it's a real kidnapping, and look at it this way. She'll be the most pampered captive in existence."

"I need to pack a bag. We should probably head out before it gets dark. Weather's already nasty."

"Go then. I'll watch over Lily while you get your stuff together."

Chapter Seven

Lily awoke to light stroking on the curve of her cheek. She opened her eyes to see Seth kneeling in front of the couch, his face close to hers. She tried to sit up, but he gently pushed her back down.

"Is something wrong? How long did I sleep?"

Instead of answering he leaned in and brushed his lips across hers. Just a simple, delicate whisper over her mouth, gone almost before he was there.

"Nothing's wrong. We were going to kidnap you. I'd rather you tell me you want to go with us."

There was light humor to his words that made her wonder if he was serious at all. She cocked her head to the side and then looked beyond him to see Michael standing in the doorway to the living room shaking his head.

"Where are we going?" she asked. Then she realized how ridiculous the question was. She flushed, but Seth only smiled.

"You're going home with us," Michael said from the doorway.

Before she could express her confusion over that statement, Seth spoke up.

"Home to Clyde. I don't want you on the streets, Lily, but I won't take you there against your will, either. I want you to come with us. I need you to come with us." He traced the line of her lips, and fire gleamed in his eyes. "Let's see where this takes us, honey. Let us take care of you."

Her mind blanked for a moment, and she stared between the two brothers. Pain was a dull throb in her arm, forgotten in breathless anticipation. Seth was close, so close, and she realized she wanted him to kiss her. Worse, the same odd longing filled her at the idea of Michael doing the same. Of touching her and letting his warm, tender voice flow over her.

It was because she'd lived too long in a vacuum. What was it they said about animals starved for affection? They'd allow anyone to pet them? That was what she felt like. Sensory deprived. Devoid of the most basic human comforts, like love and acceptance.

She didn't deserve them. But God, she wanted them.

"Lily?" Seth prompted.

Slowly, she nodded.

She expected triumph in Seth's eyes, but what she saw was relief. It warmed some of the cold encasing her soul that he worried for her. That he cared.

"Now, there are some things I need to know before we leave," Seth continued. "And I need you to be honest with me. Are you in some kind of trouble? Because if you are, I can help."

She shook her head. It wasn't any kind of trouble he was talking about. The cop in him probably thought she was a fugitive in hiding.

"Okay, are you running from someone?" His eyes narrowed as he asked, and his jaw tightened. "Is there someone who hurt you? I don't want to endanger my family by bringing you home if there's some threat I need to know about. If there is, you need to tell me about it so I can eliminate it."

Again she shook her head, and she saw frustration mirrored in both Seth's and Michael's gazes.

"There's nothing like that," she said in a low voice. "You have no reason to believe me, but I would never endanger you or your family. I'll understand if you no longer want to...do this."

Some sins weren't so black and white. No, there wasn't anyone after her. But it didn't mean she hadn't done a terrible thing. Time hadn't dimmed the guilt or the pain, but she'd become more adept at blocking it out.

"We can accept that. For now." Michael's tone warned they wouldn't allow her to avoid the issue forever. And maybe "for now" was what she needed. Just a little while to be someone else. To live someone else's life and escape her own.

Seth looked like he wanted to press, but instead he pulled up a flannel shirt and a pair of jeans that looked awfully close to her size.

"I know your arm hurts, but we need to get you into some decent clothes before we leave. The T-shirt you're down to won't protect you from zip. I noticed a few holes in your jeans, and my sister left a few of hers here so you can try them."

Without waiting for a response, Seth pushed the covers away and helped her sit up on the couch. Then he carefully pulled the flannel shirt around her shoulders. She thrust her good arm through the armhole and then slowly straightened her injured arm so that she could fit it through the other sleeve.

He buttoned the shirt up, his fingers lingering at each one as he worked down her chest. Her breasts tightened and throbbed, and it embarrassed her that her nipples thrust against the softness of the material. The shirt was large enough that he might not see, but she was acutely aware of each touch.

The awareness startled her, but it was pleasant. No, not pleasant. That was too mild a word to describe the pleasure that hummed through her veins like sweet honey. It was warm and electric and it brought her to life—into the sun after so long in the cold.

To her surprise, he didn't waste any time divesting her of her jeans. He unbuttoned the fly and helped her to her feet and then pushed the loose material over her hips until she stood in only her panties and the too-large flannel shirt hanging to her knees.

She stole a glance at Michael, her cheeks flaming, but he had discreetly looked away.

"Hold on to my shoulder," Seth directed as he held the jeans open at her feet.

She braced herself, her fingers sliding over the well muscled cord of his neck until she gripped his shoulder. Then she stepped into the pants and allowed him to pull them up her body and fasten the waist.

They fit her well with only an inch or two to spare at the waist. Her hips were slimmer but they hadn't always been.

There'd been a time her curves were lusher and she was more rounded. Living on the streets made a person lean and efficient.

A sudden thought occurred to her. It was quick and painful and cut her to the core. How long would they want her to stay with them? A day? A week? How much harder would it be to go back to the life she'd forged for herself after having a few days in the sun?

Michael caught her gaze and must have seen the bleakness she felt. He crossed the room, his lips drawn. Seth had barely stepped back when suddenly Michael was there, so close she could feel the vibrations from his body. She could smell him. His warmth enveloped her and drew her closer.

He smoothed his hand over her hair, his fingers trailing through the strands and then resting at her nape. "What are you thinking?"

It didn't occur to her to be anything but honest. "I was imagining how hard it will be to go back to my life after you..." She couldn't bring herself to say anything more. Sometimes the truth was more painful for being spoken.

Michael cursed low and hard, and then he cupped her jaw in his palm and tilted her head up as his lips came down over hers. It was a shock to her senses. A jolt that rocked her spine and sent tingling awareness in waves over her body.

It wasn't as sweet and gentle as Seth's kiss. The aching awareness she felt with Seth was more like a bomb burst as Michael fed on her lips.

Oh God, what must Seth be thinking?

She pushed at Michael with her good hand, and he stepped back immediately. Her breaths coming in ragged bursts, she wavered and stepped to the side, distancing herself from Michael as she sought out Seth's reaction.

He was there. By her side, his arm slipping around her waist in support. His lips pressed to the top of her head in a gesture of comfort—and reassurance?

She looked up, searching his gaze for any sign that he was angry, but she saw something else entirely. She saw concern for her. And something that looked remarkably like acceptance.

Michael caught her hand and rubbed his thumb over the tops of her knuckles. "This is going to sound crazy to you, Lily, but we don't want you to leave. We aren't going to keep you a few days and then toss you out. I don't expect you to believe it—yet—but I don't want you to worry."

Seth squeezed her against him and murmured low in her ear, "We want you to stay, honey. Trust in that if nothing else."

She took a deep breath and prepared herself to take the plunge. She was a little lightheaded, and at the same time a surge of...anticipation licked through her veins. For the first time in so very long, she felt alive—like she had something to live for.

There was a word for it, an emotion so alien to her that it took a moment to grasp. There, shining like a beacon at the end of a very long, very dark tunnel was...hope.

Chapter Eight

Lily dozed most of the way to Clyde. Michael had arranged a few pillows in the backseat of his Jeep and covered her in a blanket so she'd be comfortable. Seth followed in his truck.

The trip took an hour longer due to the weather and the fact that Michael didn't want to jostle Lily once they got off the interstate and onto the county roads.

By the time he pulled up to his cabin, it was already dark. Lily stirred and raised her head, the blanket sliding from her shoulders to her waist.

The rear door opened and Seth stuck his head in. "You okay, honey?"

Lily nodded, but Michael could see the wariness in her eyes. He got out and waited as Seth helped Lily from the backseat. After wrapping the blanket tightly around her, Seth hurried her toward the door, but she stopped and turned her face upward to catch the fluffy snowflakes that spiraled downward.

She closed her eyes when one stuck to her lashes, and then her entire face lit up with her smile. Michael was enchanted. He stared dumbstruck at how beautiful she looked bathed in soft moonlight as snowflakes danced around her.

Then she opened her eyes and started forward again at Seth's urging. When she reached the porch, she paused again, her gaze sweeping over the entrance.

"This is yours?" she asked Michael.

He was discomfited by her scrutiny. It irritated him that he was suddenly self-conscious about a home he was intensely proud of. It was nestled at the base of the mountain his parents lived on, purposely rural and surrounded by huge ponderosa pines. It was just minutes to town but far enough away to afford him the privacy he craved and the isolation he thrived on. But now he worried it would be off-putting to Lily. What if she didn't want to stay?

"Yeah," he said. "It's mine."

Her smiled was brilliant. "I like it. It's exactly like something I would have chosen."

The yearning in her voice made him ache. The approval relieved him.

"I'm glad you like it," he said huskily.

"It's cold. We need to get you inside," Seth said to Lily. They trekked into the house, and Michael turned up the heater. He kept the house pretty chilly when it was just him, but he didn't want Lily freezing to death.

As Lily looked around the living room, it occurred to Michael that she hadn't eaten a damn thing today. Hell, neither had he, but it was likely Lily had missed a hell of a lot more meals than he had.

"I have leftover chili in the fridge. You guys interested?"

Seth rubbed his stomach and grimaced. "Yeah, I'm starving."

Lily frowned a moment as if it hadn't occurred to her that she'd missed any meals. It bothered Michael immensely that it was normal in her world.

"Yeah, I'm hungry too. Chili sounds wonderful. Did you make it yourself?"

Michael nodded.

She smiled. "You and Seth both cook? Your mother must be so proud that you picked up the skills."

Laughter rumbled out of Michael's chest and Seth hooted as well. Lily looked at them in confusion.

"Sorry," Michael said. "Our mother can't cook to save her life. Our fathers would hurt themselves laughing at the idea we learned to cook from her."

"Oh, so they do the cooking?"

Seth nodded.

"That's cool," Lily said. "They don't mind?"

Michael smiled. "Not at all. For the most part our mother doesn't have to lift a finger. She's hopelessly spoiled and that's the way our fathers like it."

"They love her a lot," Lily said in a wistful tone.

"Yeah, they do," Seth replied.

"Have a seat and get comfortable," Michael urged. "Seth can start a fire and we'll eat in the living room. Then I'm going to check your arm. I want to keep a close watch on it to make sure infection doesn't set in."

"Anything to keep me out of the hospital," Lily said lightly.

She had lost some of the cautious reserve around them. Michael was encouraged by her ability to joke with them and indulge in casual conversation. He and Seth exchanged glances, and Seth's expression reflected the same satisfaction.

"If at any time Michael thinks you need a real doctor, you're going," Seth said.

"Real doctor?" Michael asked in mock disbelief. "You wound me, brother. I spent as many years in medical school, thank you very much."

"Vets are real doctors," Lily defended.

Her vehemence made Michael grin. She'd seemingly come alive, color flooding her cheeks and a spark of emotion in her eyes.

"I just don't want you to get sick," Seth said gruffly.

She smiled at him and then lifted her arm and poked cautiously at it. "It doesn't hurt much. I mean, I would have imagined something as dramatic-sounding as a bullet wound would have me on the floor with pain."

Seth rotated his arm and rubbed absently at his arm at her words.

"Seth would know," Michael said. "He was down for a while after he was shot."

Lily whirled around, her eyes wide. "You were shot? When did this happen? Are you okay now?"

Seth seemed surprised by her reaction but Michael was already figuring out she was loyal and protective.

"I'm fine," Seth assured. "I'll be back at work soon."

Her eyes became troubled. "You're a cop. I remember. Should you be going back so soon?"

He grinned. "Yeah. Unless I want to be unemployed."

"Where were you shot?"

He touched his shoulder and Lily's gaze followed his hand. "Was it bad?"

"Bad enough," Seth replied.

Reluctantly, Michael left the two of them to go into the kitchen to warm up the chili. When he returned a few minutes later to set up the TV trays, a fire crackled in the hearth and Lily was sitting comfortably on the couch, Seth on the other end.

It all looked utterly domestic. Bizarrely domestic. Not that he wasn't used to seeing such a scene in his parents' home, but in his cabin? Despite the family he'd grown up in, he'd never expected to have the same kind of relationship his parents did. If asked, he'd have laughed. To him, his parents were unique.

Now it looked very much like he was heading down the same road. Now he understood why his fathers hadn't been able to walk away from his mom, because he sure as hell couldn't walk away from Lily.

He set up the trays and returned to the kitchen to check on the pot of chili he'd left warming. After a quick stir, he dished up three bowls and took them back into the living room.

The three sat together eating with an ease that surprised him given the complexity of the situation. There was still so much they didn't know about Lily. He was content, however, to field her questions about his practice, Clyde and whatever else struck her fancy. He and Seth took turns answering her inquiries, but Michael noticed how careful she was not to divulge any information about herself.

By the time Michael was finished eating, Lily was listing to the side, her eyes nearly closed. Seth reached over and gently pried the spoon from her grasp and set it on her TV tray.

"Is your spare room still made up?" Seth asked Michael in low tones.

Michael nodded.

"I'll take the couch and Lily can have the guest bed."

Lily stirred and turned unfocused eyes on the two men. "No, you should take the bed, Seth. The couch is fine for me."

Seth rubbed his knuckle down her cheekbone and shook his head. "Not an option, honey. Don't bother trying to argue, because I'll win."

She cocked her head to the side. "Do you always get what you want?"

"No, but I'm sure as hell hoping I get what I want right now."

She didn't ask what it was he wanted. Neither did Michael, because he knew his brother wanted the same thing he did.

Lily.

Chapter Nine

Nervousness fluttered in Lily's chest as Seth drove the winding road toward town. Michael had made good on his desire to fashion a sling, though she'd tried hard to convince him it wasn't necessary.

Her arm was now secured to her side and dressed in a fresh bandage thanks to Michael's careful attention.

After breakfast, Seth had asked her to go into town with him. Startled, she hadn't known how to respond. Indulging in normal activities seemed so...normal. Domestic.

When they pulled into the small town of Clyde, she looked around curiously at the buildings, small shops and rustic charm. Seth parked in front of a corner pub that encompassed a third of the block. She glanced up at the sign over the entrance to see the words *Mountain Pass* in neon blue.

She glanced to the side to see the parking lot empty and then saw a closed sign against the glass of the front door. She cast a questioning look at Seth as he cut the engine.

"We'll just be a minute. There's someone here I need to talk to," he said. "Then we're going to buy you some clothes."

Heat suffused her cheeks, but before she could argue, he got out and walked around to her side. He took her free hand and helped her from the truck and then took her inside the pub.

The floor was littered with stray peanut hulls and the smell of cedar, and the lingering scent of cooked food hovered in the air.

"Callie?" Seth called.

Silence greeted him. He led Lily over to the bar and helped her onto one of the stools.

"I'll be right back. Just make yourself comfortable. Callie must be in the back."

Lily tucked her feet under the rung of the stool and rested her free arm on the scarred wood. Seth rubbed his hand over her shoulder.

"I won't be a minute."

Lily made a shooing motion. "I'll be fine. Go talk to your sister."

He leaned over and kissed her temple, his lips lingering for a minute before he backed away and walked around the counter to the door on the other side.

Michael pulled up to his parents' cabin and glanced over to see whose trucks were in the drive. The dads were either gone or out on the land because only his mom's SUV was there.

He got out and walked to the door, not bothering to knock. It irritated his mom when her sons acted like guests.

"Mom?"

He closed the door behind him as he stepped into the living room.

"Michael?"

Holly Colter hurried around the corner, her smile warm and welcoming.

He met her halfway and let her lean up on tiptoe to hug the daylights out of him. He grinned when she squeezed extra hard and then patted his cheek as she pulled away.

"Where have you been? Adam dropped by to see you yesterday but couldn't find you anywhere, and you weren't answering your cell phone."

"I went down to see Seth."

At that, his mom's eyes widened, and she latched on with both hands. "How is he? Is he doing okay?"

Michael smiled. "He came back with me."

"What? Where is he? Why isn't he here now?" she demanded.

He held up his hands. His mom could be ferocious when her chicks were involved. "He's in town checking on Callie."

"Oh." His mom's face fell and worry creased her brow. "It's good that he's talking to her. Maybe she'll tell him what's wrong."

Michael didn't tell her about Lily. He wasn't sure what he'd say anyway. He needed to talk to the dads.

"Are the dads here?"

"Ethan and Adam are down in Callie's Meadow, and Ryan is out in the barn with the horses."

Michael leaned forward to kiss his mom's cheek. "Okay, thanks. I'll head out. I need to talk to him."

"Michael?" she called, halting his progress as he made his way toward the kitchen.

He turned to look at her.

"Is everything okay? With you I mean?"

He smiled. "Yeah, Mom. Fine. I'll come find you before I leave."

"And bring your brother out for dinner tonight," she ordered.

"Yes, ma'am."

Michael went out the back door and took the familiar worn path to the barn. Ryan was inside talking in low tones to one of the horses who was nuzzling affectionately at his chest.

"Hey, Dad, you got a minute?"

Ryan looked up and dropped his hand from the horse's neck. "Michael, where the hell have you been? You had your mother all worried, and Lord knows she's worried enough about her other kids."

Michael chuckled. "Have I ever been any trouble?"

Ryan snorted. "You and Dillon. It's a wonder I survived your childhood. You tortured poor Seth endlessly and made us all crazy in the process."

He walked toward Michael and put his arm over Michael's shoulders. "What's up, son?"

Michael allowed Ryan to walk him outside into the bright sunshine. As nasty as it had been the day before, spring had won the battle once again, and it was marginally warmer.

They walked to the far edge of the fenced section that overlooked the drop-off to Callie's Meadow. Ryan leaned on the newly replaced wooden fence and glanced sideways at Michael.

He didn't say anything, but then Ryan had never been particularly verbose. He simply waited for Michael to say what was on his mind.

"I've met a woman," Michael said, surprised by how nervous he was having this conversation with his dad. Thirty years old and he still felt like a teenager crushing on his classmate.

Ryan lifted one eyebrow in Michael's direction. "You say this like it's a bad thing."

Michael ran a hand through his hair and blew out his breath. "It's complicated."

Ryan chuckled. "Meeting a woman is always complicated. So, tell me about her. How in the world did you manage to meet a woman when you spend more time with your animals than you do people?"

Michael shoved his hands into his pockets and rocked back on his heels. "I met her when I went down to Seth's yesterday."

At that Ryan frowned. "What were you doing down there? Is anything wrong?"

"No. I wanted to talk to him about Callie. Talk him into coming up so maybe he could find out what's going on with her."

"And did he?"

"Yeah, he's in town now."

"Your mom's worried about her." Ryan's eyes flickered, and he focused his gaze on the distant patch of land that was Callie's namesake. "I'm worried about her."

Ryan turned back to Michael. "So where did you meet this woman? She must have made a hell of a first impression if you only just met her and she's got you tied in knots."

"There's no easy way to ask this," Michael muttered. "I wanted to know about you and the dads. And Mom."

Ryan shot him an inquisitive look but didn't interrupt.

"I met Lily at Seth's."

He stared at Ryan, waiting for his dad to make the

connection.

Ryan's lips came together and understanding dawned. "Ah. Damn. I take it this woman is important to Seth."

"He just met her too," Michael said in frustration. "The day before I did. Christ, this is complicated, Dad. You have to know, none of us have ever batted an eye over the way we grew up. But none of us ever imagined that we'd go the same route. I mean, it sounds crazy. Two days ago I would have laughed in your face and said not only would it never happen, but it would never work. And then I met Lily, saw how Seth was with Lily, and I knew that neither of us is going to back down an inch."

"So you want to know what? If it works? If we threatened to kill each other in the beginning? What?"

"I want to know what kind of fucked-up gene you passed on to your kids," Michael grumbled.

Ryan threw back his head and laughed. He sighed and slapped Michael's shoulder then squeezed.

"It's not funny. What the hell am I supposed to do?"

"The question is less about what you're going to do and more about how Seth is handling this."

Michael sighed. "He isn't any happier about it than I am."

"Seems like you've got a problem then."

"Anyone ever tell you that you have a gift for understatement, Dad?"

Ryan chuckled. "Your mother might have accused me of not being overly helpful in the conversation department."

"Did you and the dads have...problems? When you met Mom, I mean."

Ryan shook his head. "We already knew, I mean before we met your mom, that we'd have the same wife. I can't speak for Ethan and Adam, but well, we just knew. I can't really explain it. It sounds pretty damn stupid now, but when we were much younger, we formed our business, lived together. It's the kind of situation we grew up in, so it just seemed inevitable. That and we didn't really form any strong interest in a woman, well beyond sex. Shit, I'm not having this conversation with my son," Ryan muttered.

Michael winced. "God no, I don't want to hear about your

sex lives before or after Mom."

"Look, I understand you didn't expect or even want this. But what you have to ask yourself is if this woman is worth it. If neither you nor Seth is going to budge then either she has a choice to make or you do."

"You make it seem so simple."

"It is. The decision is the easy part. Making it work is the hard part."

"I always remember you and the dads and Mom being so...in love. Did you have problems in the beginning?"

"Other than your stubborn mother deciding she needed to leave us in order to protect us?"

A scowl darkened Ryan's face. Michael smiled. Even after so many years, it was guaranteed to piss off the dads to talk about the past.

"We went into the situation with our eyes wide open. We knew what to expect. We also knew that we had to do more work than even your mother because while we only one had spouse to please, she had three very distinct personalities to contend with, and we didn't want to overwhelm her. It required some patience, some tongue-biting, but most of all it required compromise on all our parts. We all wanted time with your mom even with our unusual arrangement so each of us had to be sensitive to that and not be an asshole when one of the others wanted time with your mom away from the rest."

"You knew she was the one. I mean, the moment you saw her."

"Yeah. Kind of a cross between an 'I'm fucked' and a being struck by lightning sort of thing."

Michael's lips twisted into a rueful smile. "Yeah, that about describes it."

"So when do we get to meet this woman?" Ryan asked casually.

"It's complicated."

"So you've said. Anything I should know about?"

"She's homeless."

Ryan's face darkened. "What?"

"She's homeless. Seth served her in the soup kitchen where

he volunteers. He about lost his mind over the idea of her being on the streets. Took her home with him and then I showed up the next morning. She disappeared. We went looking for her, and she took a bullet in some drug dealer war downtown."

"Well, hell," Ryan muttered. "So you two don't know anything about this woman."

"About as much as you knew about Mom when you pulled her out of the snow," Michael said pointedly.

Ryan held up his hands. "Point taken. I just think you should be careful."

"That's all well and fine to say, but I'm already all rolled up in this thing, Dad. It's crazy, but from the moment I looked at her, I recognized her. She's mine. I can't walk away."

"Not crazy," Ryan said. "I know exactly where you're coming from."

"I just hope to hell I know where I'm going," Michael muttered.

Seth poked his head into the small office to see Callie with her head bent over a stack of papers.

"Hey, kiddo."

Her head whipped up and joy lightened the deep shadows under her eyes.

"Seth!"

She leaped up and hurled herself across the room at him. He caught her and staggered back, laughing at her exuberance.

"What are you doing here? Are you okay? How is your shoulder?"

"Whoa, one question at a time. And I'll do the asking, missy."

She frowned and stepped back. "Who ratted me out?"

"Take your pick," Seth said. "They're all worried about you, Callie. What's going on? And what's with you coming through Denver without stopping by? I didn't even know you were home until one of the dads told me."

She sighed and ran a hand through her long, dark brown hair. "I'm fine. Really."

Seth pinned her with his stare.

"Seth, don't. Okay?"

"Don't lie to me, Callie. Not me. I know you better than that."

Pain flashed across her eyes, and panic snaked down his spine.

"What happened to you, baby?"

Tears glistened for the briefest of moments before she blinked, and the vulnerability was gone, replaced by a hard shell.

"I'll be all right. I just needed...I just needed to be home."

"I understand that, and I'm glad you're here. You know you can talk to me about anything."

She smiled. "I know. What about you? Are you home for a while?"

It was then he remembered Lily, sitting at the bar by herself. He glanced at his baby sister, and whatever she saw in his expression, she latched on with both hands.

"Tell me," she demanded.

"You hold out on me and then expect me to spill my guts?"

She rolled her eyes. "I'm down, Seth. Not out. I need to get over it before I can talk about it. Now what about you?"

He sighed, knowing Callie would find out in a few minutes anyway. Better to prepare her now.

"I've met someone," he began. "Her name is Lily."

"You say that like it's a bad thing. Mom will be over the moon. I can practically hear her breathing the word grandchild."

"Yeah, well there's a slight problem."

She raised an eyebrow. "Oh?"

"Yeah. Michael met her too."

For a moment her eyes were blank and then understanding flashed and her mouth rounded in surprise.

"Oh shit," she breathed.

Chapter Ten

Lily shifted on her stool and leaned forward on the bar, keeping the arm in the sling pointed away. It actually bothered her more today than it had right after she'd gotten shot. She should have asked for more ibuprofen before she and Seth had left Michael's cabin, but she'd been too nervous—and curious—about where he was taking her.

She'd picked up enough of Seth and Michael's conversation to know that Callie was their sister, that she'd recently returned from Europe and that the entire family was worried about her.

Michael and Seth were probably the best big brothers on the planet. Everything she'd seen of them only cemented her opinion that they were generous to a fault and extremely caring.

The door to the pub swung open, and she yanked her gaze in that direction, surprised when a tall, muscular man with tattooed arms, a backward baseball cap and an earring dangling from his ear sauntered inside.

She didn't know whether to be frightened or fascinated, but he hadn't seen her yet, so she shrank against the counter, content to watch him from a distance.

He was a big man. Lean-hipped but broad at the shoulders. His tight T-shirt showed off a solid wall of muscle for his chest and the short sleeves cut into his bulging arms.

Intricate tattoos snaked down both arms and wrapped around his wrists. Other than the earring, he wore no jewelry or adornment, and his hair, which she might have expected to be long, was barely visible beneath his cap.

He was...delicious. That was the word that popped into her

head before she could ponder the absurdity of the observation. Delicious and fascinating with vivid pale green eyes surrounded by lashes that would make a grown woman weep with envy.

Then he turned and saw her. Their gazes locked, and her lips parted in surprise—at what, she wasn't sure. She felt immediately anxious, though she didn't fear the man. Maybe she should, but Seth was within yelling distance.

The man cocked his head and studied her as intently as she studied him. Then he smiled, and she was mesmerized by the dimples on either side of his mouth. Perfect, straight white teeth gleamed and he winked at her.

"Hello, sweetness," he said as he walked over to the bar.

Then he caught sight of her sling and a ferocious frown locked into his brow.

"What the hell happened to you? Are you all right?"

She glanced down at her arm, having totally forgotten that it was hurt at all. "I was shot."

"Get out! Are you serious?"

He plopped onto a stool next to her, his big frame taking up so much more space than she did.

"What are you doing in here, anyway? Is there something I can do for you?"

"Not unless you have some ibuprofen," she said ruefully as she raised her arm for reference.

He frowned. "I sure as hell do. Let me get you something to take them with. How about some OJ?"

She blinked in confusion. "Do you work here or something?"

"Or something," he said as he walked around the counter. "Actually I own it. I used to think I ran it until my sister barged in and sort of took over. I'm currently indulging her."

Lily's eyes widened. "You must be Dillon," she blurted.

He stopped in midpour. "Yeah, that's me. How did you know? Are you a friend of Callie's?"

"I haven't met Callie."

He shoved the glass of orange juice across the counter and then shook several ibuprofens into his palm. "Here, take these so you feel better."

As she swallowed them down, he leaned forward on the counter until he was awfully close. He stared at her like he could see behind the layers and defensive walls straight to her heart.

She should look away but found herself mesmerized. He was just so darn cute.

"You have me at a disadvantage, sweetness. You know my name but I don't know yours."

She swallowed. "Lily."

"Very pretty," he murmured. "Now, Lily. Tell me what you're doing here? A gorgeous woman like you shouldn't be sitting alone in an empty pub. Someone should be taking care of you and that arm."

"I came with Seth. He's talking with Callie. I think."

Dillon frowned and then straightened, his palms resting flat down on the curve of the countertop. "Seth's here?"

She nodded.

"Why am I always the last to know these things?" Dillon asked in an exasperated tone. Then he rested his gaze back on her, stroking over her skin like a paintbrush dipped in fire.

"Are you Seth's? And if so, why the hell isn't he taking better care of you?"

She blushed to the roots of her hair, but she felt compelled to dispel his belief and also to defend Seth.

"I'm not anyone's. What an absurd way to put it. Like people are belongings. And Seth has taken very good care of me. I have so much to thank him for."

A gleam entered Dillon's eyes. It was carnal and predatory. She sucked in her breath and shifted back on her stool only to unbalance herself.

Dillon's hand shot out, and he grasped her uninjured arm to steady her. For a moment he held her across the counter, and then he eased away, his gaze never leaving her.

"So you aren't Seth's."

"I didn't say that either!"

She glared at him, her cheeks warm with exertion. He grinned back at her, melting her exasperation with the warmth in his gaze.

"Come on, Lily, give a guy something to work with here. Are you taken? Otherwise involved? You fascinate me. How did you get yourself shot? And if you aren't Seth's, did my brother lose his dick when he got himself shot?"

Her mouth popped open, and then she burst into laughter. She wiped at her eyes with the back of her hand and then laughed harder.

"You're a terrible flirt," she accused.

But even as she reproached him, the realization that she hadn't had this much fun in a very long time buzzed through her consciousness. And so did the guilt over the carefree way she'd laughed and enjoyed the small moment.

She looked down and then away, hating the helplessness that held her in its grip. She was tired of feeing like she'd never be happy again. When was enough...enough?

A firm hand gripped her chin and turned. Dillon had moved around the counter and now he stood a mere breath away, his body crowding into her space, filling it with heat.

"What's wrong?" he asked bluntly. "Are you hurting?"

"Just get Seth for me. I'm ready to leave."

"I'm not ready for you to go."

Her gaze swung upward, and she had the insane idea that he wanted to kiss her. Did all the Colter men go around kissing women they barely knew? The real question was why did she let them?

"Lily?"

"Yes?" she asked in a husky voice.

"I want to kiss you. I should warn you I tend to do things I want. I'm spoiled that way. So while I'm telling I want to kiss you, the thing is I'm going to."

"You are?"

She tried to back away but he palmed her nape and held her in place as his mouth hovered invitingly over hers.

"I am. Just remember. I warned you."

Before she could say anything else, his lips found hers. The kiss was as aggressive and electric as he was, but also as playful. He danced around the corners of her mouth, pulled her bottom lip between his teeth and nipped before soothing the soft skin with his tongue.

"You taste every bit as sweet as you look," he murmured into her mouth. "Kiss me back, Lily. Taste me. Show me I'm not the only one going crazy here."

"This *is* crazy," she whispered. "Dillon, we can't. I just met you. You don't know me. I'm here with your brother...and Michael."

Dillon frowned. "Michael? What's Michael got to do with this?"

"He kissed me too," she muttered, hoping Dillon would be put off by that information. Instead he leaned back and took a seat on the stool next to her, intrigue flashing in his eyes.

"You kissed Michael, but not Seth, who is apparently taking care of you?"

She flushed until her entire face burned with embarrassment. "Seth kissed me."

"I'm hearing a lot of they kissed me but nothing about you kissing them."

"This conversation is ridiculous," she protested. "They kissed me. I kissed them. It's all crazy. They wanted to take me here." She gestured out the window toward the town as she spoke. "We stayed at Michael's last night. They say crazy stuff like they want me to stay, but we only just met. I shouldn't have let either of them kiss me, and I damn sure shouldn't have kissed them."

"If they were feeling even half of the insanity I'm currently experiencing, there wasn't a damn thing you could have done to keep them from kissing you."

She sucked in her breath until the room swam around her in bouncy waves.

"Yeah, Lily, that means I'm going to kiss you again. And I hope to hell you kiss me back."

He placed both palms on her cheeks, sandwiching her face between his hands. Then he lowered his mouth and devoured hers. Hungry and so sensual that her pulse bounded out of control.

He lapped the inside of her lip with his tongue and then thrust inward, warm and sweet, stroking over her tongue and up to the roof of her mouth.

She swayed on the stool and reached out to grab on to his chest for support. It was like meeting with a brick wall. Her fingers dug into his muscles, and she found herself tracing the dips and caressing the bulges.

When he pulled away, he put both hands at her waist to hold her in place. His breaths came in ragged bursts, and his eyes had lightened to crystal green with shimmering sparks of awareness.

"You may not belong to Seth, but you're sure as hell going to belong to me, sweetheart. From now on, I'm going to be the only man kissing you and damn sure the only one you'll be kissing back."

She slid off the stool and took a step back, prepared to either go find Seth or just go outside. Anywhere but here with this gorgeous, playful man who made her want to do crazy things like laugh. And kiss him back until he begged for air.

She'd been too long without a man. It was the only explanation for her reaction to the Colter brothers. Or maybe she'd react this way to any group of men who suddenly showered her with warmth, affection and...passion.

"Drink the rest of your OJ," Dillon said gently. "I didn't mean to frighten you away. I want you to stay. Make yourself comfortable."

"I'm going to take a stab at this one," a woman said from across the bar.

Lily yanked her head up to see Seth standing next to a petite brunette with flashing blue eyes.

"Judging by the look on my bonehead brother's face, I'd say you no longer just have Michael to worry about when it comes to your woman."

Crimson enveloped Lily. She could literally see the red as it crawled across her face. She was beyond mortified. She put her palm down and pushed away from the counter, intent only on escaping the awkwardness of the scene.

Dillon wrapped his arm around her waist as she tried to maneuver by and gently brought her against him under the shelter of his arm.

"Callie, girl, you know I love you dearly, but you seriously have to work on that mouth of yours before it gets your ass into trouble."

His sister grinned at Dillon like she didn't really give a damn what he had to say.

"I see you've already met my younger brother, Lily," Seth said. "This is my sister, Callie. The baby of the Colter family."

Lily nodded in Callie's direction, unsure of whether the other woman really was kidding or if she was ready to tear a strip off Lily's hide.

Callie smiled though, and crossed the room to take Lily by her good hand. "It's so nice to meet you, Lily. Seth was just telling me about you. I'm glad you're here."

The throb in Callie's voice made Lily wonder just how much Seth had told his sister. Lily could hear the pity and it discomfited her.

"Thank you," she said because she couldn't think of anything else to say.

Still nestled in Dillon's firm grip, Lily tried to twist away, her gaze going to Seth's. But Seth didn't look annoyed or even jealous. He looked intensely focused on Dillon, studying his every movement down to his facial expressions.

Dillon tightened his grip on Lily, not allowing her to move away, all the while carrying on a conversation with his siblings that Lily had promptly tuned out the moment she tried to escape.

"We need to talk, Dillon," Seth said in a quiet voice.

Dillon's lip curled up belligerently. "Yeah, it seems so."

"And Michael. This involves Michael as well."

Callie wrinkled her nose and then proceeded to pry Lily away from Dillon's side. "I'm going to suggest that I take Lily out to the house. Mom will love having another chick to cluck over, and I can get the dads to cook us some lunch. That way, we won't be swimming in testosterone when you buttheads have your little talk."

"I think that's an excellent idea, Callie," Dillon said. "Have Adam look over her arm while you're there. I'm still dying to know how the hell she got herself shot, but I'm sure Seth will explain it all to me, won't you, Seth?"

Seth scowled. "Lily stays with me. She's not going anywhere."

"Oh come on, Seth. Do you really want her present when you three start bitching and moaning and having your pissing contest? I wouldn't blame her if she ran screaming all the way back to Denver."

"You'll take care of her, Callie. I'm charging you with her safety. Make sure she stays with you."

"She should have been staying with you." Dillon's eyes glittered as he stared Seth down. "Don't bitch at Callie when you left her here at the bar alone. She's hurt, and anyone could have walked in here."

Seth's eyes narrowed at the insult.

Callie cocked her head. "For God's sake, both of you. She's a grown woman. She doesn't need a babysitter."

"Do it for me and my peace of mind," Seth insisted. "Okay? I need to know she's all right and more importantly that she's not off on her own somewhere."

Dillon snorted again, and Seth shot him a murderous look that told him he wasn't going to take much more from his younger brother.

Callie shrugged "Well, okay. I'll try not to overexert myself wrestling down a tiny little thing with one arm tied to her waist. I mean, I'd hate to hurt myself."

"Sarcastic little wench," Dillon muttered. "Is it any wonder I love you so much?"

Callie reached for Lily's hand and squeezed reassuringly. "Come on. I'll drive you out to the house. I guarantee you won't want to be around for this. Things are about to get messy. Men talking about their feelings are never a pretty sight."

Lily stifled her laughter at Callie's irreverence, but she also had a very real concern over what would happen in her absence. She wasn't entirely certain what was going on, but she knew it involved her, and the last thing she wanted was trouble between the brothers because of her.

"I'll pick you up later, okay, honey?" Seth said.

Lily nodded but as she walked away, she looked to both men and felt the strangest flutter deep in her chest.

Chapter Eleven

The drive was quiet, and Lily was grateful that Callie wasn't one of these people who had to fill the silence with meaningless chit-chat or ask a hundred questions.

Callie's mini SUV took the switchbacks up the mountain with ease, though Lily was still nervous about the proximity to a sheer drop-off.

Still, the view was spectacular, and Lily couldn't help the deep sighs of appreciation as they climbed higher.

When they pulled up to the sprawling cabin, Lily gasped in delight.

"This is where your family lives?"

Callie smiled. "Breathtaking isn't it?"

"You're so lucky," Lily said wistfully. "This is a beautiful place. And so private."

Callie paused as she opened her door. Then she looked at Lily. "Um, has Seth told you about our family? About our fathers?"

Lily nodded. "He said you have three fathers."

Callie looked relieved. "Okay. I just didn't want you to walk into a situation and wonder what the heck was going on. Or that maybe you were being kidnapped into a cult."

Lily laughed and eased out her side of the car. She waited for Callie to lead the way, and as they neared the front door, nervous bubbles scuttled up and down her throat.

Callie opened the door. "Mom? Dad? Anybody home?"

She motioned Lily inside, and as Lily stepped into the living room she was reminded in a lot of ways of Michael's cabin. It exuded the same homey feel but on a larger scale. The furnishings were rich and masculine looking, but Lily could see touches of femininity in the curtains and the colorful pillows arranged on the couches. Pictures of the family hung on the walls and covered every available surface of the coffee table and end tables.

Over the fireplace was a large portrait of the entire family, and Lily got her first look at the "dads".

There in the middle of all the men were Callie and her mom. They all looked so happy, and the love reached out and wrapped Lily in its warm embrace.

This was a place that screamed home. Babies and children. Laughter and good times. The knot in Lily's throat grew until each breath was agony to draw in.

"Callie, you're home early. Didn't expect you in until late tonight."

Lily turned to see who she assumed was one of the dads a few feet away.

"Hey, Dad. I brought Lily home. Was hoping you'd fix us some lunch?"

Lily smiled at the wheedling tone in Callie's voice.

Callie turned to Lily then. "Lily, this is my dad, Ethan. Dad, this is Lily. She's a friend of...Seth's."

Ethan walked toward Lily with an outstretched hand. His eyes were warm and welcoming, and he wore a gentle smile.

"Hello, Lily. It's very nice to meet you." His gaze dropped down to her bound arm, and he frowned.

"Are the other dads around?" Callie asked. "I thought Adam could take a look at her arm. And where is Mom?"

Ethan chuckled. "I'll be happy to fix you ladies something to eat. Why don't you get comfortable? I'll holler at Adam and your mother. They're out with Ryan. I think they just came back from riding."

"I'll help you," Callie said in a rush. "Lily, you take a seat. I don't want you overdoing it."

Callie followed her dad into the kitchen, and as soon as they were out of earshot, Ethan gave her an amused look.

"Okay, what's up? You never offer to help with the cooking.

Are you sick?"

Callie made a face. "I needed to talk to you and the dads away from Lily. I don't know what's been said but I don't want her to feel awkward. I think my moron brothers are doing enough of that on their own."

Both looked up when the back door opened and her mom walked in followed by Adam and Ryan.

"Callie!" her mom exclaimed, and before Callie could respond, she was swept into her mother's arms and squeezed half to death.

"Dang, Mom, you just saw me a few hours ago," Callie complained.

"But I wasn't expecting to see you for several more," Holly said with a smile. "So it's a nice surprise."

Adam ruffled Callie's hair and dropped a kiss on top of her head. "Taking things easy today?"

"Hardly," Callie muttered. "Look, I need a favor. Can you take a look at a gunshot wound?"

Ryan and Adam both scowled, and before they could explode, Callie held her hands up. "Obviously not mine. Lily is here. In the living room. Seth wondered if you'd take a look and rebandage it. Michael patched her up when it happened."

Ryan's eyebrow went up. "Michael's Lily?"

Her dads exchanged looks while her mom glanced around in bewilderment.

"Well, I think she might be more Seth's," Callie said carefully. "But they're in town sorting it all out."

"Will someone tell me what on earth is going on? Who is Lily?" Holly demanded.

"Take me into the living room," Adam said. "I'd like to meet her. I'll take a look at her wound while I'm at it."

"She's pretty," Ethan offered. "And quiet. She seems awfully reserved."

"I'd like to meet her too," Ryan said with a frown.

"Only if you promise not to scare her to death," Callie said.

Ryan's eyebrows lifted. "What?"

"If you make her run off, Seth is going to kick my ass," Callie pointed out. "I'd rather keep peace in the family."

"Will someone tell me what is going on?" Holly all but yelled.

Ryan put his hand on Holly's shoulder, and she quieted. It always amazed Callie how much could be achieved by a simple touch. She'd love to say that her parents were cheesy and gross, but the fact was, the dads were so in love with her mom that every time Callie watched them together, she was gripped by longing so fierce she ached.

"Michael and Seth have both met a woman—the same woman," Ryan told his wife. "Lily."

Holly blinked for a moment as she looked between her husbands.

"I think you can add Dillon to that list," Callie said. "He met her in town a while ago and there is some freaky chemistry going between them."

"Well, shit," Adam breathed out. "This could get complicated."

Ryan shrugged. "Not any more complicated than it was for us in the beginning."

"You mean..." Holly broke off and ran a hand through her hair.

"Yeah, that's what we mean," Ryan replied.

"Oh dear," Holly said, worry darkening her eyes.

"Ryan said she's homeless," Ethan said quietly.

"She's different," Callie offered. "I don't know her story, but there's something about her. She's...sad."

"Come introduce us," Holly said, tugging at Callie's hand. "I want to meet the girl my boys are so interested in."

Callie thought herding the entire family into the living room would probably make Lily run right out the front door, but there wasn't much she could do about it now.

"Just be...easy," she cautioned. "Lily just seems so fragile."

"Gunshot wound will do that to you," Adam said dryly.

Callie shot her dad a look and then walked ahead of her parents into the living room. Lily was still sitting on the couch, perched on the edge like she'd flee at any moment. She glanced up when they all entered, and her eyes widened.

"Lily, I want you to meet the rest of the clan," Callie said in a cheerful tone. "This is my mom, Holly Colter, and these are my other two dads, Adam and Ryan."

Lily looked cautiously at the people standing next to Callie. Adam and Ryan both stared at her like they were trying to pry every single secret she'd ever held right out of her head. Holly, on the other hand, hurried over and immediately gathered Lily in her arms.

"Oh, you poor thing. Is your arm hurting?" She turned to the others. "Adam, come check her arm, and Ryan, you get her something for pain. She's trembling."

"She's probably terrified of you," Ryan drawled.

Holly frowned ferociously at him.

"I just took some ibuprofen," Lily said softly. "Dillon gave me some at the pub."

"Oh well, good, then. Are you still hurting?"

Holly sat down next to her and gestured for Adam to come over.

"I'm okay. Really. I don't want to be a bother."

Holly made a dismissive sound and hovered as Adam sank to one knee in front of Lily.

"What happened?" Adam asked softly.

"Wrong place at the wrong time," Lily said.

"Looks like Michael patched you up good. Do you mind if I check it out?"

Despite how fierce Adam looked, he was careful to treat her gently, almost as if he were afraid of scaring her to death. She relaxed and nodded and watched Ryan out of the corner of her eye.

He also watched her. She could feel the questions being hurled at a dizzying rate. They were curious about her but so far had bitten their tongues.

Adam unwrapped the sling and then the gauze around her arm. The bandage stuck with the dried blood, and he carefully pried it away. She winced when it came free and resisted the urge to rub the ache.

"Sorry," Adam murmured.

"How does it look?" she asked anxiously. "Michael said if it got infected he'd make me go to the hospital."

Adam chuckled. "Looks like she shares your view of hospitals, Ryan. And it looks good. A little red around the wound but otherwise it looks really clean. I'll put some antibiotic ointment on it and bandage you back up."

Her shoulders slumped in relief. "Thank you. You're very kind."

Ethan ambled into the living room, hands shoved into his pockets. "Lunch is ready. Hope BLTs are okay."

"Extra bacon?" Lily asked hopefully. Then she flushed because she sounded ungrateful.

Ethan grinned. "I did happen to make some extra. Won't be any trouble at all to slap a few more pieces on your sandwich."

Lily smiled then, and the others watched in fascination as the young woman in front of them transformed from merely pretty to absolutely stunning.

Chapter Twelve

"So, what's going on with you and Lily?" Dillon asked.

Seth leaned against the counter and eyeballed his younger brother. This was a hell of a note. "Michael will be here any minute now. Let's just wait on him so there's no rehash."

"Tell me about *her*, then."

Seth saw the tension in Dillon, how he curled his fingers and flexed them in and out at his sides. Dillon...Dillon was usually laid back and had a complete I-don't-give-a-fuck attitude about life in general. Seth had never known him to get his underwear in a knot over a woman.

Until now.

"She's in trouble," Seth began.

"What kind of trouble?" Dillon demanded.

"I'm not entirely certain."

"Someone after her?"

Dillon's expression had grown stormy, and he looked for the world like he wanted to kick someone's ass.

"No. I don't think so, anyway. Hell, I don't know."

"What do you know, then?" Dillon asked impatiently.

"I served her in a soup kitchen two days ago. She's homeless."

Dillon's scowl grew darker. The muscles in his arms rippled and his jaw tightened. "She's what?"

"She was living on the streets. I talked her into going home with me. Michael arrived the next morning. I don't know if he spooked her or what, but she took off. Michael found her in an alleyway, and when he got her back to my house, he discovered she'd been shot during a turf war downtown. We brought her here. It was Michael's idea. He said everyone was worried about Callie, and well, I wanted Lily somewhere I didn't have to worry about her running off into the city."

The front door jangled and Michael stepped inside. He looked at his two brothers and his lips twisted as if he knew all too well what had happened. Hell, he'd probably been expecting it.

"I take it he met Lily," Michael said.

"Yeah, I met her. I want her," Dillon said bluntly. But then leave it to Dillon to be a caveman when it came to such matters. To him everything was black and white. No in-between. And when he wanted something, he never took no for an answer.

"Yeah, well, there's a problem with that," Michael said, surprising Seth.

"She said you both kissed her," Dillon said casually.

Seth looked sharply at him. "Why were you discussing us kissing her?"

"Because I kissed her too. I think she was warning me off," he said with a shrug that clearly said it didn't matter to him whether she was warning him off or not.

"Don't be an asshole, Dillon," Michael admonished. "Even you can't be this dense. Think about it. All three of us meet her and have this baffling, insane reaction to her?"

Dillon gripped the back of his neck and stared Michael down like he was a bug he was about to crush. "You aren't convincing me that the three of us are destined to have the same sort of relationship with Lily that our dads have with Mom. That's crazy."

Even though Seth found it pretty crazy himself, he felt compelled to speak up. "Why is it so crazy? I mean obviously it's happened in the past."

Dillon shook his head. "You've lost your fucking mind. Think about what you're saying. Since when have we ever planned on something like this? I mean yeah, I thought about it like when I was twelve and wondered if we were headed down the same road as the dads, but then I grew up."

"Look, I didn't plan on this either," Michael snarled. "But I'll be damned if I stand by and allow you or Seth to walk away with Lily. If you want to walk, fine, say the word."

"Christ," Seth muttered. "We're taking a lot for granted here. We're sitting around deciding Lily's fate and not one of us has asked her what she wants. We know nothing about her past."

"I don't recall the dads asking a lot of dumb, sensitive questions when Mom hit their radar," Dillon growled.

"Thought you weren't considering a relationship like they had," Michael snapped.

"I'm saying their method worked just fine."

Seth stared hard at Dillon. "Yeah, well, they're lucky Mom didn't kick them in the balls. The caveman act might work for you, but it's not what I'm doing with Lily."

"You two are actually considering sharing this woman?" Dillon asked incredulously.

Seth's breath caught. It had been hinted at. He and Michael had danced around the subject, but here it was in black and white.

"Let me ask you this," Michael said. "If we make her choose. If she even did choose one of us, are the other two ever going to be content to watch their brother have a life with her? This isn't some passing attraction—at least not for me. What is it going to do to our family for her to be with one of us or none of us? Can either of you really walk away?"

Seth pressed his lips together and ran a hand through his hair. Then he looked up at Dillon.

"This is crazy," Dillon muttered. "People don't fall in love at first sight. And definitely not with the same woman."

"Tell that to the dads," Michael said. "Tell that to yourself."

"You want me to decide. Right here and now. I've spent ten minutes with her, and you want me to commit to sharing her with my brothers?" Dillon asked incredulously.

"No," Seth said shortly. "But if we don't handle this right, there won't be a decision to make. She's already run once. I don't want her out there alone. Cold and scared. Hell, she could have died."

Michael nodded.

"Jesus," Dillon bit out.

"I'm going out to the house," Seth said. "You two do what you want."

He walked past his brothers and out the door, never looking back.

Thirty minutes later, Seth pulled into the drive of his parents' home. Anticipation quickened his steps as he headed toward the front door. It had been too long since he'd been home. This was where he was most comfortable.

Before he could open the door, it swung open and his mom flung herself at him, wrapping him in her embrace. He braced himself and chuckled.

"For such a small woman, you pack a wallop, Mom."

"I've missed you," she said fiercely. "You waited entirely too long to come home."

He winced at her admonishment. "Yeah, I know. But I'm here now."

She smiled and patted his cheek. "Yes, you are. Come in. Your fathers will be thrilled to see you."

She tucked her arm through his and herded him inside. His dads were sprawled in the living room, and the television was on. Adam punched the mute button on the remote and tossed it aside while Ethan and Ryan both stood.

"It's about damn time," Ryan said as he walked toward Seth, his arms outstretched.

Ryan hugged him and then scrubbed his hand over Seth's head. "How are you, son? How's the shoulder?"

"Good. I'm good. Should be back on the job soon."

Ethan enfolded him next and caught him in a headlock. Seth laughed and allowed himself to be led over to the couch. Adam stood and locked arms with Seth before yanking him into a hug.

"Damn good to have you home," Adam said gruffly.

Seth pulled back and frowned as he stared around the room. "Where's Lily?" he demanded.

"Callie took her riding," Adam said.

Seth's mouth fell open. "Have you lost your minds? You let Lily go riding? Hell, she's been shot!"

"Calm down," Ryan said. "Callie's not stupid. She put her on a good ride. Adam tended her arm."

Seth grabbed the back of his neck and shook his head. "You all are crazy. Would you have let Mom on a horse right after she was shot?"

Ethan scowled. "Of course not."

Holly rolled her eyes.

"Then is there any reason you let Lily go riding?"

"Relax," Adam said. "I lifted her onto the horse. She's got the gentlest mount we own, the one we reserve for kids when they come with their parents hunting. She can totally hold the reins one-handed and Callie's horse will lead. They're just going down to the meadow and back. Lily was so damn excited about the prospect of riding, I couldn't tell her no."

Seth sighed. "How did she take the family? Was she overwhelmed?"

Ethan chuckled. "A little nervous maybe, but not overwhelmed." He paused for a moment and then looked up at Seth. "I like her, son. Ryan told us about her situation."

"Yeah, it sucks. I don't want her out there. I want her with me."

Adam raised an eyebrow. "As does Michael, apparently."

"And Dillon," Seth murmured. "It's so crazy I can't even wrap my brain around it. I left Dillon and Michael in town because we were getting nowhere. I get so pissed off at them because they only just met her, so how the hell can they be so convinced? But then I have to remind myself that I only met her two days ago."

His mom looked at him with worry in her eyes. "She means a lot to you already."

"Yeah, she does." He moved toward his mom and then sank onto the couch in front of her. "Tell me something, Mom. We've all heard the dads' version over the years. We know they knew you were the one and that they took over, took charge, all that not very politically correct stuff men aren't supposed to do. Did it scare you? Did you ever think about walking away? I'm scared to death of pushing Lily too hard, and yet I can't let her just go back to her life without showing her what her life could be like with me—us."

She sat beside him and wrapped her arm around his waist. "I don't know that I was frightened. I never got the idea that your fathers would ever hurt me. Quite the opposite. I felt very safe with them. They made sure I felt safe. I was nervous and confused, though. I didn't understand what they wanted from me, and when I did, I didn't know how it could possibly work."

"So how did you get through all that?"

"It came down to trust. And they simply asked me to give them and us a chance. It sounds so basic, but when put like that, what else could I say but yes? They weren't making demands of me. They weren't forcing me to make decisions I didn't want to. They just wanted to take care of me and for me to give our relationship a chance. And so I did."

"You do make it sound simple, like I've completely over-thought every aspect of this," Seth said ruefully. "Maybe that's all anyone can do is ask for a chance."

"I just want you to be happy," his mom said in her gentle, sweet voice. "I want all my children to be happy, no matter how it has to happen. I don't doubt for a moment that the three of you could make Lily happy. But I want you to make sure *you'll* be happy with this kind of arrangement."

He leaned over and kissed her cheek. "I love you, Mom. And thanks. It helps to get your point of view."

"Where are your brothers now?" Adam asked.

"Probably right behind me. Michael's pissed. Dillon isn't much better. Dinner ought to be interesting tonight."

His mom rolled her eyes. "Like the three of you bickering and carrying on at the dinner table is anything new?"

"I was your good child," Seth reminded her. "Michael and Dillon were the demon spawn."

"We can't even argue that point," Ryan said wearily. "Those two. I hope to hell Lily knows what she's getting into."

"How long have they been out riding?" Seth asked. He tried not to be anxious, but he was eager to see her again and see for himself that she was all right.

"Walk with me out to the barn and we'll wait on them," Adam said. "I need to talk to you anyway."

Seth followed his dad out to the back, and they leaned on the fence so they could see the path the girls would take back up from the meadow.

"Have you given any more thought to taking over Lacey's term as sheriff?"

"Hell," Seth muttered. "I haven't thought about it at all. This thing with Lily happened so fast. I mean one day I was looking forward to next week, getting my psych evaluation done with and getting back to the job. The next thing I know, I'm bowled over by a woman who's in the worst sort of circumstances, and worse, I don't know anything about her. And yet, she's mine. And if that's not crazy, I don't know what is. So no, I haven't given any thought to Lacey's job."

"Well, it seems to me it might be a godsend and fell into your lap at just the right time."

Seth's brow furrowed as he stared back at his dad.

"Think about it. Dillon and Michael are here. They both have businesses here. You're three hours away in Denver. How the hell is that going to work if you're all trying to work things out with Lily?

"I know enough about your brothers to know they're tenacious as hell. No way they'll let Lily go back with you. They'll want her here with them. Your only choice might be to compromise."

Seth swore long and hard under his breath. "You're right. I mean, I know you're right. But sheriff? That's always been Lacey's job. I can't even imagine her not there. She's well liked and respected here. She's got tough shoes to fill."

"If anyone can, it would be you. The folks around here would need a familiar, friendly face. They get nervous when outsiders come in and take over the job of protecting their interests. You lived here all your life. You grew up with these people. They trust you."

Seth settled his elbows on the wood railing and pondered his dad's suggestion. Leave his job on the force? Even after being shot, he hadn't considered leaving, even for a moment. It seemed cowardly to quit at the first sign of adversity and come home to take a sheriff's job that for the most part never involved anything more serious than livestock disputes or the occasional disorderly conduct.

"Let me ask you something," Adam said. "What would make you happy? Staying in Denver in your current job, or coming home where your family lives, where you've lived all your life?"

Put that way, it was pretty much a no-brainer. This was home no matter the years he'd spent away. This was his life. His family. The people he loved. And now Lily. He didn't want her back in Denver. She could have a fresh start here. With him. With his brothers if she so chose.

"Think about it and go talk to Lacey tomorrow. She's going to be pissed when she finds out you were in town and didn't stop by to see her."

Seth grinned. "Yeah, but she'll forgive me."

"Here they come now," Adam said, gesturing toward the trail.

Callie appeared first, keeping her horse to a sedate pace while Lily bobbed into view a few moments later, a ridiculous smile plastered across her face.

It hit Seth right in the stomach, and for a minute he forgot to breathe.

"Now you know why I couldn't tell her no," Adam murmured. "She's beautiful, son. But skittish as a newborn colt. You're going to have to tread a very careful path with her."

Seth nodded. "I know, Dad. Believe me, I know."

Chapter Thirteen

When Lily and Callie hit the top of the trail that ended at the Colter barn, Lily saw both Adam and Seth standing by the fence waiting for them.

"Uh oh, you're busted," Callie muttered. "Seth looks like he swallowed a lemon."

As they approached, Seth's gaze found Lily, and his lips twisted into a slight frown. Her horse came to a halt behind Callie's and Callie slid easily from the saddle. Seth walked up and put his hands on Lily's waist.

"You ready?" he asked. "I don't want to hurt you."

She smiled and reached down for his shoulders as he gripped her hips. She landed in front of him, nearly swallowed by his much larger frame.

"Where the hell is your sling?" he demanded.

"I asked your dad to take it off," she said. "I didn't need it, and I wanted to be able to move my arm."

Seth cupped her shoulders and stared intently down at her. "Honey, you were shot. You need the sling and you need not to be out riding horses. You should be inside on the couch."

Her nose wrinkled and she squinted up at him. "It's a cut. If I'd hurt myself on a tree branch, or maybe a piece of glass, you wouldn't be freaking out over this minor a wound. But because it was a bullet, it's more dramatic. The end result is the same. I'm fine. I don't need a sling. It actually feels better when I can move it around."

"Michael's going to have a cow," Seth muttered.

She smiled. "No, he's not."

Seth framed her face in his palms, his thumbs brushing over her cheekbones. She had the crazy idea that he was going to kiss her, right here, right now, with his sister and father looking on.

She realized she didn't mind at all.

This time she kissed him back. His lips slid over hers, feather light, and then he came back, harder this time, his tongue probing at her mouth to open.

She sighed and allowed her lips to part. His taste flooded over her tongue just as his warmth seeped clear to her bones. He wrapped his arms around her and pulled her so close into his body that she felt absorbed by him.

One hand splayed over her back, holding her against him, while the other cupped the side of her neck and jaw as he tilted her head for better access.

Where before he'd given her soft kisses, almost teasing, or restrained even, now he possessed her mouth. There was no other word for it.

Chill bumps raced down her spine and back up again, spreading over her shoulders and down until her nipples tightened and pressed into his chest.

Desire was a thrill ride she hadn't been on in a long time. She'd forgotten the joy in a single kiss or touch, how her skin reacted to the gentle coaxing of a man. How her breasts swelled and tightened, and how much she liked to be touched there.

Or how much she simply loved to be kissed. And held. Some comforts were never forgotten no matter how long they were denied.

"You taste so damn sweet," Seth murmured against her lips. "I want you so much, Lily." He pulled away and then rested his forehead against hers. He ran the tip of his finger over the line of her jaw and let it linger over her lips.

Forgotten were his father and his sister, though when she glanced sideways she saw they'd already taken the horses into the barn, leaving her and Seth alone.

She raised her gaze to meet Seth's, her thoughts jumbled by the morning's events.

"Seth, Dillon kissed me earlier. I don't understand why. I

mean, he'd only just met me. But I also kissed him. I don't know what's going on. I'm confused by...all of this. But I thought you should know, that you had the right to know."

Seth pulled away, his eyes troubled. But she didn't see anger. Or jealousy.

"Come walk with me, Lily. There are a few things we need to talk about."

He put his arm around her and led her away from the barn down a stone path that led through a cluster of aspens. There was a bench in a small clearing, and he settled her onto it, but he remained standing, his body language tense and unsettled.

"You probably think we're all crazy," he said. "My family. My brothers. The way things are with my parents."

She shook her head. "Not crazy. Just different. It's obvious your fathers love your mother very much. It works for them."

"I want it to work for *us*," he said bluntly.

She stared back at him, sure she hadn't understood. He ran a hand through his hair and blew out his breath.

"Something happened when I met you, Lily. Something powerful I'm at a loss to explain. All I can say is that I knew you were meant to be mine. The problem is, the same thing happened with Michael and then Dillon."

She looked down, uncertain how to respond. What did anyone say in a situation like this?

"You felt it too, Lily. I watched you with my brothers. You responded to them like you responded to me."

"I don't know what to say," she murmured.

He knelt in front of her and took her hands in his. "I'm going to ask you for the same two things my fathers asked my mother when they met her. Your trust and a chance."

She met his gaze, her heart beating so hard, it made her lightheaded.

"There are things you don't know."

"And we'll get to them. In your time," he said softly. "I want you to be able to trust us, and more than that, I want a chance. Give us a chance to make it work."

The past still had her firmly in its grip, but what if this was her chance to change her future? She couldn't change what was done, but she *could not* spend the rest of her life paying for her mistakes over and over.

But what if when they knew the truth they no longer wanted her? It was natural that they'd want a family. They'd grown up in a large family. That was the one thing she couldn't give them. Could they accept that?

And then it sank in. She was sitting here calmly considering a relationship with three men. Three men she barely knew. There were so many unanswered questions her head hurt.

"I know you're overwhelmed," Seth said. "Hell, who wouldn't be? But this is where the trust and the chance come in, Lily. We have a lot to work out, and it won't be easy. But we can do it."

"Can we?"

He stroked the side of her head, the curls springing back after he flattened them.

"I'm falling in love with you, Lily. I feel stupid even saying it, but it doesn't alter the inevitable."

Her breath stuttered and hiccoughed until she thought she'd choke. Love? Even as she shook her head in mute denial, he was nodding, reaffirming his words.

His eyes were so serious. An intense blue that seemed to sear right into her soul.

How could he love her, or *think* he loved her?

"Oh God, Seth. You don't know. You just don't *know*."

"Then tell me," he said gently. "When you're ready, I'll listen, and we'll face it together."

"Something tells me that if I agreed to...try...that it would be taking the easy way out."

"Easy?" He laughed. "I don't expect any part of this to be easy. Easy would be walking away. Hard is going to be staying and making it work."

Walk away. Could she do it? It was what she'd done before and it hadn't been easy. But maybe it had been easier than facing her reality. She'd been a coward for too long. Maybe it was time to grow a backbone and start living again. Maybe it wouldn't be with these men, but how would she know if she didn't try?

She frowned then, because Michael and Dillon had said nothing to her of this.

"Are you speaking for Michael and Dillon?" she asked hesitantly.

Seth rocked back and then rose. "No. I'm speaking for me. I can't and won't make their decisions for them. I didn't pull this out of my ass if that's what you're asking. They're aware of the way I feel. Michael... He was the first to bring this up. I'll be honest, I fought it. I wanted you. I still want you. But it'll be up to them to speak their minds and up to you to accept or reject what we're offering."

"Oh."

He reached for her hand again and pulled her to her feet. "I've given you a lot to think about. I don't want to overload you. For right now, I only want you to promise me you'll stay. No more running. Let's see where this takes us. Okay?"

She took a deep breath and wrapped her fingers tightly around his. Anticipation and fear curled within her chest and fluttered around in her stomach like a crazy amusement park ride.

Then she met his gaze and saw the hope reflected. And the same mirroring fear. She let out her breath in a long exhale and said, "Okay."

Chapter Fourteen

Lily was a little dazed when she and Seth returned to the house. It hadn't settled in. Yes, she'd told him she'd try it. But how innocuous did that sound? It was as if she'd told him she'd try some new dish. But what she'd agreed to was a relationship—a *relationship*—with three men.

Nervous laughter bubbled and fizzed in her throat like a shaken-up soda. She was out of her mind. She had no business entering a relationship with one man, much less three. And while she had at least gathered some idea of Seth and Michael, she knew nothing of Dillon. She'd spent all of half an hour in his presence. He'd kissed the daylights out of her, but a kiss did not a relationship make.

She shook her head as she and Seth entered the kitchen through the back door. She hadn't agreed to a relationship. She'd agreed to give them a *chance*, and she'd agreed not to leave.

Most women in her position would leap at a chance to leave a life on the streets and allow a tender and caring man to shelter her.

She wasn't most women.

Seth's hand settled possessively on her hip as they walked through the kitchen and into the living room. To her surprise, Dillon stood by the fireplace, one leg kicked up and his shoe planted against the wall as he leaned back.

She was struck again by his presence. In a family of conservative-looking...cowboys—she was convinced they all looked like the typical western, mountain family—Dillon stuck out like a steel blade among plastic knives.

Thick, muscled arms with intricate tattoos. She was dying to study the patterns, to trace them with her fingers and see how far over his body they ran. Did they extend to his chest? His back?

He fascinated her. He exuded confidence and self-satisfaction, as if he was right where he wanted to be in life and couldn't care less if anyone else found him lacking.

She glanced around, searching for Michael, but didn't see him anywhere in the living room, though it was pretty crowded with the rest of the Colter family. They were all watching her, some more subtly than others, but she felt the weight of their stares as they measured the situation.

Tension spiked and held thick in the air. Seth's hand was a brand on her hip while Dillon's gaze burned her with its intensity.

She pulled away from Seth, putting a bit of distance between them. There was already so much focus on her, and the entire family seemed to be watching and holding their breath to see what would happen between Dillon and Seth.

Already she regretted her hastily given promise. This was a close-knit family, and she was a nobody. It was already uncomfortable, and she hadn't even exchanged more than a few words with Dillon. The last thing she wanted was to be a bone of contention.

Her throat narrowed and the air felt too hot squeezing through her windpipe. Her instinct was to flee, and she only fought the compulsion for the barest of seconds before she murmured a faint excuse and turned back toward the kitchen.

She'd said she needed something to drink, but she didn't even pause. She opened the back door and stepped into the crisp mountain air. Inhaling sharply, she savored the tang of pine and the cool relief as air flowed easily into her lungs.

When had she become such a mouse? This nervous, hesitant person was a stranger to her. She'd become someone she no longer recognized. A shell of the young woman who'd once held the world in her hands.

The truth of the matter was, she was angry. Angry at herself. The instant she'd walked into the living room and faced the Colter family, saw Dillon staring at her so intently and knowing of the conversation she'd just had with Seth, she'd immediately felt unworthy.

Unworthy.

And why?

"You deserve to be happy, Lily," she whispered. "Quit punishing yourself for past sins."

"Very sound advice."

She jerked her head around to see Dillon standing just behind her. She hadn't even heard him come out the door. Warily, she edged sideways, her gaze never leaving him.

His eyes darkened with regret, and he ran a hand through his short, spiky hair. "I didn't mean to frighten you, Lily."

She frowned slightly, unsure of how to take his apology.

He took a step forward. "At any time. Before in the bar, and now. I've made you uncomfortable and that's the last thing I ever want to do. Seth's ready to kick my ass, and the truth is, I deserve it."

"Seth said..."

"What did he say?"

"He said a lot of things. About him and you and Michael. About your family. About your...feelings...for me."

Dillon shoved his hands into his pockets and rocked back on his heels. Then a slight gleam entered his eyes, and he glanced back toward the house. "Want to go take a ride with me? On my bike?"

She blinked. "Your bike?"

"Yeah, I drive a Harley. Well, I have a truck too, but the bike is a hell of a lot more fun to ride when the weather's good."

She hesitated. This became more surreal by the minute. She expected at any moment to wake up from a dream. Everything seemed so random. Something different at every turn.

Embrace it, Lily. Live, for God's sake. Two days ago you were living alone in an alley with the knowledge that you'd always be alone. Now you don't have to be. Even if it's only for a little while, savor it.

"I want to spend some time with you, Lily. Just you and

me. No Seth. No Michael. Nothing to confuse the issue. I don't want to know what Seth said about me or my feelings. I don't care. What I care about is exploring this thing between you and me. Because my feelings—whatever they are—will be explained by me. Not my brother."

"And no one will mind if we just...disappear?"

He grinned—a cocky, self-assured grin—that did funny things to her insides. In that moment she caught a glimpse of the mischievous rebel that was part and parcel of his image.

"Do we need their permission?"

She smiled. "No, I suppose not. Although I don't want Seth to worry. He wasn't happy that I went riding with Callie with my arm."

Dillon's eyes darkened as his gaze swept down her shoulder and then he frowned. "Where is the sling?"

She rolled her eyes. "I took it off. I don't need it."

"I'll be careful with you. All you have to do is hug tight to me and keep your shoulder against my back."

The idea of being so intimately pressed to him sent a flutter of awareness through her veins. Her belly clenched and adrenaline spiked, sending a warm flush over her skin and deeper until she was aware of the slow thud of her pulse.

Dillon tilted his head in the direction of the house. "They're used to my craziness. They won't even blink. Seth might get uptight, but he's already had you to himself. If he's so keen for this to work, he's going to have to deal."

He held out his hand, and for a moment she stared at it, studying the long fingers and the roughness of his palm. Carefully she slid her hand over his, absorbing the sensation of the spark that leapt between them.

He curled his thumb over the top of her hand and rubbed up and down before tightening his fingers around hers.

"Come with me, Lily."

His voice lowered and there was sensual enticement in the simply stated plea.

"If you'll let Seth know where we're going," she said by way of agreement.

Again the cocky smile flashed and he tugged at her hand.

"All right then. Let's go face them together. Did the dads feed you?"

She nodded.

"Okay, then I'll feed you dinner later. I'm a pretty good cook and not just the bar food we serve up at the pub. I'll promise Seth to have you home at a decent hour."

He grinned as he said the last, and she smiled in return at the playfulness in his voice.

He guided her inside, barely touching her except for his grip on her hand, but the heat from his body hovered and invaded her until she leaned into his side, wanting that wonderful jolt of awareness all over again.

Conversation stopped when she and Dillon re-entered the living room, and once again there was open speculation on the faces of the Colters.

Seth's gaze dropped to her and Dillon's linked hands. His expression remained neutral, but his eyes told a different story. There was uncertainty there, and forgetting that Dillon was going to inform him that she was taking a ride with him, she dropped Dillon's hand and went straight to Seth.

She hovered close, wanting to touch him, wanting to go into his arms, but she didn't know how to handle situations like this. She wished the others weren't there because she felt like a performer in a bizarre scene. Like everyone was waiting to see the big reveal.

"Can you come outside?" she whispered to Seth. "With me and Dillon?" She looked back at Dillon as she spoke, worried that he would think she was asking for the very permission they'd joked about. It wasn't about permission. It was about respect, and in her own way she wanted to reassure Seth.

Seth nodded and touched her arm as he turned her in the direction of the front door.

"We'll see you guys later," Dillon announced as he followed Seth and Lily out. He stopped to ruffle Callie's hair. "Don't be late for work tonight, kiddo. And try not to hurt my customers."

There were murmured goodbyes, and Lily was already out the front door, but then she turned, not wanting the Colters to think her rude. She grasped the door frame and smiled at Seth and Dillon's parents.

"Thank you for your hospitality. You were very kind." Then she looked to Callie. "I enjoyed the ride very much. Thank you for taking me."

The Colters looked a little dazed, and who could blame them? Lily had burst into their well-ordered lives and turned things upside down in a matter of hours.

She bit her lip and prayed she hadn't made a decision that was going to hurt what was obviously a very close family relationship.

As if sensing her worry, Holly smiled and crossed the room to stand in front of Lily just moments before enfolding her gently in her embrace.

"You're very welcome, Lily. It was wonderful to meet you. You're welcome here anytime. I expect we'll be seeing more of you soon."

Her eyes twinkled as she pulled away, and Lily returned her smile.

Dillon stopped to plant a noisy smack on his mother's cheek before all but pushing Lily out the door.

"I'm taking Lily for a ride and we'll grab some dinner later," Dillon announced as they approached the parked vehicles out front.

Seth's only reaction was the slight twist of his lips, but he glanced at Lily. "Are you up for that? You shouldn't be running all over the damn place with your arm hurt."

There was an accusing note in his voice, almost as if he was criticizing Dillon for not taking better care with her.

She put her hand on Seth's chest and left it there as she stared up at him. "I'm okay, Seth. A ride sounded nice. And...well...if what you said is true, then I need..." She struggled to say the words, but she had to be as honest and upfront with them as they were with her, and if that meant expressing her needs, then she had to do it.

"I just met Dillon. There is an obvious attraction there, but I have to know. He has to know. We *all* have to know," she added for emphasis. "You asked for a chance, and I agreed to give you that chance, but we all have to make sure this is right."

Seth pulled her into his arms, a slight smile tugging at his lips. "Way to turn my words back on me. I just worry. I want you safe." He glanced sideways at his brother but there was no heat in his gaze. "Dillon's a maniac. I don't want him to get you killed."

Dillon smirked and rolled his eyes. "C'mon, big brother. Let her go. You were the one preaching time and patience and how we need to do this and that. Time to walk the talk."

Seth kissed her but relinquished her without further argument. "I'll meet you at Michael's later, okay?"

She nodded and smiled. Dillon looked over at her and then gestured toward his truck. "You ready?"

She took a deep breath and started toward Dillon's flashy red Dodge truck. She glanced back at Seth and their gazes connected for one last moment before she slid into the passenger seat of Dillon's vehicle.

Chapter Fifteen

Lily cast sideways glances at Dillon as they drove into town but never could figure out anything to say, so she remained silent.

She had that nervous, edgy feeling like people got on first dates, and she supposed for all practical purposes this was.

She kept expecting him to initiate conversation. She figured he had any number of questions about her. His brothers had to have filled him in on how they met her and the circumstances of her life. But he never said a word. She didn't know if she was grateful or if she was annoyed he wasn't more curious about her.

Then she had to stifle her laughter. No, she wasn't ready to divulge the reasons why she'd been homeless, and she should be grateful they seemed willing to wait. They didn't press, and maybe that's why she was willing to venture down this unconventional path with them.

She'd been reassured after meeting the Colter family. She'd been wildly curious and apprehensive, knowing the dynamics of their relationship beforehand. But they'd made it seem so normal. So acceptable. It was obvious that the older Colter men adored Holly and that they were at ease with their relationship.

Maybe she'd expected tension. Jealousy. Something overt to signal disquiet with the arrangement. Instead she'd walked into a very normal household and been surrounded by the feeling of warmth and love. And happiness. True contentment, and maybe that was the biggest draw of all for her.

She was ready to move forward. Put away the awful guilt

and grief that had been a daily battle for so long now. How much time had passed? She found that time had little meaning when the goal was just to survive another day on the streets.

But that wasn't her life. It hadn't been. It had been her choice to walk away even though at the time she hadn't felt or wanted to feel any alternative.

It seemed silly to her now, and she was a little shamed by her willingness to simply give up. Could anyone possibly understand the impetus for her actions?

Maybe it was time to close that chapter on her life and open the door to another. All she could do was try.

Dillon drove down the main street of Clyde, passed his pub and turned onto a paved road that climbed above the town. It turned to dirt and rock after a mile or so, and she looked curiously around as they rode higher.

"You live up here?" she asked.

He nodded. "It's not much, but it suits me."

They rounded the bend and the road dead-ended into a clearing. She caught her breath as she saw the gorgeous cabin. There was maybe an acre of cleared grassy area broken up by rocks, but the area beyond was densely forested, a mixture of aspens and pine.

"Not much? It's beautiful!"

He cast her a sideways smile. "Glad you like it. Want to have a look around before I pull the bike out?"

She nodded eagerly and opened her door. The first thing she became aware of was the silence. Only the occasional rustle of tree limbs from a gentle breeze disturbed the peace and tranquility that blanketed the area.

She inhaled deeply, enjoying the crisp pine-scented air. Not waiting for Dillon, she wandered forward, drawn to the cedar porch and the rocking chair that swayed gently every time a breeze blew through. As she got closer, she heard the light creaking noise the chair made. She paused at the steps and drank in the homey, rustic feel of the house, felt it wrap around her and draw her closer.

Dillon came to stand beside her and curled his arm around her waist. "This is it, home sweet home, or the bachelor pad as my mom calls it."

"It's awfully big to be a bachelor pad. I can't wait to see the inside."

He took her up the steps and opened the door then gestured for her to go ahead of him.

"You don't lock your door?" she asked.

He smiled. "No reason here. No one comes up unless they're here to visit. I'm the only person who lives on this road. I had to have the second half built for access."

She glanced around the living room and was taken by the richness of the woodwork and the large stone fireplace that was the centerpiece of the cozy area.

"It all looks custom. Did you have it designed and built to spec?"

A hint of color dusted his cheeks. "I did it all myself. Well, the dads helped me, but I designed it and did most of the woodwork myself. Took me two years, but it's exactly as I wanted it."

Her eyes widened. "It's gorgeous, Dillon. You're very talented."

The large overstuffed sectional sofa beckoned. It looked so inviting and comfortable that she couldn't resist trying it out. As soon as she sat, the cushions enveloped her and sucked her into the couch.

She kicked off her shoes and curled her feet underneath her. The sigh escaped before she could call it back.

Dillon stood several feet away, his eyes dark as he watched her. "Can I just say how natural you look sitting on my couch in my living room all curled up like you're at home?"

It was the first time he'd said anything directly to her that hinted at a desire for her to stay. He'd kissed her—boy had he kissed her—but while Michael and Seth had been more vocal and forthcoming, Dillon had been quiet. Until now.

"I like seeing you here, Lily," he said in a husky voice. "You belong here."

He moved forward, slowly, like he didn't want to frighten her. Then he sat next to her on the couch and turned to face her. He put his hand just over her knee and leaned toward her, his hand sliding up to her thigh.

"Kiss me, Lily. This time *you* kiss *me*."

She sucked in her breath and then glanced at his hand still resting on her thigh. Tentatively she reached out and slid her palm up his arm, and then down to his wrist where his tattoo began. She traced the lines with her fingertip until she reached the sleeve of his T-shirt.

"You're killing me," he said. "Kiss me."

Using his arm for leverage, she leaned forward, nervous but fascinated by the intensity in his gaze. He had a sensual mouth. Full lips that looked utterly kissable. And just enough shadow on his jaw to make him damn sexy.

She touched his cheek with her other hand and skimmed her fingers down to feel the rasp of stubble against her skin.

He closed his eyes and leaned further into her touch just as she pressed her lips to his in the lightest of kisses. He tensed beneath her fingers but held still, content to allow her to be the aggressor.

"I want to see your tattoo," she whispered against his lips.

"I want you to see a hell of a lot more than that," he muttered.

He pulled away and tugged his T-shirt out of his jeans and then rolled it up over his head. He had two sleeves from the wrists up. Matching designs that curled over his shoulders and licked toward his neck. There wasn't an actual image—an identifiable picture—but a series of intricate lines and shapes. It looked exotic but still unfamiliar.

"How did you come up with this?" she asked as she traced over his shoulder until her finger came to rest in the hollow of his throat.

"Callie and I went to India and Nepal one summer. We saw some amazing art and tattoos. Callie took pictures and when we got back, we took the photos to an artist in Denver who incorporated the designs into a larger one that was reflective of all the places we'd been."

"That's amazing. And what an awesome experience. That must have been so fun."

"Callie's our free spirit. She's traveled a lot. Sucks when

she's gone so much, but she's been to some awesome places."

Again Lily traced the colorful patterns with the tips of her fingers, but this time she allowed her hands to wander over his broad chest.

The muscles tightened and bunched under her palms, and his eyes narrowed to slits. He reached up and caught both her hands, holding them at the wrists, still over his chest.

"I have a better idea," he murmured. "I vote we ditch the bike ride and I take you into my bedroom and let you explore my tats all you want while I'm inside you."

Chapter Sixteen

Lily's eyes widened, and her breathing sped up until little puffs of air blew over Dillon's neck. He watched, gauging to see if he was moving too fast, too soon, but it wasn't fear he saw in her gaze. There was interest. And answering desire. A little hesitancy but not fear.

Her hands trembled in his hold and little goosebumps spread across her neck and shoulders, making him want to lick every last one.

He burned for her. His skin was itchy and alive, and he knew he wouldn't find relief until he was buried deep inside her. He wanted to hold her and soothe away the shadows and watch while she came apart beneath him.

"Do you want that, Lily?" he prodded. "Do you want to make love with me as much as I want to make love with you?"

She swallowed and then licked her lips in a nervous gesture he found endearing.

"What about Seth and Michael?" she asked in a low voice. Her lips turned down into a worried frown. "How is this supposed to work? I feel like I'm cheating on them."

She tugged her hands free and rubbed over her face in a frustrated gesture. "I don't know how this works. What I'm supposed to do. I don't want to screw up before it even begins."

Dillon's chest tightened and then went soft. He reached out to take her hand again, pulling it away from her face. Then he kissed each of her fingertips to soothe some of the tension flowing from her.

"There's no right or wrong way, Lily. If I'm moving too fast for you, just say the word. I just know that when I saw you, I had to touch you. I know my brothers felt and feel the same. If you've talked to Seth, and if he explained what they're proposing, then you know they'll be okay with this. They have to be. It's the only way it works. I won't ask their permission every time I want to make love to you."

"You said they," she said quickly. Her eyes narrowed as she stared at him. "You said what *they're* proposing. You didn't say *we*."

He sighed. "Yeah, I can see how that might look to you. Like I'm only going along for the ride and aren't fully on board. Maybe I'm not at this point. It's hard to tell. Things have happened so fast. What I do know is that I have an undeniable attraction to you. I never used to believe in hokey love-at-first-sight stuff. My dads always said it was that way with Mom, but I didn't really believe it."

"And now?"

He blew out his breath. "Now I know that you can meet someone and want them with every breath in your body, mentally and physically. Is that love? I don't know. Maybe. Maybe it's the foundation being laid. Relationships have begun with a hell of a lot less, that's for sure."

"You have to wear a condom," she blurted.

He blinked at the whiplash her statement caused.

Her cheeks colored, but her lips were set into a determined line.

"I'm not on birth control," she rushed on to say. "I mean it's not something I've been able to afford nor have I had the need, but I don't want to get pregnant. I won't take the risk."

Now there was fear in her eyes. Dillon eased back but kept firm hold on her hand. He squeezed and massaged, trying to ease the tension.

"Baby, I'd never not protect you," he said gently. "Of course I'll wear a condom. And I'm sure you know condoms aren't foolproof, so I'll make an appointment for you at the clinic in town so you can get on birth control if that's what you want."

She looked down, avoiding his gaze. "I don't have insurance—or a way to pay."

The shame in her voice nearly killed him. God, he hurt for her. But he needed to make it clear from the start that they were damn well going to take care of her, and the last thing she needed to worry about was having the money for birth control.

"Lily, we need to get a few things straight, okay? I'm assuming you and Seth had a long talk in which he laid out the fact that he and Michael and me all want one thing. You. And I'm sure he laid out just what that would mean if we all agree to see where this takes us. I'm also assuming you agreed, or you wouldn't be here with me right now. Part of the arrangement, if you will, is that we take care of you. We wouldn't have it any other way. That means providing for your needs both emotionally and financially."

She raised her gaze to meet his. "It's easy to see what I get out of this. But what about you? And Seth and Michael? What could you possibly get out of this relationship that you can't get somewhere else?"

He raised an eyebrow. "You think all we want is sex?"

She flushed and looked down again. He slid his hand underneath her chin and prompted her to look back at him.

"No, I don't think that," she said when he continued to stare at her. "If that's what you wanted, you could certainly find better elsewhere."

"I don't agree, but that's not the point. I'm not attracted to every other woman out there. I'm attracted to you. If sex was all I wanted, I'd have you naked and underneath me right now instead of having one of those sensitive conversations that make men's testicles shrink."

A smile hovered on her lips and her eyes gleamed, losing the dull shadow of shame.

"I did agree, I mean when Seth talked to me before about...us...all of us, I said okay."

"Then you have to give us that chance," Dillon said as he stroked her cheek with his hand. "And you have to give us your trust that we'll take care of you and provide for you."

She turned her face into his palm and brushed her lips over his skin. "I'll try."

He felt his insides give this peculiar squeeze, and he knew in that moment that he was in it for the long haul. No, he damn

115

sure hadn't ever considered that he'd share his woman with his two brothers no matter how they'd grown up. But his parents had made it work, and he was just as committed to making this relationship work with Lily and his brothers.

"I'm in this, Lily. Maybe I wasn't sure before, but now I am. I'm not going anywhere. We can make this work."

Her eyes brightened, and her smile lit up her entire face. She was so astonishingly lovely that he ached. His hand shook against her face, and it hit him how badly he wanted to make love to her. Not sex. He wanted to savor and cherish her and make her feel undeniably loved.

"Every time I think this can't possibly work and that I'm stupid for trying it, one of you says something to make me believe. I want this too, Dillon. So much that it scares me because I'm afraid it's all a fantasy that I'm going to wake up from."

He touched his thumb to her lip and rubbed back and forth over the soft, full bottom. "Believe it, Lily. This isn't something we'd take lightly. Ever."

"I also want you to believe me," she said. Her gaze caught his again and sincerity burned bright in her blue eyes. "I don't want any of you to think that I'm latching onto the first way out of my life and that it could be anyone. That's not it, I swear."

He covered her mouth with his fingers. "Shhh. I don't think that. None of us thinks that. Do we want to help you and take care of you and make damn sure you never have to spend a day out on the streets again? Hell yes. All we want in return is you. Just you. It's enough."

Tears glistened, making her eyes go wet and shiny. But she smiled underneath his fingers and then she kissed the tips.

"Tell you what," he said, before his selfish nature completely took over. It was obvious she was unsettled with things moving so quickly and not having Michael and Seth to reassure her that they weren't going to lose their minds if she was intimate with Dillon. "Why don't you and I spend the afternoon on the couch. We'll watch a movie or two, or just lay here and talk. I'll call my brothers and tell them I'll cook dinner here tonight for all of us. It'll give the four of us time to spend together, and hopefully that'll put you at ease. Michael's probably convinced I skipped town with you anyway."

Lily grinned and put her hand over her mouth to stifle her laughter. "I'd like that. I'd like that a lot."

He leaned in to give her a quick kiss. "You get comfy then. I'll go let them know."

He left her on the couch but watched as she snuggled deeper into the cushions. She looked so damn cute that he couldn't wait to get back and wrap himself around her. It was pretty pathetic when he opted for an afternoon of cuddling on the couch over taking a woman to bed, but he was so eager to have her in his arms that it didn't matter how it had to happen.

He called Seth first since he already knew where Lily was, although Dillon was pretty sure Michael knew by now. Seth sounded a little surprised when Dillon gave him the run-down— maybe he was the one who thought Dillon would skip town with Lily. He suppressed a smile and rang off after telling Seth to show up at six. That gave him a few hours alone with Lily before he had to be gracious and share.

Next he dialed Michael's cell since the odds of catching him in his office were slim.

"Hey man, what's going on?" Michael said as soon as he came onto the line.

"I'm with Lily."

There was a slight pause. "Yeah. I know. Everything okay?"

"Yeah, fine. We didn't go riding after all. Going to spend the afternoon here. Catch a movie or two. I thought it would be a good idea for you and Seth to come here for dinner tonight. I already called Seth and he'll be here."

"How is her arm? Have you been taking care of it?"

"Yeah, it's fine." He hoped to hell he hadn't lied. He wasn't going to admit that the last thing on his mind had been her injury, which probably made him a complete asshole, but it was the truth.

"She's uneasy about how you guys are reacting to her being with me and I'm sure it's the same when she's with one of you. I thought if we could all be together in the same room, it would ease some of her insecurities."

There was another long period of silence that had Dillon

fidgeting.

"So does this mean you're on board with this?"

There was a note of caution in Michael's voice that Dillon wasn't sure how to take.

"I wouldn't be inviting you over for dinner if I wasn't."

Michael sighed. "Look, Dillon, you have to admit you didn't sound like you were open to this the last time we spoke."

"I'm not the one who stormed out," Dillon pointed out. "And excuse me all to hell for not being able to make a life-altering decision in a split second."

Michael made a disgruntled sound. "Okay, you got me there. This is just important, and I don't want us to fuck it up because we can't get our shit together."

"You may not realize it, but this is damn important to me too, Michael," Dillon said in a low voice. "This is the biggest decision we'll ever make. I've made mine. I think you and Seth have made yours. Now the hard part starts."

"Yeah, I hear you. I'll be over at six provided I don't have any call-outs. Tell Lily... Tell her I'll see her then."

"Will do," Dillon said as he ended the call.

He slowly lowered the phone to the kitchen table and stood there a long moment, coming to terms with what he'd just committed to.

Any sane person would be heavy into the what-the-fucks right now, but he was at complete and utter peace with the decision. He didn't think for a minute it would all be a bed of roses and they'd live happily ever after in the clouds. But what he did know was that the Colters believed in family above all else. And now Lily was a part of that family. He and his brothers would go to the wall for her each and every day of their lives.

Seth left his parents' house early to drive into town to see Lacey. He parked in front of the sheriff's department, and before he made it out of his truck, Lacey stood in the doorway, a hand cocked on her hip as she stared him down.

"Want to tell me why you're only just now making it in to

see me?" she asked. "Word is you hit town yesterday."

Seth grinned and held out his arms for a hug. "Still as bossy as ever, I see."

She hugged him fiercely and then all but pulled him into her office. After shoving him into a chair, she circled around her desk and took her seat.

"I won't beat around the bush. I'm sure your dad has talked to you already. I'd like you to take over the rest of my term. I'm going to retire as soon as I find a replacement."

"Okay."

She blinked and then reared back in her chair, suspicion darkening her eyes. "Okay? That's it? You're not going to argue and list ten reasons why you're not the right person for the job?"

He fought back a smile. "Nope."

"Well, hell. I was prepared to have to spend an hour arguing you down, and you come in and take the wind out of my sails."

This time he laughed. "Dramatic as ever, Lacey."

She leaned forward, her expression serious. "What changed your mind? Adam told me you were reluctant to even consider it."

"I want to come home," he said simply. "Law enforcement is what I do. I could never imagine you not being the sheriff, but if you're going to retire, I want the job."

"Is your arm healed up? Is everything okay in Denver?"

He smiled at the anxious note in her voice. "Everything is fine. Quit worrying. I met someone. Someone I want to have a life with here."

Lacey's eyes sharpened. "Anyone I know?"

Seth shook his head. "No, and you aren't going to run a background check on her, either. She's says she's not in any trouble, and I believe her. But there is definitely a lot of hurt in her past, and I don't want to push her too hard. I have to tread a very delicate line with her—we all do."

Lacey didn't look happy with his decree. "So who is she?"

"Her name is Lily," Seth said quietly. "And you should also know, because you'll hear sooner or later, and I know I can count on your support, that Michael and Dillon are also involved with Lily."

Lacey sat back again, her eyes round with shock. "Oh shit. Is this a joke?"

He shook his head.

"Well I'll be damned," she murmured. "I never would have imagined. It's certainly worked well enough for your mother and your dads, so I guess you know it's possible. But still... Damn."

"Lacey, I'm sorry about Dan. Dad told me. How is he doing?"

Her expression crumbled for a moment before she smiled brightly. "He's doing good. We've been driving back and forth to Denver so he can get treatment. I'd like to move there, though, because it's wearing on him. Plus we have that place on the mountain and it's become more than we can keep up. All the kids are gone, so it just makes sense to move ourselves."

"If there's ever anything I can do, you know all you have to do is ask."

She reached across the desk to put her hand on his. "I know, Seth. And thank you." Then she leaned back, all business again. "I've already spoken to the city council about the possibility of you taking over the job."

He raised an eyebrow.

"Well I had to prepare," she said defensively. "No one wants to bring in an outsider. My deputies are young and too inexperienced to take over as sheriff, and Jimmy is too old. He just wants to get in another few years so he can take his retirement. If you want the job, it's yours. The vote will just be a formality, but you already have them in your pocket."

"How soon?" Seth asked quietly.

"As soon as you can fill out an application so it's official. There's paperwork to do and the council will hold a meeting where they vote. I figure we can have it done in a few days, and you can take over in two weeks' time. That'll give me enough time to hand in my resignation and get my ducks in a row."

"I'll be sad to see you go, Lacey."

She smiled. "I'll be back to visit. I'll always consider this my town."

Seth paused for a moment and then glanced back at her. "Do you think my...relationship...with Lily is going to cause problems with me in this job?"

Lacey leaned back and studied him for a moment. "I'll be honest, Seth. I just don't know. Most folks around here are familiar with your upbringing and your mom's relationship with your fathers. There was a lot of talk when it became obvious all those years ago, but it quickly died down and people here tend to mind their own business. Your mom is dearly loved and your fathers are very well respected in the community.

"You'll have a few folks who raise their eyebrows but most will take it in stride, but you just never know. My thought is, you keep quiet for now, finish my term and by the time you come up for re-election, let the chips fall where they may. If you do the job, I think that's all that's going to matter, and as I said, the people here really don't want some hotshot from the outside to come in and take over the town. You'll have two years to prove your mettle. Then you're just going to have to let the voters decide."

Seth nodded. "I guess you're right. I'm not going to keep Lily as some dirty little secret, and I know my brothers will feel the same. If it doesn't work out, I'll just have to find something else to do, even if it's helping the dads out with their guide business."

"Just do the job, Seth. Really that's all you can do. And I have every confidence that you'll win the support of the community in short order. You'll have a few busybodies who'll consider it their personal duty to stick their noses where they don't belong, but fuck 'em. You don't get to be sheriff here without alienating a few along the way. Nature of the job."

Seth grinned. "Damn but I'm going to miss you, Lacey."

Her office door opened and Linda stuck her head in. "Lacey, you're needed over at old man Witherspoon's place. Grundy's dogs got out again and Witherspoon is raising hell and waving his shotgun around."

Lacey sighed. "I'll be right there." She rose and walked around her desk but stopped to hug Seth. "I'm glad you're coming home. I'll feel a lot better about leaving if I know the town is in your hands."

He hugged her back and felt the first tingle of excitement snake up his spine. His town. It had a nice ring to it. He knew everyone here. Had grown up a part of a tight-knit community. The idea that he'd come back home and have not only this job, but Lily... How quickly things changed. He found he didn't mind one bit.

Chapter Seventeen

Michael pulled into Dillon's drive and parked beside Seth's truck. He was running late and it was nearly dark. It figured that on an evening when he was hoping like hell to get out early, he'd been flooded with last-minute "emergencies".

He mounted the front steps, and not bothering to knock, he pushed open the front door. He was instantly flooded with the smell of good food. Whatever Dillon was cooking, Michael couldn't wait to eat. His stomach rumbled as he glanced over to see Seth and Lily on the couch.

Seth was reclined on his side and Lily was nestled in his arms, her eyes closed as Seth stroked his hand up and down her hip. Michael didn't want to wake or disturb her, but he wanted to be the one wrapped up with her.

As if sensing his presence, Lily stirred and opened her eyes. Her bleary gaze settled on him and her eyes widened in pleasure as recognition dawned.

"Michael," she whispered.

She pushed herself upward and Seth caught her hand to help her. She was off the couch and hurrying for Michael in the next moment. Surprise and pleasure swept over him when she flew into his arms and hugged him fiercely.

"I'm so glad you're here," she said close to his ear. "I thought you weren't coming."

He brushed a short curl over her ear and kissed her temple, letting his lips linger there for a long second. It crushed him that she was here and so happy to see him. That she'd waited for him. Had worried he wasn't coming.

"I wouldn't miss it or you," he murmured. "Sorry I'm late."

"I see the doctor made it," Dillon drawled from the kitchen door. "Why don't you let Lily lie back down and you come help me a sec."

Michael cast a wary glance in Dillon's direction. When Dillon was in the kitchen, it was his domain. No one entered.

Dillon tossed his head toward the kitchen, and Michael leaned down to kiss Lily again.

"Go get comfortable. I'll just be a minute."

She clung to him a moment and returned his kiss before backing toward the couch. Michael stood long enough to see her settle next to Seth before he headed into the kitchen to see what was up with Dillon.

"Damn that smells good, whatever it is," Michael said.

"Crawfish étouffée courtesy of the Cajun cooking show I watched last week," Dillon said as he stirred the contents of the skillet. "It'll be ready just as soon as the rice is done."

Michael took a seat on one of the barstools and leaned on the granite countertop. He had to hand it to Dillon. It had taken him two years to build the place, but it was exquisitely crafted and looked high end and custom from top to bottom.

"So what's up? You don't ever let anyone into your kitchen when you're cooking."

Dillon cast a glance toward the doorway and stopped stirring. "You're friends with Dr. Burton over at the clinic. Think you can pull some strings and get Lily an appointment ASAP?"

Michael frowned. "What's going on? Is her arm worse? Damn it, I knew no one was taking it seriously enough."

Dillon held up his hands. "Whoa. Slow down. Nothing's wrong. She needs birth control."

Michael's mouth formed an O.

"She insisted I, or I guess *we*, use condoms. She seemed stressed about the possibility of getting pregnant. I can't say I blame her. She was worried because she doesn't have insurance, or money for that matter."

Michael swore under his breath. Dillon held up a hand again. "I took care of that. Told her we'd damn sure take care of her and we'd make sure she had everything she needs. I don't want her stressed so I was hoping you could get her into the clinic quickly so we have that out of the way."

"Yeah, I'll make a call in the morning. Are you working tonight?"

"I was supposed to be behind the bar, but Callie's covering and I have Kenneth pulling bouncer duty. I don't want Callie mixing it up with any more customers. We're lucky it was just a bunch of stupid college students and she didn't get hurt."

"I was hoping Seth could talk to her, but obviously we've been focused on Lily."

"I'm not sure she'd talk to him anyway. She's been tightlipped ever since she got home. I know she and Seth are tight, but Callie and I are buds and she shuts me down every time I start asking questions."

"I wish to hell I knew what happened to her."

"You and me both, bro."

Dillon picked up the lid on the rice steamer and then let it fall shut again. He clapped his hands together and then hollered toward the living room, "Soup's on!"

"Anyone ever tell you how subtle you are?" Michael asked.

Dillon grinned. "Subtlety is for pussies."

The brothers looked up when Lily entered the kitchen with Seth right behind her. She offered both Dillon and Michael a tentative smile, and Michael reached his hand out to her.

When she took it, he pulled her onto the barstool next to him and wrapped his arm around her waist. He nuzzled against her temple, inhaling her sweet scent.

"I missed you today," he whispered.

She turned and gifted him with a broad smile and then leaned her forehead to his. "I missed you too. I met your family. They're all so great. You're lucky to have them."

"They'll be your family too," he pointed out.

Her eyes widened as if she hadn't considered that aspect. There were equal parts fear and longing in her eyes. And then she smiled again. "I guess that makes me lucky too, then."

"Break it up, you two," Dillon grumbled as he plunked plates down in front of them. "Time to eat up."

Seth pulled out the barstool on the other side of Lily and

took his seat while Dillon finished fixing the plates. He took a seat on the end next to Seth.

"Dig in, guys. Hope it's good."

Lily took a bite and then let out a sound of pleasure. "It's wonderful, Dillon. I think I could make myself sick on it."

"It's damn good," Seth agreed. "It's obvious you didn't inherit Mom's cooking ability."

Michael snorted with laughter while Dillon grinned.

"I used to cook," Lily said in a wistful tone. "I loved it."

"My kitchen is your kitchen," Dillon said. "And whatever's in my pantry is yours anytime you want to fool around in here."

Seth cleared his throat and everyone looked in his direction. "Speaking of kitchens and places. We need to talk about our arrangements. I spoke to Lacey today. I'll be taking over her job in a couple of weeks as soon as all the paperwork is finalized."

"Hey, that's great," Michael exclaimed.

Lily shot Seth a puzzled look. "You're not going back to Denver?"

Seth smiled in her direction. "No. I'm taking the sheriff's position here in Clyde. If we're going to make this work, I can't be in Denver. Michael and Dillon are both established here. It only makes sense that I make the move."

"Which begs the question of where you're going to stay," Michael said. "For that matter, where we're going to stay. Together."

"Here," Dillon said.

Lily looked like she had no idea what they were talking about. Michael put his hand over hers and squeezed reassuringly.

"It makes the most sense," Dillon continued when no one responded. "It's bigger than your place, Michael, and Seth doesn't have a place here. There's room for expansion, and most importantly, it's private."

"What about Michael's house?" Seth asked.

"He could turn it into his practice instead of that tiny-ass office he has in town."

Dillon's idea was solid. Michael did need more office space, and Dillon's place was ideal for the four of them.

"What do you think, Lily?" Seth asked. "Are you up for staying here?"

Michael laced his fingers with hers and glanced over to see so much longing in Lily's gaze that it hurt him. He lifted her hand and turned it over to press a kiss into her palm. "Stay with us, Lily. You won't regret it."

Lily in turn looked at each of the brothers, warmth shining in her eyes. "Do you really all want...me? Do you really want to do this?"

Both Dillon and Seth nodded.

"Absolutely," Michael said.

"Okay then," she said softly. "I'll stay here with you—all of you."

Michael hadn't realized his grip was so tight on her hand until he felt her flinch. He released her immediately and then rubbed his fingers apologetically over hers.

Then he glanced over at his brothers, silently asking for their commitment. There was determination in their faces, and their focus was entirely on Lily. But when they looked up at Michael, he knew they were every bit as committed to making this work as he was.

Chapter Eighteen

Dinner was fun. For Lily it was glimpse into the days ahead, something that filled her with hope and excitement. The brothers joked and ribbed each other mercilessly, but there was also a solid thread of loyalty and love. The same feeling she'd had when she first walked into their parents' house.

She longed to be a part of that. Something solid. To be a part of a family unit again. To know there were people she could count on.

Dillon refused to allow her to help with the dishes, and instead he corralled Seth into helping with the chore while Michael returned to the living room with her.

As soon as they were away from the kitchen, Michael halted and pulled her into his arms. His lips found hers in a hungry, urgent kiss. Warm and so smooth. He nibbled at her lips and then slid his tongue between them, stroking sensually along her tongue until all she could taste and feel was him.

"It made me crazy today," he murmured. "Knowing you were with them and I couldn't be with you. It was the longest damn day of my life."

"You're with me now," she said as she feathered her fingers over his temple and then through his hair. "It's fascinating. I would have imagined Dillon with his rebel image to have the long hair and you with the staid image of a country vet to have short, very neat hair." She pulled her fingers to the ends of his hair.

"You don't like it?" he teased.

"I do. It's just surprising. Like you, I guess. Seth seems so quiet and focused and then you came along and it was like being hit by a tornado. And then Dillon. I can't decide, but something tells me that you're more of a rebel than Dillon is, and that at heart, Dillon is really a homebody."

He blinked in astonishment and then laughed. "Don't ever tell Dillon that. He'll take it personally that you find me more exciting and dangerous than him."

"Well, I didn't say that."

"But you're thinking it," Michael said with a grin. "That's good enough for me."

"You're incorrigible."

"Don't call me things I can't spell."

She laughed and leaned further into him. They were still standing in the middle of the living room, but they could be anywhere and it would be magic.

That was the word—the feeling—in a nutshell. It was magic. A miracle that she didn't deserve but was so grateful and gobsmacked over.

Three men who seemed too good to be true. Three loyal, strong, devastating men. And they all wanted her. They wanted to make a *life* with her.

"I'd pay a lot to know what you're thinking right now."

She realized she was smiling—no, *beaming*—from ear to ear. "I was thinking about you. And Dillon and Seth. I'm still just processing it all. It seems too good to be true."

"Believe it," he said just before capturing her mouth again.

Oh, but she ached. Her breasts tightened against his chest and her nipples formed hard, tingling points that begged for his touch—his mouth. Her body was awash with heat. Her skin was flushed and desire pooled low in her belly, simmering to a slow boil.

She swayed in his arms. Her knees buckled and he caught her waist, hauling her firmly against him. It seemed she'd spent the entire day in a state of heightened awareness. She wanted to make love with these men, but she was at a loss as to how.

She twined her arms around his neck and slid her mouth down his jaw line to his neck where she nuzzled and licked at the area over his pulse.

He groaned and went tense against her, his arms like iron bands around her body. His erection bulged against her belly, and she rubbed enticingly, causing sweet friction between them.

She felt alive. Electric. Coming to life after a long period of dormancy. Forgotten was the past. Sorrow. Regret. Here, with these three men, she'd found herself again.

She turned when she heard a sound and saw Dillon and Seth standing in the doorway to the living room. Their eyes glittered, and Seth's mouth was drawn into a tight line. She could feel their need across the room. It mirrored her own.

She glanced back at Michael and knew what she needed to do.

It wasn't as if she had experience with this kind of thing. Honestly, the idea terrified her. What if they were appalled by what she wanted? She'd never been in such a precarious position. She felt like she was sticking one foot over a drop-off and praying for all she was worth that she found purchase.

Slowly, she backed away from Michael and her hands fluttered nervously to the hem of her shirt. Before she lost all her nerve, she raised the material over her head and dropped it to the floor.

It seemed important to her that this first time—*especially* the first time—they made love for it not to be a choice between one brother and the other. Now, she was glad she and Dillon hadn't given in to the overwhelming heat and desire between them earlier in the day.

She wanted to give herself to all of them on equal footing. She wanted to show them she accepted and wanted the three of them and not one more than the other.

When her hands dropped to the waistband of her pants, she felt the sudden inhalations around her. The brothers glanced between each other, seemingly as hesitant and unsure as she was herself.

She eased her clothing from her body in slow, unrushed movements until finally she stood naked and painfully vulnerable in the middle of the room.

Three sets of eyes burned into her flesh. She could feel the tension, hovering heavy in the air. An electric current buzzed in her ears, warmed her body to the point of discomfort.

Lust. Desire. Need.

They were tangible in the close confines of the room. Heavy and almost suffocating.

She sucked in air through her nose and then wrapped her arms protectively around herself as she waited for their response. She had no idea what to do next.

Seth was the first to move. He strode across the room and wrapped his arms around her as if to shield her from the world.

"You don't have to do this, honey," he said softly. "You have nothing to prove to us."

She shook her head. "You don't understand. It's what I want. Together. The first time. It seems important that we do this together, don't you think?"

Seth turned to his brothers as if gauging their reaction. Dillon's gaze was ablaze with lust and desire. Michael looked a little less certain, but there was no denying the clear curiosity—and excitement—in his eyes.

Seth turned back to her and ran his hands up her hips and then underneath her breasts to cup the small mounds in his palms. His thumbs stroked over her nipples until she was twitchy with intense arousal.

"What I think is that we want you any way we can have you, and that if this is what you want, then we want it too," he said, his voice full of sensual growly vibrations.

"I don't know how," she whispered. "I don't know what to do."

Seth's heart softened as he gazed down at the beautiful, brave woman standing in front of him. She'd risked a lot by taking the initiative. She wanted to show the three of them that she accepted them. Equally. And to her credit, it would have eaten at him if Michael or Dillon had made love to her first, just because he would have imagined them having a bond that somehow excluded him.

This way...it might not be the most conventional, and he damn sure didn't have any experience with multiple partners, but it was a forced reality of their new circumstances.

There were plenty of nights he remembered his parents

sharing the same bed, and he was reasonably certain they weren't just snuggling.

He just hoped like hell he didn't have performance anxiety issues now of all times.

Wanting to allay her insecurities, he bent and swept her into his arms. Then he turned to Dillon. "She'd be a hell of a lot more comfortable on a bed."

Dillon bolted into action and started down the hall to his master suite. Michael followed behind Seth as he carried Lily into the bedroom. In the center was a mahogany four-poster king-sized bed. Seth gently set her down and positioned her so that she was in the center, but he pulled her until her legs hung over the edge.

He wasn't going to direct a damn thing. His brothers could figure it out on their own. All Seth knew was that he wanted to make Lily feel impossibly cherished, and he planned to love every inch of her.

She was exquisitely lovely, naked against the covers, her pale skin flush with desire. He honestly didn't know where to start. He was captivated and wanted to taste every inch of her.

Her thighs were parted just enough that he could see the soft, pink flesh of her pussy. He bent and grasped her knees, parting her further as he pressed a kiss to the inside of her thigh.

Her reaction was instantaneous. She shivered and twitched against him.

He kissed his way to the soft patch of curls that guarded her femininity and then crossed to the other side to kiss his way back down to her knee.

She moaned and twisted restlessly beneath him.

The bed dipped and Michael crawled onto the mattress next to where Lily lay. Seth watched in fascination as his brother palmed one breast and then bent his head to suckle her nipple.

Lily's hand tangled in Michael's hair, bringing him closer, holding him there as he fed gently at her breast.

Seth lowered his head once more and slid his fingers over the lips of her vagina, pushing until they parted under his insistence.

The pink, delicate flesh called to him. He wanted to taste her. To lick every part of her until she was writhing and begging for mercy.

He kissed the softness of the inside of her thigh just a breath from her pussy. Then he nipped lightly, eliciting another full-body shiver from her.

Using his fingers to part the folds, he hovered over her clit, blowing a warm stream of air before he finally closed his mouth over it.

Her hips arched off the bed as he sucked gently, flicking his tongue over the tip. He closed his eyes, savoring her taste, the delicate sweetness that was so much a part of her.

He dipped lower, lapping and licking his way to her tiny entrance. He rimmed the edges, teasing with shallow little thrusts before plunging his tongue inward, absorbing her essence.

The bed dipped again, and Seth looked up to see Dillon on Lily's other side. Dillon carefully placed a few packets of condoms next to Lily's hips, a subtle reminder to Seth about protection.

Then Dillon leaned over to touch Lily's cheek before lowering his mouth to hers.

"Did you tell them?" she whispered to Dillon. "About the condoms."

Dillon caressed her cheek in a tender motion and kissed her again before saying, "We'll always protect you, Lily. You have my word."

Her smile was brilliant and did funny things to Seth's insides.

It was a little unreal, this woman stretched beneath the three of them, Michael at her breast while Dillon devoured her mouth. Their hands coaxed up and down her sides, cupped her breasts, their mouths never leaving her skin while Seth stood between her legs.

Her eyes were drowsy and glazed, infused with passion. She made sweet little sounds of contentment that were about to drive Seth beyond all control.

He eased a finger into her, watching as her eyes widened.

He stroked the slick walls of her vagina with the tip, withdrawing and then sliding back into her warmth.

He couldn't wait to get inside her. His cock throbbed and was so damn swollen it was a wonder he hadn't split apart at the seams.

There was something intensely erotic about seeing her in complete surrender. Giving herself to the care and regard of him and his brothers. Trusting that they wouldn't hurt her and that they'd cherish her trust.

He reached for a condom and hastily tore away the wrapper. Then he left her long enough to tear at his clothing. He tossed his shirt aside then ripped at his pants, suddenly desperate to feel her against his skin.

He rolled the condom on, wincing at how tight the latex was around his straining erection. Then he leaned into her, rubbing his length up and down her slit before fitting himself to her opening.

He reached for her hand that lay next to her hip and laced his fingers with hers just before inching his way forward into the hot clasp of her pussy.

She squeezed his fingers and made a helpless sound of pleasure around Dillon's mouth.

She was tight. Impossibly so. He didn't want to hurt her, but with every passing second, he battled the urge to bury himself as hard and as deep as he could go.

He clenched his teeth together until the pressure in his jaw made him ache. He withdrew and then carefully pressed forward again.

Her silken, swollen tissue grasped wetly at him, trying to push him back and holding him so tight that he fought not to come then and there.

"Sweet Jesus, Lily, you feel so good," he whispered. "So damn good."

"Take me," she said in low, velvet tones. "Don't hold back, Seth. You won't hurt me."

He pulled back once more, enjoying the ripple over his cock, and then he drove hard and fast, burying himself to the balls inside her.

She gasped and arched up, her muscles contracting and jittering until he had to hold her down to keep her from unseating him. Her fingers flexed and dug into his, and a strangled cry erupted from her lips.

He stood there, leaning into her, feeling her contract and squeeze around him. Then he withdrew his hand from hers and looped her legs over his arms, pulling her higher so he had a better angle of entry.

He withdrew and plunged inward again. Fire erupted, burning a path from his balls to the tip of his cock. His orgasm built, rising hard and fast, boiling inside him to the point of pain. Every nerve ending screamed. Electricity arced and flowed, heating his veins until his blood sizzled.

He began to thrust. Hard. Fast. Driving into her until he was mindless—helpless against the rising tide.

He was aware of his brothers soothing her, caressing her, murmuring in low voices as they worshipped her body. But for Seth, it was only him and Lily in this one moment. Joined so intimately, him an irrevocable part of her.

He claimed her. He possessed her. He told her without words that she was his—would always be his—and that she held his heart and soul in the palms of her hands.

And then he heard it. His name on her lips. Torn from her throat as release rushed upon them both. It wasn't a gentle ride to completion. It was like riding a tornado, tumultuous and so dizzying that he lost all awareness of everything but her. Lily. His woman. His.

He jerked against her, his hips pumping spasmodically as the first jet of his release burst from his cock. He cried out. It was part pain and all pleasure. So intense that the room was black around him.

He heard the vague sounds of his brothers removing their clothing, and he slumped forward, gathering Lily into his arms as he continued to pump against her.

She wrapped her arms around him, rubbing up and down with her soothing touch. Her lips brushed over the scar on his shoulder, lingering as she pressed tiny kisses over the puckered skin. She followed her mouth with her fingers, tracing the outline. When he lowered his gaze, he saw that her lips were turned down as she stared at the wound.

He lowered his head to kiss the frown away, and she slid her hands around his neck, holding him lovingly as the last vestiges of his release shook from his body.

Chapter Nineteen

Lily moaned when Seth eased off her and withdrew from her body. She floated, the world hazy around her. She felt listless and completely sated. She smiled in Seth's direction, and then Dillon moved between them, blocking her view.

Dillon's eyes were fierce, dark orbs that had her catching her breath. He leaned over, pressing his body to hers until she felt every muscle ripple and coil against her breasts.

He kissed her once. Hot and breathless. Not the kiss of a patient man bent on wooing his woman. No, this was a demand for a response, and she gave it, wrapping her arms around him as she pulled him down to meet her lips again.

"Tell me, Lily, can you take me and Michael at the same time?" he rasped against her mouth.

Arousal coiled and tightened low in her belly. Her breasts ached, and her nipples drew into tight points that dug into his chest.

"How?" she whispered.

He drew away and extended his hand to help her up. He pulled her into a sitting position and then prompted her to get up on her knees.

Michael climbed onto the bed in front of her, and she caught her first glimpse of his long, thick cock. Michael's body was a thing of beauty. All lean lines, tight muscles, narrow hips. His erection jutted outward and bobbed in front of her lips.

As Dillon kissed the small of her back, Michael fisted his erection in his hand and slowly guided it toward her mouth.

She wet her lips and then parted them as he entered. For a

moment he rested there, with the head barely past her lips. Then he thrust further and his taste exploded onto her tongue.

Salty. Tangy. A hint of musk. All male. Rugged and masculine like him. He still had his hand wrapped around the base, and he was inside her mouth as far as he could go.

Dillon teased the seam of her ass, running his finger up and down and then lower to ease into her pussy. Still swollen from Seth's lovemaking, she flinched when her tissues clasped Dillon's finger as tightly as if it were a cock.

"Easy baby," Dillon murmured. "I won't hurt you. We're going to take this nice and easy. You have all the time in the world to take me, and if I ever hurt you, you let me know. I'll back off immediately."

She closed her eyes and allowed Michael to work deep inside her mouth again. He was gentle and patient, keeping his strokes shallow and slow to give her time to adjust.

Dillon eased his finger inside her again, but this time he did so with ease. She felt the cool slide of lubricant as he carefully moved his fingers until her passage was completely coated.

Then he pulled away, and a moment later, the tip of his cock breached her entrance. There was a burning, stretching sensation as he pushed inward. Even with the lubricant, it was a tight fit.

But he was achingly tender, moving in increments, giving her time to adjust to his size and his possession. She stretched wide around the base of his cock until she was impossibly full.

The restless, edgy build was back. She pushed against him, wanting more, wanting the delicious friction of his cock burning through her pussy.

His hips finally met her ass and pressed against her, holding firm for a long moment. Then he withdrew until she squirmed and tried to push back to take him again.

He rocked forward again, gripping her hips to hold her in place. Michael cupped her jaw and fed her his cock, inch by delicious inch.

The two men moved in rhythm, buffeting her body between theirs. She was overpowered by them. Awed by them. Completely consumed by her need for them.

At one point Michael pulled away, his breaths coming in harsh spurts. His chest heaved with exertion, and he held his cock away from her as he caressed her cheek with his other hand.

"I'm close," he murmured. "But I want to be inside you when I come. I want to make you come again."

"Kiss me," she begged softly. "Kiss me while Dillon takes me."

Michael lowered himself until he was on eye level with her. She reached up to cup his face and then fused their mouths together. Their tongues tangled and dueled while Dillon fucked her with increasing force.

Dillon's fingers dug into her sides, tighter until she was sure she'd bear his marks.

Faster and more frantic, he pushed himself inside her until she felt his balls slap against her clit. Then he went tense all over and strained, holding himself as deep as he could go. A huge shudder rolled through his big body, and he spasmed against her.

He leaned over and pressed his lips to the center of her back. "Did I hurt you?"

She shook her head. "No," she whispered. "I know you'd never hurt me."

"This might be a little uncomfortable," he said, regret in his voice. He leaned back and then eased himself from the tight clasp of her body.

Her knees shook so badly that she threatened to buckle. Michael caught her shoulders and gently turned her until she was on her back again.

He lowered himself until he half covered her, his body warm and flush against hers.

"Where do you like to be touched?" he asked softly. "Tell me how to please you, Lily."

Heat brushed her cheeks, but she met his gaze, emboldened by the approval and true desire to please her she found in his eyes.

"Here," she whispered as she cupped her breasts and rubbed her thumbs over her nipples. "And here." She gestured toward the spot on her neck below her ear—the part that drove her insane when it was nibbled at. "And here." She lowered her hand to delve between her legs and rub over her clit.

"Mmm. I can't wait to taste all three," Michael said throatily.

He angled his head and grazed his teeth along the column of her neck until her entire body was bathed in goosebumps. He nipped and sucked and kissed, tormenting her endlessly until she writhed uncontrollably beneath him.

Then he turned his attention to her breasts, blowing air over her nipples and watching them pucker into taut little beads.

He flicked his tongue out and licked lightly at the tips, taking turns going from one to the other. She whimpered and raised her chest, trying to make him take them into his mouth.

He chuckled and merely nipped at them, teasing and taunting her until she growled her frustration.

"I want you so on edge that the minute I slide into you, you fall over," he murmured against her nipple.

"Oh God, I'm already there," she said in a strangled voice.

"No. But you will be."

He started at her breastbone and licked his way down to her navel, rimmed the shallow indention and then continued down until he kissed the sensitive skin right above her soft curls at the apex of her legs.

"Open for me, sweetheart."

She parted her legs, her breath hitching in her throat when his dark head dipped and his mouth found her, hot and wet. Her pussy ached from Seth's and Dillon's loving, but Michael's mouth soothed the discomfort away. He licked and sucked, driving her swiftly up the rise to another orgasm. He tongued her entrance and slid inside with gentle little pushes.

His mouth was pure magic. He had infinite patience and excellent instinct for what made her feel good and what drove her crazy. And he was committed to making the experience all about her.

Her fingers curled into the sheet, and she closed her eyes when warm hands smoothed over her belly and up to her breasts. Her eyes flew open to see Seth and Dillon on either side of her, their hands coaxing over her skin.

As Michael continued his sensual feast between her legs, Dillon and Seth lowered their mouths to her breasts. They each took a nipple between their teeth and sucked inward until both began a rhythmic pull that had her completely mindless.

She was hovering on the edge, so close to going over, when Michael pulled his head away. She moaned her protest and he smiled down at her.

"Just a minute, sweetheart. I promise. I have to get you ready to take me. I don't ever want to hurt you."

He picked up the tube of lubricant that Dillon had used and spread a liberal amount in his hand. He rolled on a condom with his other and applied the lubricant to the entire surface of his cock. Then he pressed his fingers between her legs and dipped inside her, easing the passage with the remaining gel.

When he fit himself to her, she realized he was bigger than both Seth and Dillon. He stretched experimentally, and she held her breath as she battled the intense pleasure and anticipation as well as the slight discomfort his entry caused her.

Michael paused and held still, but she could feel him so big and swollen within her. "Breathe, baby. I'm taking it slow. Look at me."

She found his gaze and stretched her arms high over her head. She arched upward, pushing her breasts more firmly against Dillon's and Seth's mouths. Her sensual cat-like movements pushed a growl from Michael's throat. Did she even know how beautiful she was? Did she know that with only a look he was completely and utterly lost?

"Move with me," he whispered. "Come with me, Lily."

She wrapped her legs tightly around him and tilted her hips to receive him more deeply.

Slowly. So tenderly that tears crowded her eyes, Michael rocked into her. Each push stretched her to accommodate him. Each retreat tugged at her insides as her pussy gripped him, reluctant to let go.

Dillon nipped sharply at her nipple while Seth sucked with hard tugs. Michael worked himself deeper until he was so fully lodged inside her that moving was near an impossibility.

Then he slipped his fingers between them and found her clit. He thumbed over it, rotating in a tight circle as he inched back and forth.

The friction of his cock stroking through her tight tissues combined with the pressure on her clitoris and the dual assault on her breasts was more than she could bear.

She came apart in a sudden burst, sharp and unrelenting. She tumbled over the edge and began a freefall that was dizzying for its speed and height.

She went liquid around Michael's cock, and suddenly he could move with much more ease. He stroked harder and faster until she was sobbing with the enormity of her orgasm.

Time slowed. The room blurred. She lost awareness of everything but mind-bending pleasure that bordered on very real pain. Never before had she been taken on such an intense sexual ride. Her experience to now had been sweet. Soft. Unthreatening. Comforting, even. Predictable.

She didn't know it could be this way. Didn't realize that she could lose control so completely.

She flew. This was what it felt like to be free and to face the wind. She never wanted to go back. She wanted to grab on to this—to them—and hold on forever.

Air blew cold on her face, and she realized her cheeks were wet with tears. And still she could make no sense of her surroundings.

Gradually she became aware of soothing hands and gentle voices saying such sweet things to her. She was beautiful. She was incredible.

She smiled and closed her eyes as she absorbed the feeling of being at peace. For the first time in so very long, she could feel the hole in her heart close just a little bit.

Healing and forgiveness were necessities of life. And in the arms of the Colter brothers, she began to believe that she just might have both.

Chapter Twenty

Lily was still sleeping soundly, curled into a ball in the middle of the bed, her head buried in a mound of pillows when the brothers dressed and crept silently from the room the next morning.

Michael avoided making eye contact with Seth and Dillon as they walked quietly to the kitchen. Dillon took out ingredients for a quick breakfast while Seth sat at the bar. The silence was so smothering that even the slightest noise Dillon made was like a cannon shot.

Michael sighed. "Okay, so who's going to bring it up first?"

"Bring what up?" Dillon muttered.

Seth glanced sharply at Dillon. "Don't be an ass. We might as well get it out in the open now before Lily wakes up. If we have issues, now is the time to discuss them so they don't cause problems later."

Dillon shrugged. "Look, I don't have a problem. Am I always going to want to make love to her with you two in the picture? Hell no. But I doubt you want that any more than I do. It was important to her that she not show preference by making love to one of us first. If that makes her feel at ease with the situation then I'm all for it. I'll do whatever it takes to make her happy."

"Never thought I'd say this, but I agree one hundred percent with you, Dillon," Michael said.

Seth nodded slowly. "So do I. Right now, I'll do anything to make her more comfortable. We have plenty of time to work the kinks out of our relationship as we go."

"So what's on everyone's agenda this morning?" Dillon asked as he dished up the bacon and eggs onto plates.

Dillon always was the planner. It was why he was so damn successful at everything he tried. He planned to the nth degree, and he followed through. He didn't know the meaning of the word fail. If he wanted it, he went after it.

"Lily needs to get into the clinic if you can arrange it, Michael, but the problem is, I can't take her. I've got a meeting with my accountant that'll probably take most of the day. I have to get my taxes squared away and take care of my quarterlies while I'm at it. Going to be a long damn day."

Michael grimaced. Dillon got downright cranky when it came to money. Funny, considering how easily he seemed to be able to make it. He had a Midas touch when it came to enterprise. He could take any business and turn it around or get it off the ground. Not everyone knew it, but Dillon damn near owned most of Clyde in one way or another.

"I can probably get her in, but I'm full up with appointments today. Seth, can you take her?" Michael asked.

"Yeah, I could take her and go by to fill out all the necessary paperwork for the new job. At some point this week, I'm going to have to go back to Denver to give notice at my house and move my shit."

Dillon rubbed his jaw thoughtfully. "What if we got Mom to go with her? It would accomplish a few things. One, Lily might be uncomfortable over the nature of the visit if one of us goes. Plus, I know she's ashamed of the fact that she can't foot the bill. If Mom took her, she might relax a bit about it all. It would also give Mom some time with her, and I want Lily to feel like she's part of the family."

"Not a bad idea," Michael said. "Why don't you give her a call while I call Dr. Burton. It might be later this afternoon when he can work her in, but I'm sure he'll do it if I ask him to."

"I could run Lily over to Mom's so she wouldn't have to tag along with me to fill out paperwork," Seth said. "She'd probably be bored out of her mind, and if Callie's around, she might like to go riding again."

Michael scowled. "She's not going riding until I check her arm again and make sure the wound isn't showing signs of infection. I swear everyone acts like she didn't just get shot a few days ago."

"I didn't see you worrying about that last night," Dillon drawled.

"Fuck you. I was very careful with her."

"Cut it out, you two," Seth said.

Dillon and Michael both held up their middle fingers at the same time, and Seth just shook his head.

"I swear you two always did share the same twisted, demented brain."

Michael raised an eyebrow in Dillon's direction. "I think he just tried to insult us."

Dillon shrugged. "I suppose we're going to have to put up with him since he did bring Lily to us. I'm sure he'll be smug about the fact that if it weren't for him we'd never have met her."

"I hadn't even thought about that, but you're right," Seth said with a grin.

"You and your mouth," Michael grumbled in Dillon's direction.

Slight movement from the corner of Michael's eye had him turning in the direction of the doorway of the kitchen. Lily stood there looking delectably rumpled. Her sleepy eyes took in the three brothers, and she fidgeted nervously in the doorway. It was obvious she'd dug out one of Dillon's button-up shirts. The problem was it hung clear past her knees and she had rolled up the sleeves several times just to get them over her wrists. She looked so darn cute that Michael had to smile.

"Good morning," he called out to her. He held out his hand and waited for her to come to him.

Dillon and Seth both turned to look in Lily's direction, and she gifted them with a shy smile.

She walked barefooted across the floor and slipped her hand into Michael's. He pulled her into his side and gave her a long, leisurely kiss.

When he pulled away, he stroked the hair from her eyes and trailed his fingers down the strands, tucking them over her ears.

"Sleep okay?"

She blushed. "Yes. Wonderfully. The bed is like sleeping on a cloud. I didn't want to get out of it."

At that, Dillon and Seth both frowned at the subtle reminder that just days before she'd been sleeping on thin cardboard. Hardly a barrier to the rough concrete of an alleyway.

Michael's own jaw twitched because he remembered all too well the sight of her huddled in the alleyway, scared out of her mind. As God was his witness, she'd never spend another day unprotected from the harsher realities of life.

"I have to go soon," he told her regretfully. "I have a full day of appointments."

She snuggled into his chest and wrapped her arms around him, hugging him tight to her. "I'll miss you. Will I see you tonight? I mean, I don't even know where I'm staying or where you're staying."

"You're staying here," Dillon growled.

"Yes, you'll see me tonight," Michael said, ignoring Dillon's outburst. "You'll be here, as will Seth. It'll take me a little time to arrange things with my house, but I'll be around for sure."

"I have an appointment with my accountant that's going to tie me up for most of the day," Dillon said to Lily. "Michael's going to get you in to see the doctor at the clinic, and I thought Mom could take you so Seth could get all his paperwork started for his new job."

Lily stiffened against Michael, and she chewed nervously at her bottom lip. "I don't want to bother her. I could go myself. I mean if I could ride into town with Seth, I could just wait there."

Michael rubbed his hand up and down her back, soothing away some of the tension. "First of all, you're not a bother. Mom will be thrilled to get to spend some time with you. If I know her, she'll have you spoiled in no time at all with the dads' help."

"We'll take care of all the arrangements, honey," Seth cut in softly. "There's not a damn thing you need to worry about. I thought I'd run you out to Mom's. If Callie's around, you two could go riding again, and then Mom can take you into town when it's time for your appointment."

Michael felt her hesitation, but he also saw the longing in her eyes. He squeezed her to him and kissed the top of her head. "Our mom's going to love you, Lily."

She smiled. "If you're sure she won't mind, I'd love to go out to the house and maybe ride with Callie again. I'll even let you check my arm so you can reassure yourself that it's not about to rot off."

He smacked her lightly on the bottom. "Smartass. I'm also going to make sure Dr. Burton gives it a thorough exam when he sees you this afternoon."

"Make the call so I can talk to Mom and let her know what's going on," Dillon prompted. "Lily, bacon and eggs okay?"

She sniffed and licked her lips. "It's perfect. I love bacon. Bacon makes everything better."

"Girl after my own heart," Seth said with a grin.

Michael dug out his cell and punched in the private number for Dr. Burton. He never asked for favors, and Michael had treated Dr. Burton's kids' animals on short notice on more than one occasion, so Michael hoped he'd return the favor now.

As he spoke to the doctor, he watched Lily laugh and interact with Dillon and Seth and marveled at how natural it all played out. Maybe it was because he had so many memories of his own parents laughing and loving in such a way, but it felt right.

After gaining Dr. Burton's assurance that he'd see Lily that afternoon, Michael rang off. "Two thirty," he told Dillon.

Dillon picked up the phone and dialed their parents' number as the others continued to eat.

"Hey, Mom," Dillon said. "How are you?" He grinned as he listened to whatever she was saying and then he said, "Hey, can you do us a favor? Seth thought he'd run Lily over to the house so she could hang out there, maybe go riding with Callie again. We all have a pretty full day and Lily has a doctor's appointment with Dr. Burton this afternoon. Do you think you could take her?"

Dillon smiled and after a moment said, "Thanks, Mom. We really appreciate this. I'll be sure to tell her. I'll see you later.

Love you."

He hung up and laid the phone down. "Mom said to tell you she'd be thrilled if you came over to visit and that she'd love to go to the doctor with you."

"She's so nice," Lily murmured.

"Yeah, she's pretty great," Seth agreed. "There aren't many people who don't think the world of her."

Lily snuck a piece of bacon from Dillon's plate, and Michael stifled his laughter at the look of sheer innocence on her face when Dillon noticed that his last piece was gone.

"Who the hell took my bacon?" he demanded. He scowled at Seth who was the closest and then his gaze settled on Lily who looked decidedly guilty. "You little thief," he said with a laugh. "Bacon stealing is a crime punishable by death in these parts."

Lily glanced over at Michael and then down to his plate. "Are you going to eat that last piece?"

Her tone was so hopeful, he couldn't possibly tell her yes. He picked it up and held it to her mouth. She grinned just before taking a big bite of the strip.

She sighed as she chewed. "Heaven. Just heaven."

Dillon chuckled. "Well, I know how to keep her happy. Just make her bacon every day."

Lily nodded vigorously.

Michael checked his watch and then pushed away from the bar. "I have to go, baby. I wish I didn't, but the patients await. Come into the living room so I can take a look at your arm before I go."

He urged her into the other room and onto the couch. He unbuttoned the shirt enough that he could slide it down her shoulder. He frowned when he saw the bandage had either fallen off or she'd taken it off since the night before.

But when he examined it, it was only slightly pink. The wound had closed. He palpated the area around it, watching her closely for signs of discomfort, but she didn't so much as flinch.

"Okay," he conceded. "It looks like you're all better. I'll back off and quit worrying so much now."

She smiled but threw her arms around his neck and

hugged him fiercely. "I love that you worry about me. It's kind of nice." Then she pulled away and raised her mouth to his.

He kissed her and soaked in her gentle sweetness.

"I'll see you this afternoon," she said.

"You betcha. Have a good day with Mom, okay?"

Michael said his goodbyes to his brothers and then headed for his Jeep. The morning air was chilly and the sky was overcast. It looked like snow. He frowned, realizing that they'd never taken Lily to buy clothes. Things had gone awry the minute Dillon had entered the picture.

She needed everything, including a coat and things that would keep her warm and comfortable. She couldn't continue to wear Callie's old stuff.

As he got into his Jeep, he picked up his cell to call his mom. She'd take care of the matter, and if he knew his mom, Lily would be outfitted head to toe in just a few hours' time.

Chapter Twenty-One

When Seth and Lily pulled up to his parents' house, Lily saw Callie standing in the distance overlooking the expanse of land below the cabin.

Seth cut the engine but sat in the truck watching his sister for a long moment.

"She looks sad," Lily observed.

Seth sighed. "I'm not sure what's going on with her. Something happened on her last trip overseas, but she's not talking. I hate to see her down. She's always the cheerful, upbeat one in the family."

"Maybe she just needs some space," Lily said softly. "It's not always easy to talk when wounds are still so fresh."

Seth turned his gaze on her, unpeeling her layer by layer. "Is that what happened with you, Lily?"

She hesitated and gripped the handle to the door. "Some wounds never heal."

"You'll heal," he said quietly. "You'll have me and my brothers and our family. Family heals even the worst hurts."

Warmth spread into her heart until her smile reflected the sheer joy his words brought her.

"That's a beautiful sentiment, Seth. And you know, I believe you. I really do. I feel...I feel like maybe everything is going to be okay again."

He leaned over and cupped her cheek and then he kissed her. "You can count on it, honey. Now let's go in and find Mom. She'll be looking forward to seeing you."

Lily opened her door and stepped into the chilly air. It was colder now than it had been earlier in the day. She turned her face upward to see the white sky lined with shades of gray.

"Bet it snows before the day's out," Seth said.

She shivered but secretly hoped it would. Before, snow had been a dreaded event when she lived on the streets. With no way to stay warm, snow could mean death. But here where she could sit in front of the fireplace with hot chocolate and watch the snow fall through the window? She couldn't think of anything more heavenly.

Seth opened the door and called in, "Mom? Dads? We're here."

He ushered Lily inside and closed the door behind them. One of the dads entered the living room—Ethan? She was fairly certain he was Ethan. She been a little befuddled and overwhelmed the first time she'd met them all, but he'd been the one to prepare lunch for her and Callie.

He smiled gently in Lily's direction. "Hello, Lily. How is your arm today?"

"Oh, I'm fine. Michael even gave me a clean bill of health this morning."

Ethan chuckled. "If you got by Michael, I'm betting you're just fine."

"Where's Mom?" Seth asked.

"She'll be along in a minute."

The peculiar look in Ethan's eyes made Lily think that she and Seth had interrupted a private moment. Her suspicion was confirmed a moment later when Holly entered the living room, her face flushed and her lips swollen.

Ethan's gaze was drawn to his wife, and he pulled her to his side. The tenderness that he displayed and the obvious love in his eyes made Lily's heart melt.

Holly's eyes lit up when she saw Lily, and she hurried across the room, her hands extended. "Lily! I'm so happy you came over. How are you doing? Is your arm all right?"

As she spoke, she did very motherly things like smooth Lily's hair from her face and stroke her hand down Lily's arm. Lily couldn't help but be drawn to the other woman. There was just something so warm and infectious about her.

"I'm good," Lily said, returning her smile. "Thank you for having me. I appreciate you being willing to go with me to the clinic."

Holly beamed back at her and then turned to Seth. "And you. You're going to get all the paperwork done so that your coming home will be official?"

Seth smiled and nodded. Holly latched on to Seth and hugged him senseless. "Oh, I'm so happy that you're going to be home." As she pulled away, tears shone brightly in her eyes.

"Aw, Mom, don't cry."

"I'll cry if I want to," she sniffed. "I hate that you've been away for so long. It'll be so wonderful having all my children back home where they belong. I pray that Callie doesn't decide to go back to parts unknown."

Seth grinned and rolled his eyes. "Admit it, Mom. You'd rather we all still lived here under your roof driving you and the dads crazy."

"Well, yes. I refuse to apologize for that."

Lily's chest tightened as she watched the obvious love and affection between them. She glanced up to see Ethan watching her with those soft brown eyes. She squirmed and looked away, worried that they were still wary of her and her intentions.

Holly shoved Seth toward the door. "Okay, so off with you. I'll feel a lot better when you've filled out all your paperwork and it's all official. Don't worry about Lily. Callie and I will take good care of her."

Seth turned to kiss his mom on the cheek. "I know you will, Mom." Then he looked up at Lily and his features softened. "I'll see you later, honey."

Lily smiled and gave him a small wave as he walked out the front door.

Holly turned her attention to Lily. "Okay. You and I have some shopping to do."

"Oh hell," Ethan muttered. He backed away, hands out. "I'll leave you to it."

"What are you leaving them to?" Ryan asked as he entered the room. He smiled at Lily as he came to a stop next to Holly. He bent and kissed his wife full on the lips until she emitted a breathy sigh.

"Shopping," Ethan replied in a voice that suggested Holly had said they were going to murder someone.

Lily couldn't suppress the giggle when Ryan took a hasty step away.

"You two are such wimps," Holly muttered. "In the early years, you were all about shopping and providing for your woman."

"That was before you turned it into a survival sport," Ethan said dryly.

"Lily needs clothes, and Callie and I are going to take her to get what she needs. We don't need you anyway."

"I'll drive you as long as I don't have to go in," Ethan offered.

Holly rolled her eyes and looked over at Lily. "You'd think after thirty-something years that I could drive somewhere by myself. Ethan still has a kitten when I want to drive into town without one of the menfolk."

"The weather's supposed to get worse," Ryan said with a frown. "It's not a bad idea for him to take you ladies. Snow's supposed to start in an hour or so, and there's a chance of it worsening as the afternoon progresses. Could get more than a foot accumulation."

"Then I'll let Callie drive," Holly said.

Ethan and Ryan both winced.

"I'll take you in the Rover," Ethan said. "There's plenty of room for everyone and you ladies can take your time. I'm in no hurry."

Holly looked at Lily as if to say, "See what I have to put up with?"

Lily smothered her laughter, but the sound still escaped.

Holly's gaze narrowed. "Just you wait, Lily. If you think you're going to have it any easier with my sons, you've got another think coming. They're chips off the old block for sure, and I'll tell you right now that Michael and Dillon have two of the hardest heads I've ever encountered. It's a wonder any of us survived their childhood."

"Amen," Ryan muttered.

"I think you're all pretty great," Lily said in a low voice.

Holly beamed at her and walked over to pull her into a hug. "And I think you're pretty great too. If you make my sons happy, this family will love you forever."

Ryan frowned. "Lily needs a coat. Do you or Callie have something she can wear into town?"

"Oh, of course. I'll get her one from the closet. If one of you will holler at Callie, we can go."

Holly hurried away, leaving Lily in the living room with Ethan and Ryan.

"I'll get Callie and warm up the truck," Ethan said. "Tell Holly to come on out when you're ready."

Lily waited in nervous silence for Holly to return. She could feel Ryan watching her.

"Lily," Ryan said in a soft voice.

She looked up to meet his gaze.

"You don't have to be nervous around us. I think you'll find we're pretty laid back around here. You're important to my sons, so that makes you important to me. You're part of this family and that means you have our support. All of us."

"Just like that?" she whispered.

He smiled. "Just like that."

She smiled back. "Thank you. I don't know what else to say. It's all so hard to believe. How did I get so lucky?"

He walked over to her and held out his arms. After only a moment's hesitation, she went into his embrace. He hugged her tightly.

"I think my boys would say they're the lucky ones. No reason to dissuade them of that notion, is there?"

She laughed and absorbed the wonderful feeling of home and acceptance.

"I think this will be perfect for you, Lily," Holly said as she hurried back into the room carrying a heavy coat. "It might be a little big on you, but it'll do until we get you a new one in town."

Lily took the coat, enjoying the feel of the warm sheepskin lining.

"You don't have to take me shopping, Mrs. Colter," she said. "Just taking me to the clinic is more than enough."

"First, call me Holly. Mrs. Colter sounds so...old. And second, you need clothes. My boys have given me strict instructions to buy you whatever I think you need. Notice, they were sure to say what I thought you needed and not what *you* thought you needed." Her eyes twinkled merrily as she teased. "And since I don't want my boys to think I fell down on the job, you're going to be fully outfitted head to toe by the time I'm finished."

Ryan let out a groan. "Thank God Ethan volunteered for chauffeur duty."

Holly elbowed him in the gut.

"And speaking of, Ethan said for you two to go on out when you were ready. He's warming up the Rover."

"You ready?" Holly asked. "Get your coat on and we'll hit the road. I don't want you to be late for your appointment."

Ethan drove them into town, and as they pulled into Riley's the first snow flurries started to swirl.

Holly climbed out of the front while Callie and Lily got out of the back.

"Riley's has been around forever," Holly explained as they walked into the general store. "More shops have opened over the years and I'll take you there for clothes, but this is the best place to get coats and boots and jeans."

Callie grinned. "In other words, if you want something cute, you'll need to hit the boutiques on Main Street."

"You should know that Callie's idea of cute isn't most people's idea," Holly warned.

Lily smiled. "I like her clothes."

"Oh, I dress to fit in here," Callie joked as they started browsing the racks of jeans. "Anyone not in jeans, boots and western wear gets the eyeball from the locals."

Holly picked up a pair of jeans and held them up, looking skeptically at Lily. "You can try these on but they look a little big to me. You're smaller-waisted than me and Callie. I figure you're at least a size smaller if not two. We'll start with these, though and see how they fit you."

Lily was hustled into a dressing room and never had to come out. Callie and Holly kept handing stuff in for her to try.

In an hour's time, she had an armful of jeans, two coats, one heavy and one a lighter windbreaker, plus two pairs of boots and two pairs of loafer-style shoes.

"It's too much," Lily protested as Callie and Holly hauled the clothing to the register.

Callie held up a hand. "Oh please, this is a drop in the bucket compared to some of the shopping trips I've made Seth take me on. They'll be happy the bill was only this much."

Holly laughed but nodded. "Callie was a born shopper, much to her fathers' and brothers' dismay."

Lily joined in their laughter, enjoying the companionship of other women. Friends. God, how she'd missed having good times and social outings. Shopping trips.

Holly checked her watch. "Okay, we need to get to the clinic. We can either hit the boutiques after your appointment, or, if you trust Callie to pick up a few things for you, she can walk over while we're at the doctor's."

Lily glanced over at Callie who raised her hands in defense. "I swear I'll do right by you. I have a pretty good eye for what will look good on you. And it will give me immense pleasure to go shopping on my brothers' dime."

Lily laughed. "I trust you. I'm sure your taste has to be better than mine."

Holly hustled the girls out of the store and into the truck where Ethan waited. They stuffed their bags in the back and piled in.

"Get everything you need?" Ethan asked.

"Take us to the clinic," Holly said. "Callie's going to do some shopping across the street while Lily is at her appointment."

Two hours later, Lily and Holly walked out of the clinic, Lily clutching the bag with the starter pack of her pills and a prescription for several months' worth. Callie was waiting in the truck with Ethan when Holly and Lily climbed in.

"I've had calls from all three of my sons demanding to know how things went with your doctor's appointment," Ethan said to Lily.

"Oh, everything is fine," Lily said. "He looked at my arm and said it was healing nicely. No cause for alarm. It doesn't even hurt anymore."

She wasn't about to tell any of them what the true reason for her appointment had been, although she was pretty sure Holly had a good idea.

Callie leaned forward and rested her arms over the back of Ethan's seat. "I vote we go home and have the dads fix us dinner while Lily hosts a fashion show for me and Mom."

"Spoiled much?" Ethan asked dryly.

"I'm not going to deny it," Callie said with a grin.

Holly laughed. "Well, I could cook, but somehow I don't think anyone wants that."

"No, that's okay," Ethan said hastily. "I'm sure any of us would be more than happy to cook for our women." He glanced back at Lily as he started to pull out of the parking space. "Were the guys expecting you for dinner?"

"I'm not certain," Lily said hesitantly. "They were all so busy today. They said they'd see me tonight, but I don't know when."

"Don't worry," Holly soothed. "Ethan will call them and tell them all to come to supper. It's been a long time since we all had dinner together, and I can't think of a better occasion than now."

In truth, Lily was excited about the prospect. She smiled and nodded and then leaned back, squeezing her arms over her chest and holding her happiness close, as if any moment it would be torn away from her.

Chapter Twenty-Two

Seth and Michael pulled up to their parents' house at the same time.

"How did it go?" Michael asked as he got out and walked around to the front of his truck to meet Seth.

"Got everything filled out. Spoke to a few members of the city council. They're pretty excited that I've agreed to come on board. They're calling a special meeting on Monday, but it's just a formality."

"Are you comfortable with the decision?"

Seth paused for a minute as he stared around the place he'd grown up in. "Yeah. I'm good. Glad to be coming home."

They walked into the house and were greeted by the sounds of women's laughter. Michael exchanged grins with Seth as they entered the living room to see Lily modeling in dramatic fashion in front of Callie and their mom.

Seth held a finger to his lips and motioned Michael to stay back. The sight of Lily so carefree and uninhibited and having fun was enchanting.

He watched her twirl and strike outrageous poses as Callie and his mom cheered her on. Lily's face was flush with pleasure, her eyes alive and bright, and her smile was about ten thousand watts.

His dads had gathered in the doorway behind Lily, clearly as entranced as Seth and Michael were. But no one made a move into the room, not wanting to ruin the obvious delight of the women.

"Oh hell, they're drinking," Michael muttered.

Holly and Callie poured wine from a nearly empty bottle, handed Lily a glass and set the bottle down by two other empties on the coffee table.

"Jesus, and the dads allowed this?" Seth whispered.

"They look pretty amused."

Amidst giggles and calls of encouragement, Lily struck another outrageous pose, and at the same moment, her gaze lifted and she saw Seth and Michael in the doorway.

Color rushed to her cheeks, and for lack of a better word, she looked appalled. She stumbled, then righted herself and quickly plopped into a chair across the couch from their mom and Callie.

The dads began clapping, perhaps to break up the awkward moment. Lily whirled to see them standing in the doorway, and her face only got more crimson.

Then she buried her face in her hands and let out a groan.

Callie hurried from the couch, shoved into the chair with Lily and slung an arm around her shoulders. She hugged her tight and then glared at first the dads and then Seth and Michael.

Holly stood, but from all appearances, she was more than a little tipsy. She waved her glass in the dads' directions and scowled.

"Go away. We're having girl time here. The last thing we need is a bunch of Neanderthals interfering."

"Even if the Neanderthals have cooked dinner and have it ready to eat on the table?" Adam drawled.

Holly hesitated, wobbled a little and then said, "It depends on what you cooked."

"Good answer, Mom," Callie crowed.

"We might have grilled steaks, baked potatoes and all the fixings," Ethan said in a casual manner.

"Good enough for me," Callie said as she rose. "Ready to eat, Lily?"

Lily tried to stand and promptly plopped back down. Then she giggled and rubbed a hand over her eyes as if trying to clear the cobwebs. Holly tried to go over to help her, but nearly stumbled over the edge of the carpet.

"For God's sake," Ryan muttered as he hurried forward to steady Holly. He looked up at Seth and Michael. "You might want to come help Lily to the table. I think they tried to see how much wine they could drink before they started puking."

Seth chuckled and started toward Lily while Ryan helped Holly toward the kitchen.

"Hey, what about me?" Callie demanded.

Michael tweaked her on the nose. "The day you can't hold your liquor is the day I check you into the hospital."

She rolled her eyes and headed for the kitchen after the others.

Lily still looked embarrassed and sat quietly at the kitchen table as the dads set the table and dished up the large steaks.

Everyone had taken their seats and were about to dig in when Dillon hollered from the front door.

"In here, son," Adam called.

Dillon entered the kitchen and sniffed appreciatively. Then his gaze settled on Lily, and without saying anything further to anybody, he headed straight for her, inserted himself between her chair and Michael's and kissed her long and hard.

"Everything go okay today?" he murmured.

She smiled and nodded and Dillon reluctantly pulled away from the table to go take a seat down at the end.

Holly cleared her throat and everyone looked in her direction. "I just want to say, before we all eat, how wonderful it is to have my family home again. I miss my children when they're gone."

"And a big welcome to the newest addition to our family," Adam said as he held up a glass in Lily's direction. "To Lily."

"To Lily!" the rest chorused.

Lily looked as if she was battling tears. Her eyes glistened, and she raised her table napkin to wipe at her face several times.

Dinner...was just like old times. Loud. Boisterous. Seth was a little worried at first that they'd overwhelm Lily, but she looked to be enjoying herself as her gaze bounced back and forth between the noisy conversations.

Seth's homecoming dominated the dinner conversation.

Though his mom had been the most vocal, it was obvious that his dads were every bit as thrilled that he was coming home. Adam smiled every time he looked in Seth's direction, and he wrapped an arm around Holly and held her close as they surveyed the gathering at the table.

At one point, Adam leaned over to kiss the side of Holly's head and murmured something in her ear. Her face lit up, and she smiled down the table, her face glowing in happiness.

Seth looked to his brothers and found the same satisfaction on their faces. The same contentment. Only Callie seemed withdrawn, her smile strained. He could see the shadows under her eyes and faint pain in the depths.

It had to be hard when everyone else was so happy and she was dealing with whatever had driven her to seek refuge.

"Are you ladies sober enough to make it back into the living room?" Ethan joked.

"Oh we're fine," Holly said in exasperation.

"Hate to eat and run," Seth said as he rose. "But we really need to get on the road. The snow was coming down pretty hard and we don't want to get stranded."

"It might be better if you stayed over," Adam said, concern darkening his voice. "It's after dark and it's been snowing for a while now."

"We'll take Michael's Jeep and leave mine and Seth's trucks here," Dillon said. "We have a lot to talk about and work out. We'll visit again soon."

Dillon stood and walked to stand behind Lily. He clasped her shoulders and rubbed gently. "You ready?"

She glanced up at Seth and then Michael and nodded.

There was a chorus of hugs and goodbyes, and Seth smiled as Callie and his mom both fussed over Lily. The women joked and laughed about their afternoon together, and then Holly recruited the dads to help bring all of Lily's packages out to the Jeep.

"Are you sure there's going to be room for all of us?" Dillon joked as he and Seth stood back watching all the bags being stuffed in the back. "How much of our money did Mom spend today, anyway?"

"You don't want to know," Callie said cheekily. Then in a lower voice, "Don't give Lily a hard time about it. It was like pulling teeth to get her to agree to all the stuff, and she needed everything."

Dillon pulled her into a hug and kissed her forehead. "Thanks for doing it for her. You're the best."

"I like her, Dillon," Callie said in a low voice. "So do Mom and the dads. Don't fuck this up."

Seth chuckled next to Dillon. "Leave it to Callie to take us all to task."

Michael bundled Lily into the front seat and then motioned for Seth and Dillon. "Come on you two, before Lily freezes to death."

Seth and Dillon brushed the snow from their shoulders and heads and climbed into the Jeep.

"Did you have fun today?" Seth asked as Michael pulled out of the drive onto the snow-covered road.

Lily turned and smiled. "I did. Your mom and sister are so great."

"How did it go at the doctor?" Dillon asked. "Did you get everything you need?"

Lily ducked her head and Seth shot Dillon a glare for embarrassing her.

"I did," she said in a low voice. "It's good timing actually. I start the pills the first Sunday after my last period. That's day after tomorrow."

Seth reached up and squeezed Lily's shoulder. "As long as you feel like you have what you need, honey."

It took longer than normal to make the drive through town and up to Dillon's place. When they stomped onto the porch to shake the snow from their boots, Dillon opened the front door to let them all in.

"Give me a minute to get a fire built," Dillon said.

"I'll make some hot chocolate," Seth said.

"That leaves you and me to snuggle on the couch," Michael said to Lily.

She smiled and kicked her shoes off and piled them with the others by the door. Then she padded across the floor and curled into the plump cushions of Dillon's sectional.

Seth heated milk and then added the chocolate mix to the cups. He wasn't sure whether Michael or Dillon would want a cup, but he made enough for the four of them. He arranged the mugs on a tray and carried it into the living room where a hearty fire already blazed in the hearth.

Dillon and Michael were sitting on either side of Lily, and she looked adorable all but lost between the two men and the fluffy cushions.

Seth set the tray down on the coffee table and handed around the mugs. Then he leaned back on the couch and propped his feet up.

"You get everything ironed out, Seth?" Dillon asked.

Seth nodded. "Yeah, I'm going to go back to Denver tomorrow and tie up all my loose ends there. Shouldn't take me more than a few days."

Michael turned to Lily. "Want to come hang out with me at the office while Seth does his thing? Lots of critters to see."

Lily's face lit up. "That sounds fun. I love animals."

As Seth settled back to sip at his hot chocolate, he looked around at a new family in the making, and despite his initial reservations, hope and anticipation, and most of all, *satisfaction* gripped him.

Chapter Twenty-Three

Three days later, Lily held a pitifully mewling cat in her arms while she waited for Michael to complete his assessment. She stroked her fingers over her ears and murmured nonsense words in an effort to soothe her.

The poor thing was bedraggled, cold and hungry to boot.

"What will happen to her?" Lily asked anxiously.

The cat had been dumped at the door of the clinic in a box a few minutes after Michael had closed for the day. By the time they heard her plaintive wails, the cat had been half dead from the cold.

Michael grimaced. "We'll feed her, make sure she's healthy and no serious problems and then we'll try to find a home for her. But I'll be honest. I get a lot of castoffs here, and I simply don't have the room to board them all. I usually have to call the shelter over in Gunnison."

"But don't they put animals to sleep if they can't find homes?"

She tried to keep the stress from her voice because she knew Michael wasn't any happier about this than she was, and he was right, he couldn't take in every stray that came across his doorstep.

Michael's eyes softened. "They'll try to find a home for her first. Euthanization is a last resort."

Lily looked down at the bundle of fur and felt tears crowding the edges of her eyes. She stroked the cat and felt the answering vibration of purring.

Then she looked back up at Michael, her expression

pleading. "Couldn't we take her? I mean home? I don't want her to die just because someone didn't want her anymore."

Michael blew out his breath and then looked between her and the cat. Then he lifted his gaze to hers again, his eyes troubled. He touched her cheek and softly caressed.

"Is that how you felt, Lily? Like no one wanted you anymore?"

The ache grew in her chest as she struggled with her emotions. "Maybe I just didn't feel like I deserved to have people to love me," she whispered.

"Aw, Lily. You have such a big heart. I can't imagine anyone not loving you, and furthermore, if it's the last thing I do, I'm going to make damn sure that not only do you know you deserve it, but that you expect it."

She dropped her gaze to the cat who'd snuggled into her arms.

"She deserves a home and someone to love her too."

"I have this feeling that you're going to be impossible to ever win an argument with," he said ruefully. "I can't think of a single reason to tell you no."

Lily lifted her gaze back to Michael. "So I can keep her?"

He dragged a hand through his hair and pulled it behind him in a makeshift ponytail. "Yeah, you can keep her. God help me. Dillon's going to have a coronary."

"Dillon doesn't like pets?"

"More like the thought of a cat scratching up his custom wood is going to give him a seizure," Michael said with a grin.

"I'll take good care of her and keep her off Dillon's wood," Lily said solemnly.

Michael pulled her in and kissed her hair. "I'm just giving you a hard time, baby. We'll pack her up after I've finished my exam. She'll need worming I'm sure and we should treat her for fleas before we take her into the house. I have cat food here and we can bring a few bags home so she'll have what she needs."

"And a litter box?" Lily asked. "I don't want her to be outside in the cold. She needs to stay inside."

"And a litter box," Michael agreed. "She can take up residence in the mud room."

Lily clapped her hands together in delight and then threw her arms around Michael, scaring the cat in the process. She leaped to the neighboring counter and stared suspiciously as Lily danced around the room, holding tight to Michael.

Michael laughed. "Easy there. You're making me dizzy."

"Thank you," Lily exclaimed. Then she reached up and kissed him full on the lips.

He caught her against him, cradling the back of her head in his palm as he kissed her. His tongue slid along the seam of her lips, demanding entry. With a breathless sigh, she opened and let him in. His taste seeped into her mouth and floated through her veins until all she could breathe, smell or taste was him.

When he drew away, his eyes were half-lidded and glittering with desire. His hands wandered idly over her hips and up her sides to her breasts.

Then he walked her back until the small of her back met the edge of the exam table. He planted his hands on the table on either side of her, effectively trapping her.

"Shouldn't we be going?" Lily asked innocently.

"Kiss me again, and I'll take you and your cat home for dinner."

"Bully," she grumbled, but she melted against his chest and wrapped her arms around his neck.

He smelled good. Tasted even better. She delved her fingers into his hair, letting the strands slide over the tips as he kissed her senseless.

They were both hungry and breathless. His arousal pressed into her belly, hard and urgent.

The cat meowed and jumped back onto the exam table to rub against Lily's side. Michael drew away with a muffled curse when the cat sank her claws into his arm.

"Damn cat. Already encroaching on my territory," he grumbled.

Lily giggled and leaned into Michael. "Take me and our new kitty home and feed us. We're hungry."

Lily fussed over the food and water bowls and then made

sure the litter was situated just right before locking the cat into the mud room until she was better acquainted with her surroundings.

When she went back into the living room, Michael was standing in front of the couch, his eyes hooded. She was immediately wary. Arousal was heavy in the air. Thick, so thick it prickled up her nape.

She stopped in the doorway, her hand resting on the frame. He was looking at her like he was about to pounce. Her pulse raced and her breath caught in her throat until her lungs burned.

He crooked his finger in her direction. The power in his gaze and the command in his eyes sent a shiver down her spine.

Her legs wobbling, she took halting steps toward him, stopping a mere foot in front of him.

"Tell me, Lily," he said in a silky voice. "Just how grateful are you that I let you bring your cat home?"

She battled a smile, but played along. Then she leaned up on tiptoe and brushed an innocent kiss over his lips. "Thank you. I'm very grateful."

"Then get on your knees," he growled.

Her eyes widened and fire pooled low in her belly and tightened every muscle in her groin. Erotic images buzzed through her mind as she imagined precisely what he wanted to do.

Nervous bubbles scuttled around her stomach as she slowly went to her knees in front of him. His expression was fierce, demanding, his face drawn into harsh lines.

He slowly unzipped his jeans, the rasp loud in the silence. He loosened the waist, shoved them just over his hips and pulled out his cock.

Letting his pants fall to just below his waist, he reached out with his free hand and grasped her behind the neck.

"I can be demanding, Lily," he whispered. "I like control. Don't let me overpower you, though. If I ever go too far, say the word. I'll back off."

Heat rushed through her body, weakening her to the point

she swayed on her knees. The words purred from his throat, so erotic and sensual. She gazed up at him, all the trust she placed in him shining in her eyes.

She was wildly intrigued by the command in his voice. His hand massaged her nape, but his grip never lessened. His fingers were firm, applying pressure as he guided his cock toward her mouth.

"Open," he rasped.

As soon as her lips parted, he shoved into her mouth, deep and rough. A moan rippled from her throat and vibrated over his cock. Her lips met his knuckles and then he slid his fingers from around his cock underneath her chin as he fed his erection even deeper into her mouth.

"Swallow, baby. Swallow against the head. Milk it."

She obeyed, awkwardly at first, but she quickly mastered working her throat against his huge shaft. One silky rope of semen filled the back of her throat as pre-come slipped from the probing tip.

His hands tangled in her hair, pulling her closer. Then they slipped to the sides of her head and held her in place as he began thrusting harder into her mouth.

"Holy fuck, is this what I'm going to come home to every night?"

Michael paused, his cock buried in her mouth. Lily glanced sideways to see Dillon standing in the doorway to the living room. His eyes were glazed, and judging by the bulge at his groin, he wasn't the least bit put off to find his brother's cock buried in Lily's mouth.

Michael eased out to give her breath but kept his hands on her head. He thrust shallow, keeping her mouth open and drawled lazily in Dillon's direction.

"She's showing her gratitude for my generosity."

"Oh? And what pray tell did you do that warranted a blowjob?" Dillon demanded.

"I let her bring home a cat."

"You did what?"

Lily flinched at the tone of Dillon's voice but Michael caught her and soothed his hands over her face, still rocking his hips back and forth in short thrusts.

"We're the proud new owners of a cat left on the clinic's doorstep," Michael explained.

"Well hell," Dillon muttered. "What possessed you to bring something with claws into my house? The damn thing will shred my furniture."

Michael withdrew and caressed her cheek, rubbing his thumb over her bottom lip. "Lily thought she needed a home, and I agreed. I'm finding that our lady here has a way of asking that makes it impossible to turn her down."

Lily glanced over at Dillon, worried that he was truly angry. Maybe some of her fear showed in her eyes, because Dillon's expression immediately softened but then became quickly calculating.

It was the slow smile that told Lily she was in deep trouble. Dillon advanced, his eyes gleaming with a predatory light.

"It seems to me that since I wasn't party to this agreement that you should throw a little gratitude in my direction."

"Her mouth is busy right now," Michael said. "I have plans for it for quite a while."

"But not her pussy," Dillon purred. "Strip, Lily. I see no reason why you can't accommodate us both at the same time."

Goosebumps raced across her skin with lightning speed. Every nerve ending jumped. Her breasts swelled and her nipples beaded so tight that her shirt abraded the tips painfully.

"You heard him," Michael said tightly. "Undress and get on your knees on the L of the couch."

He reached down a hand to help her, and she grasped it tightly, hoping her knees didn't buckle on the way up.

Her fingers clumsily grasped at the buttons on her shirt. Several times she missed and had to go back to unfasten each one. As she pulled the shirt away, she walked toward the sectional where the side resembled a long, rectangle ottoman.

She loosened her bra, dropped it away and then quickly shed her pants and underwear. With a nervous glance over her shoulder, she carefully crawled onto the cushion, positioning herself as Michael had directed.

Michael walked around in front of her while Dillon came up

behind her and slid his hands over the globes of her ass. Then he leaned down and ran his tongue up the seam of her behind to the small of her back, eliciting a violent shiver from her.

Michael cupped a hand underneath her chin and tilted her head upward as he grasped his cock with his other hand and brought it to her lips. For a moment, he teased her, running the tip over her mouth, from one corner to the other.

More pre-come seeped from the slit, coating her lips. She flicked her tongue out, licking the moisture. Michael's breath escaped in a hiss, and she smiled, knowing he liked the erotic image of her licking his fluid from her lips.

Dillon ran his thumb over the opening to her pussy and pushed inward as his fingers found her clit. She closed her eyes and wiggled her hips as he rubbed over her sweet spot just the way she liked.

Then he positioned his cock at her opening and pushed in a few inches. Her pussy locked down, protesting the invasion. He caressed her buttocks and her hips and continued his shallow thrusts as he coaxed her body into accepting him.

Michael grasped her jaw and guided his cock past her lips and into her mouth once more. Then, as soon as he was positioned, he moved his hands down her chest to cup her breasts.

He pinched her nipples gently between his thumbs and forefingers. Her body tightened and she went liquid around Dillon's cock.

With a moan, he slid deeper until she was snug all around him and his balls rested against her mound.

"Damn," Dillon muttered. "Whatever the hell you just did, keep doing it because she just went all silky on me, and she's wrapped around me to the nuts."

Michael continued to thumb and carefully tweak her nipples as he thrust deeper and harder into her mouth. She was so on edge that the room was a haze around her. She was riding a cloud of intense sexual heat, and each stroke brought her higher and closer to a razor's edge.

Neither man was small. She was completely and utterly filled. Overwhelmed by their power and trapped by their hands. Impaled on their cocks as they rocked her between them.

They knew how to touch her. Knew her sweet spots and they teased her mercilessly, determined to bring her the ultimate pleasure.

She rolled her tongue around the head of Michael's cock as he withdrew. He made a strangled noise, paused, but then powered forward over her tongue. She swallowed as he'd taught her, drawing him deeper and working the back of her throat around his head.

"Jesus. I can't last, baby. God, you're so sweet. So good. I've never felt anything so good."

He withdrew and held his straining erection to her lips. "I'm going to ride you hard, Lily. And I want you to swallow every drop. I won't hold you, though. The choice is yours. If you get overwhelmed, or you aren't comfortable, you can pull away at any time."

She stared up at him and then slowly licked over her lips, her stare as sultry as she could muster. He pumped his erection once with his hand and then guided it back into her mouth. He gave her a moment, as if to make sure she was on board, and then he began pumping into her mouth with rapid, hard strokes.

Dillon thrust deep into her body and then held tight to her hips, holding himself against her while Michael worked her front. Dillon continued to hold still, absorbing Lily's backward motion against the force of Michael's thrusts.

She needed to come. Was desperate for release. But she knew that as long as Dillon remained still, she'd hover there on the edge.

Michael felt enormous. He was so rigid that it was like an iron bar crowding her throat. His hands found her breasts again, cupping and molding them as his hips worked spasmodically.

The first hot stream of semen splashed against the back of her throat. She swallowed as he thrust again and it spread over her tongue and filled her mouth faster than she could swallow. She held it, allowing it to coat his cock and lubricate his thrusts.

He slowed and his movements eased until his thrusts were slow and measured. She swallowed the remainder of his release and sucked gently as she licked the remnants from his softening erection.

When he finally pulled away, Dillon eased back, rippling through her swollen pussy. He powered forward, gliding like a warm knife through butter.

Michael continued to caress her breasts, and he captured her nipples between his fingers, twisting and pinching lightly as her orgasm mounted with rapid, aggressive intensity.

"Please," she begged. "Don't stop."

"I'm not stopping," Dillon growled. "Come for me, Lily. Bathe me with your heat. I want to feel you come apart around my dick."

The explicit words sent her straight over the edge. Her entire body tightened. Michael pinched hard at her nipples, and with a harsh cry, she threw back her head and pushed frantically back against Dillon as wave upon wave of intense, agonizing pleasure rippled through her body like a tidal wave.

Just as soon as her orgasm ripped into her, Dillon began thrusting hard and deep, his fingers digging into her hips. He was so big, and she was so tight. She felt every part of him, every ripple, every thrust until she was to the point of over-stimulation.

As her orgasm subsided, she whimpered at Dillon's thrusts over her hypersensitive flesh.

"Shhh, baby," he soothed, but he let up and thrust more gently even in the throes of his own orgasm.

He leaned into her and worked slowly in and out, taking care not to hurt her. He shuddered one last time and held himself inside her as his hands wandered over her body, touching, petting and caressing.

And then he eased away, and she all but collapsed over the couch, her body heaving with exertion.

Michael smoothed the hair away from her face and bent to kiss her cheek, smooching gently up to her ear. Then he gathered her in his arms and picked her up, swinging around to walk toward the bathroom.

"Why don't you take a soaking bath or a hot shower while we cook dinner," he said as he kissed her forehead.

She snuggled into his arms for a moment before allowing herself to slide down until her feet hit the floor.

"I'll just take a quick shower," she said in a slurry voice. "If I get into the tub, I'll be asleep in two minutes."

Michael smiled. "Okay, then. Take your time. We'll be in the kitchen."

Chapter Twenty-Four

Lily lingered in the shower and turned the water cool so that it would rid her of the lingering heat still simmering through her veins. She was deliciously sore, and she could still feel the imprint of their hands on her body.

Her pussy throbbed and pulsed, and her clit was so hypersensitive that even brushing a washcloth over it sent shards of aftershocks through her groin.

She leaned against the wall and let the water rain down over her head and back as she took deep, steadying breaths to ease some of the tension coiled in her muscles.

When the water grew too cool for her to bear, she stepped shivering from the shower and quickly wrapped herself in a towel to warm up.

She towel dried her hair and ran a comb through the curls until they held some semblance of order. Then she quickly dressed, eager to return to Michael and Dillon.

As she walked into the kitchen, she inhaled the aroma of cooking food and her mouth watered.

"It smells great. What are we having?" she asked as she slid onto a barstool beside Michael.

"Spaghetti," Dillon said. "Not too fancy, but I was later getting home than I wanted. This is something that's quick to whip up."

"Mmm, it smells yum and I'm starving," she admitted. "Michael promised me food. He said nothing about me having to service him."

She worked to keep the betraying grin from her face as

Michael turned his heated gaze on her.

"Servicing me. I like the sound of that. Maybe I should make a rule that you have to service me at varying intervals of the day."

Dillon snorted. "You'll wear her out."

"On the contrary. I have a feeling she'd have me exhausted inside of a day," Michael teased.

"And when do I get serviced?" she asked innocently.

Dillon's gaze smoldered. "Any damn time you want, sweetness. I'm at your beck and call any time you find yourself in need."

She'd have to be dead not to respond to that. Her nipples tightened all over again and desire that she'd thought completely satisfied pooled in her belly and swelled outward at alarming speed.

Dillon finally dropped his gaze and fished a noodle from the pot of boiling water to test it. Then he picked up the pot and went to the sink to pour it into the colander.

"Seth called earlier to say he'd be in tonight," Dillon said.

"Oh that's wonderful!" Lily exclaimed. "I think I'll stay up for him. Did he say when he'd get in? And did he get everything settled in Denver?"

She hadn't realized how anxious she sounded until Michael slid his hand over her shoulder and squeezed reassuringly.

Dillon smiled as he piled three plates high with spaghetti and ladled the thick sauce over the top.

"It'll be after supper sometime. He was leaving as I left the pub. He didn't have much stuff to move so he's dragging a trailer with his truck. He said he gave notice and gave his landlord the keys, so it looks like he'll be back for good."

Lily clapped her hands together in delight, joy and such deep contentment squeezing her heart.

"I'm so glad. Now we can all be together."

Michael and Dillon exchanged smiles. "Yeah, sweetness. We'll all be together now," Dillon said.

It was late when Seth pulled into Dillon's drive. He parked

way over to the side and didn't even bother unhooking the trailer. He was tired and more than a little eager to see Lily after being gone for three days.

He got out and headed toward the front door. The outside light had been left on for him, but the interior looked dark. Disappointment gripped him at the thought of her being asleep already.

He let himself into the living room and quietly closed the door behind him. A lamp burned in the corner and it was there in the soft illumination that he saw Lily curled on the couch, her head resting softly on the arm.

He smiled. She'd waited up for him but had fallen asleep.

Tenderness filled him as he walked slowly in her direction. For a long moment, he stood over her, simply watching the slight rise and fall of her chest.

Then as if sensing his presence, she stirred and opened her eyes. Her smile was immediate and warmed him through. Her face lit up, and she shot to her feet before he could put out a hand to stop her.

She threw her arms around him and hugged him fiercely.

"I'm so glad you're home," she whispered. "I missed you so much."

He gathered her in his arms and just held her, enjoying the feel of her against his body. He kissed the top of her head and laid his cheek against her hair.

"I missed you too, baby."

To his utter surprise, she pulled away and then leaned up to take his mouth in a fierce, possessive kiss. Her mouth was hot and wet against his and then moved to kiss a path down his jaw and to his neck.

She sank her teeth into the column of his neck and nibbled her way further down his chest. She tore impatiently at his shirt as if she couldn't wait to touch him.

"Take your clothes off," she urged in a husky, passion-filled voice. "Hurry."

He was already hard—painfully so, and he wasted no time shucking his shoes, pants and shirt. Before he could reach for his underwear, she was there, sliding her hands into the waistband and pulling downward to free his cock.

Her hands closed around his length and then her mouth, hot and lush, covered the head, sucking him deep.

He slid his hand into her hair to steady himself. His knees shook so badly that it was a wonder he didn't hit the floor.

She sank onto the couch, pulling his hips forward so he remained in her mouth. He leaned, propping his hands on the back of the sofa to brace himself, forcing her back.

"Damn," he murmured. "If this is the kind of homecoming I can look forward to, I'm going to make it a point to leave more often."

Her hands were everywhere, over his ass, stroking down his sides then back to cup his behind, squeezing and kneading as she sucked him with her wicked mouth.

"Do you have a condom on you?" she asked hoarsely around his cock.

"Back pocket," he managed to grind out.

She left him long enough to retrieve the condom from his jeans and then she pushed him down to the couch. He sprawled against the cushions, his legs splayed out and his cock so erect that it lay back toward his belly.

She yanked off the long T-shirt she wore and to his delight, she didn't have on a stitch underneath. His gaze was riveted to her small, curvy body, rounded hips and plump small breasts that just begged for his mouth.

She tossed him the condom, and he wasted no time tearing it open and rolling it over his dick. As soon as he was done, she crawled onto the couch and straddled his thighs. Using his shoulders for leverage, she lifted herself then reached down to guide his cock to her pussy.

There was no light tease, no work up to the big moment. She took him hard and fast, and he was inside her so quickly that he momentarily lost awareness of everything but her liquid heat surrounding him and gripping him like a fist.

She wrapped her arms around his neck and began to ride him, squeezing him like she was eager to take him into every part of her being.

"You're going to have to slow down," he gasped. "I'm not

going to last long like this, and I want it to be good for you."

"You're good for me," she said as she dipped her head to fuse her mouth to his.

He slid his body forward so that she could straddle him more effectively, her feet reaching toward the floor. The movement sent him deeper and they both gasped at the exquisite fullness.

"Damn it, Lily, I don't want to hurt you."

"You need to worry that I'm going to hurt *you*," she murmured.

She fisted the hair at his nape in her hand and yanked him to her, taking him with savage abandon. She was hungry and wild, her pussy clutching desperately at him with each thrust.

He laughed, the sound light in the air. "Hurt me. Please. Have your evil way with me. I won't complain. I swear. I'm yours."

"Oh yes, you're mine," she breathed. "All mine."

She twisted above him, taking him whole as she bucked over his hips. She threw back her head, her breathing coming in harsh, ragged spurts.

With one hand on his shoulder, she slid her other hand between them, her fingers finding her clit.

"Last one there is a rotten egg." She looked at him, her eyes glittering with intense arousal.

He gripped her hips and ground her downward. It was fast, and she was slick. His worry of hurting her disappeared as she met him thrust for thrust.

Her fingers slid rapidly over her clit and she tightened around him.

"Oh no you don't," he muttered.

Her throaty laugh flowed over his skin, frying every one of his nerve endings. He felt her in the deepest part of himself. With a shout, he surged upward, just as she let out an intense cry of her own.

His release exploded from his groin, so fast and so furious that he lost focus. He acted instinctively, taking her, owning her in the most primitive way a man could own a woman.

But it was her doing the possessing. She had his heart in

her hands. She owned his soul.

He arched one last time. Her hands flew to his shoulders and her fingers dug painfully into his skin as her body shook and trembled violently over him. Then he gathered her tight in his arms and collapsed back against the couch. They were sprawled, a tangle of bodies and arms and legs, and he struggled to catch his breath.

"I think we have to call that one a tie," he said raggedly.

She smiled against his neck and then kissed his pulse point. "I'm good with that."

"Thank God. I'd hate to think we had to call a do-over. You damn near killed me," he groaned.

Her body shook with laughter but neither made an effort to move.

Finally she lifted her head so that she could look into his eyes. "I missed you."

He was suddenly so overwhelmed by the depth of his feelings for this woman. The days he'd been away all came to this. Her back in his arms. There was such a sense of rightness and belonging that he found the words tumbling out.

"I love you, Lily."

Her eyes widened but joy burst into her expression with the radiance of a Colorado sunrise over the mountains. If he lived to be a hundred, he'd never forget the shine in her eyes as she stared wordlessly back at him.

It hadn't come out the way he wanted. He would have preferred a moment where he could better put to words his feelings and his utter contentment. But there it was, in the aftermath of the best sex he'd had in his life. His woman in his arms, warm and sweaty from loving. Maybe there was no better time than right here and right now.

"Oh Seth," she whispered.

She hugged him to her, holding on for all she was worth. Her heart beat wildly against his chest, and she squeezed. He could feel the emotion boiling within her as she struggled to maintain her composure. For some reason that satisfied him all the more.

She didn't return the words, and he wasn't threatened by

that. He knew they had a lot to work through. It was enough that he'd offered her the gift of himself. In time she'd come to trust in that offering and she'd return it in full measure.

Chapter Twenty-Five

"Lily! I'm so glad to see you," Holly exclaimed as she opened the door.

Lily smiled, now quite used to the other woman's exuberant hugs.

"Come in, come in. Hello, son," Holly said as she gave Seth a kiss on the cheek. "Your fathers are waiting for you out in the barn. They need help rounding up the stuff they're taking to Michael's to start work on his house."

"I know when I've been dismissed," Seth said with a grin. He bent to kiss Lily. "We'll probably be gone all day. Dillon's going to meet us out there after the lunch crowd dies down at the pub."

"Oh, I'll take good care of her," Holly said.

"Where's Callie?" Lily asked after Seth had left.

"She's still sleeping. She didn't get off work until after two this morning. I try to let her sleep as long as she will. It's not good for her to keep running on only a few hours of sleep a night," Holly said with a frown.

Lily took a deep breath and worked up the nerve to ask Holly, "Would you happen to have a notebook or blank paper and maybe some colored pencils? Or even just a pencil would do."

Holly looked curiously at her. "Oh, I'm sure we do. I still have a ton of stuff left over from when the boys and Callie were children. The guys tease me about never throwing away anything, but I figure one day I'll have grandchildren and all that stuff will come in handy."

Lily flinched and hoped that Holly didn't hear her quick intake of air.

"I'd love whatever you have," she said softly.

"Have a seat and give me a minute. I have it all boxed up in one of the storage closets."

Holly hurried away and Lily sank onto one of the couches in the spacious living room. All around her were signs of the big, boisterous family. Pictures—tons of them—all laughing. Surrounded by big smiles and loving gazes. Everyone looked so happy. She wanted that. Now more than ever.

And then she smiled because she was happy. Seth loved her. Michael and Dillon wanted her. She wanted them. It was okay to be happy. Her grin grew broader until her cheeks hurt from the sudden attack.

Not only did she have three wonderful, delicious men, but she had a large, close-knit family who seemed to think nothing of pitching in when they were needed.

That was what families were all about. They didn't bail at the first sign of adversity and they didn't place blame.

After a few minutes in which Lily sank back on the couch and hugged her newfound knowledge to her like an overstuffed teddy bear, Holly came back in carrying an armful of papers, notebooks, art books and a box full of colored pencils, crayons and markers.

She dumped them onto the coffee table in front of Lily and said, "It's all yours."

Lily latched on to a large tablet of blank paper. A child's art book. But it was perfect for what she wanted. Then she grabbed a handful of the colored pencils, examining the points of each.

"Would you mind too much if I walked down to Callie's Meadow?" Lily asked. "There's a surprise I want to do for Callie."

It was obvious that Holly was dying to ask at least a dozen questions, but instead she smiled and said, "Of course. You know the way. Just don't be gone too long. I'll have lunch ready for when Callie gets up."

Lily raised her eyebrow.

Holly frowned ferociously. "Okay, okay, so Ryan made

lunch and left it for me to warm up."

Lily laughed and then Holly joined in.

"One would think after thirty-plus years I'd learn to cook, but I think my husbands are determined for it to never happen. They're too afraid I'll either burn the house down or poison someone."

"I like cooking. I was pretty good at it."

"Oh, then you and Dillon should have fun. That boy loves to create new masterpieces as he calls them. He's always experimenting and putting new things on the menu at the pub. The locals love to go in to try out his new recipes."

Lily gathered her stuff and rose from the couch. "I won't be long."

Holly smiled. "Be careful."

Lily stepped outside into the sunshine. Though just days earlier the ground had been covered by a layer of snow, now it was as if spring had always been here. Flowers bloomed along the stone path that spiraled down the Colter property and the trees were leafing out. Some of the flowering species already had buds that were opening.

When she topped a slight rise that overlooked the meadow, she stopped and sat on a large boulder just off the pathway. The view was simply perfect, and the meadow spread out before her, covered in wildflowers. The mountain peaks jutted upward on all sides, still snowcapped against the bright blue sky.

For a long time she simply stared, absorbing the peace and beauty that seemed to cover the entire landscape. Then she began to draw.

She was totally ensconced in her creation. From time to time she would pause and mutter under her breath and then frown when a line didn't look just so. She paid careful attention to color, blending when she didn't have the one she needed.

Her back ached, but she continued on. Once started, she couldn't stop. It was a compulsion. Her fingers felt alive. She was energized as her hand flew across the page.

Her wrist was stiff and her fingers had curled rigidly around the pencils, and still she continued on, in pursuit of perfection.

The sun had started to fade over the horizon when she heard her name carried on the wind. She straightened and nearly fell over when every muscle in her body screamed in protest.

"Lily!"

That was much closer. She frowned. That sounded like Dillon. She reached behind her to rub a kink out of her throbbing back and when she tried to stand, her knees buckled and she plopped back down onto the rock.

"Well hell," she muttered.

"Lily!"

That one sounded like Michael.

"I'm over here," she shouted back.

And then remembering the scattered pencils that now lay on the ground, she got off the rock and went to her knees, grabbing at them to stuff in her pockets.

"Lily?"

"Here," she called again. "Just a minute. I'm coming."

She was just slapping the art book closed when both Dillon and Michael rounded the corner.

"Where the hell have you been?" Michael demanded. "Everyone's been worried sick about you."

Dillon raised a radio to his mouth and said, "We've found her. She's all right."

She blinked in confusion. "Your mom knew where I was going."

Dillon frowned in exasperation. "Lily, that was hours ago. You missed lunch."

"I did?"

Michael raised his hand toward the sky that was now ablaze with pink, purple and golden hues. "You've been gone for over six hours."

"I'm sorry. Really, I am. I had no idea."

Dillon glanced at the notebook clutched in her arms. "What were you doing?"

"Just passing time," she murmured. "I wanted to make Callie a surprise."

Michael cocked his head to the side. "What on earth could

you have been doing for Callie that made you lose track of time so that you were gone for six hours?"

She ducked her head and shifted her feet, but when she did, the pencils spilled out of her pocket and tumbled to the ground.

Both Michael and Dillon bent to gather them up and Lily backed up a step, her bottom lip caught firmly between her teeth.

"Lily?" Michael asked softly. "What's going on? Is everything all right?"

"I was drawing," she said in a low voice. So low that both men leaned forward to hear. "I wanted to draw Callie's Meadow for Callie. It's not much. It's not very good, but I know she loves it here, and I thought it might cheer her up."

"Can I see?" Dillon asked cautiously, holding out a hand for the notebook.

She hesitated for a long moment but then handed over the notebook, nausea rising in her stomach. They would hate it. Think it was a waste of time. And she'd worried their mother on top of that. All while doing something frivolous.

Dillon flipped it open with Michael looking over his shoulder and both froze. Their eyes widened in shock and then Dillon glanced over the edge to Lily, his mouth wide open.

"I shouldn't give it to her, should I?" Lily rushed to say. "I'll just tear it up. It was a stupid idea anyway."

"Holy fuck," Michael breathed.

"Lily, this is amazing," Dillon said in awe. "Absolutely fucking amazing. You did this? All today?"

She felt like a deer caught in the headlights. She didn't know what to say so she nodded instead.

Michael took the notebook from Dillon and examined it again, his expression incredulous.

"This is the most beautiful drawing I've ever seen," Michael said. "It looks exactly like the meadow. The colors, the landscape, the trees and the mountains. It's like looking at a photograph. It's damn well perfect."

She flushed until her cheeks burned, and she ducked her head as shyness gripped her.

Dillon tucked his fingers underneath her chin and nudged upward. His eyes were questioning, and anger lurked in the depths. "Why didn't you want us to know?"

"It's not very good," she said lamely. "And you were angry because I worried your mom. Time just got away from me. I tend to do that when I'm drawing. I know it's silly."

Dillon placed his hands on her arms and guided her down to sit on the same boulder where she'd sat to draw for so many hours.

"We need to get a few things out in the open here. First of all, you don't need our permission or approval to do a goddamn thing. If you want to sit around and paint yourself purple, that's your prerogative.

"Second, you have an amazing talent. The drawing was absolutely brilliant.

"Third, don't ever sell yourself short or worry that we're not going to approve. I'm so goddamn proud of you right now I could burst. I can't even wrap my head around the fact that you came out here and created this spectacular replica of a piece of land that means so much to this family. You thought Callie might like it. Hell, she's going to die when she sees this. You have no idea what that piece of property means to her—to all of us. She was born there. She was raised there, running hell-bent all over these mountains. And you've found a way to encapsulate that so that she can look at it no matter where she is and be at home. Lily, that kind of gift is priceless."

"Oh," she breathed.

"Oh? That's all you can say?" Michael said with a laugh.

"I'm sorry I worried you," she murmured. "I promised your mom I'd be back for lunch. She probably thinks I'm a complete flake or that I did something stupid like get lost."

"We were the ones worried," Dillon corrected. "Give us a break. We're still getting used to having you, and we still worry you're going to take off at a moment's notice. The old adage about being too good to be true is my paranoia."

She smiled then and rose to her feet, stepping forward so that she could wrap her arms around Dillon's waist.

"I'm not going anywhere. I promise."

He squeezed her back and then she backed away, looking cautiously at the drawing still in Michael's hands.

"You really think it's good? That it's not a waste of time?"

Michael shook his head. "I don't know where you get your ideas from, Lily, but I'm going to drum some sense into that head of yours. I wouldn't care if it was the worst drawing ever crafted. If you enjoy it and it gives you pleasure, then it's certainly not a waste of time."

Her smile was more brilliant this time and the tightness in her chest eased. Butterflies flitted round and round in her belly until she was dizzy from the sensation.

"So you think I should give it to Callie? I thought she could frame it or something."

"I think Callie is going to so bowled over that she's not going to have words," Dillon predicted. "I can't wait to see her face when you give it to her."

Dillon's radio crackled and Seth's irritated voice came over the receiver. "Goddamn it, Dillon. Where the hell are y'all? You said you'd found her. Is everything all right?"

Michael chuckled. "We better get back before Seth has a kitten and calls out search and rescue."

He slung an arm around Lily's shoulders and then carefully handed her back the drawing. Then he kissed her temple and squeezed her against his side.

When they arrived back at the house, Seth was pacing back and forth in front of the porch steps, dragging a hand over his already short hair. When he turned and saw them approach, he strode over, his expression grim.

"Where the hell have you been?" he demanded.

Lily frowned. "What's it to you?" she asked belligerently.

Dillon and Michael threw back their heads and laughed as Seth blinked in surprise and halted in midstep.

But then Holly ran out behind Seth, and Lily's frown disappeared. She pushed past the men and hurried toward Holly, already apologizing before she ever got there.

"I'm so sorry," she blurted. "I completely lost track of time. I didn't mean to worry you. It was inconsiderate."

Holly surprised her by laughing. "I told your guys that you

were probably just enjoying the view, but they lost their minds and hauled out their fathers to look for you. Callie and I weren't worried. You don't strike me as the type to just wander off and get lost."

She tucked her arm into Lily's and guided her into the house, leaving her three sons openmouthed in the yard.

"I bet you're hungry now, aren't you?"

"Starving," Lily admitted.

"Ethan was setting the table when Seth harangued him into looking for you. Callie and I finished up, so we can sit down to eat."

Lily flushed. "I'm so sorry everyone went out looking for me."

"I'm just glad it wasn't me this time," Holly teased. "I'm a bit of a klutz, and I've had some doozies before."

"Lily, you're back," Callie said as she rounded the corner of the kitchen. "I can't stay long. Have to be to work in a few."

"I wanted to give you something first," Lily said shyly.

Callie reared back in surprise. "Me?"

Lily slowly opened the art book and carefully eased the paper free of the binding. Then she handed it to Callie.

With a curious glint in her eyes, Callie took the paper and then when she glanced down at the drawing, she looked dumbstruck.

At that moment, Michael, Seth and Dillon along with their fathers tromped into the kitchen. Michael and Dillon smiled knowingly and held up a finger when the others would have questioned the stunned look on Callie's face.

Tears gathered and pooled in Callie's eyes. Her hands shook, making the paper jump and wobble in her grasp. Then she raised her gaze to Lily.

"How did you do this?" she asked in wonder. "It looks just like it. It's perfect."

The dads and Holly and Seth gathered around, looking to see what Callie held. Only Dillon and Michael remained back. Dillon slung an arm around her shoulders while Michael slid his arm around her waist.

"Told you," Michael whispered in her ear.

Lily fidgeted between them while the others looked on with stunned amazement.

"Oh Callie," Holly whispered. "It's your meadow." She looked up at Lily. "Did you draw this? Is this why you wanted the paper and colored pencils?"

"Yes," Lily murmured. "It would be better with oils or even more vivid pencils. I had to mix some of the colors to get the right shade. It's not my best effort."

"It's perfect," Adam said so bluntly that Lily jumped.

Emotion glimmered in the older Colters' eyes as they stared at the drawing in their daughter's hands.

"That's where our baby was born," Ethan said.

"I just thought that since Callie loved it so much that she could take it with her wherever she goes so she can feel close to home," Lily said.

Callie carefully handed her mom the drawing and then she walked over to Lily and pulled her into a hug.

"Thank you," she whispered. "You have no idea how much this means to me. I'll treasure this always."

Lily's entire face warmed under the open and frank praise of the Colters. She smiled back at Callie. "I'm so happy you like it. It's been so long since I've drawn something. I miss it," she said wistfully.

"You'll have whatever supplies you need tomorrow," Dillon said fiercely. "Even if I have to drive to Denver to get them. I want you to make a list of everything down to what kinds of brushes, pencils and paints. You have an amazing talent, Lily. And it obviously makes you happy."

"It does," she said softly. "I didn't remember how much until now."

"Let's eat," Holly said, breaking the awkward silence. "Then you guys can take Lily home. She looks like she's about to fall over."

Chapter Twenty-Six

True to Dillon's word, by the next afternoon, there were so many art supplies piled into his office at the house that Lily was at a loss as to where to start sorting.

"We need the extra bedroom, however, the office would make a perfect studio for you," Dillon said as he carried in the last box. "Lots of natural light with the windows and skylights. As soon as we get Michael squared away with converting his house to the new clinic, we're going to tackle the addition to this house."

"I can totally take the couch," Lily said. Then she blushed. "That is on the nights that I'm not with one of you."

Dillon grinned. "Like that's going to happen. We have enough bedrooms until we can add on. Someone will be the odd man out, and when you want us all out of your hair, then one of us can take the couch."

"I'll always want to be with y'all," she said softly. "I don't want to be alone. I've been alone for so long. I know what it's like. I'm tired of being lonely."

Dillon's smile faded and his eyes dimmed as he pulled her into his arms. "You'll never have to be alone again, Lily. You get to call the shots here. You can have as much or as little of us as you want. We're never going to push you beyond your limits."

She kissed him hungrily, snuggling further into his embrace. She loved the feel of the solid wall of muscle. He made her feel so protected and cherished. Loved.

"I'm going to leave you to it," Dillon said. "Have fun with all your stuff and use as much of my space as you need. I need to run out to meet the dads at Michael's right quick. They want me to eyeball their plans."

"I'll be fine. I tend to lose all sense of time when I'm messing with my art stuff. I'll probably still be here when you get back."

Dillon gave her a quick kiss, patted her on the ass and then walked out of the office.

With a satisfied smile, she turned in a circle. She really didn't know where to start, but she was ready to dive in and immerse herself in the joy of putting to canvas the images that had sustained her during the long weeks and months on the streets.

"Dad, you got a minute?" Dillon asked Adam.

Adam put down his measuring tape and glanced at the doorway. "I assume since you waited until your brothers left the room to talk, this is a private matter?"

"Got it in one."

"Take a walk with me," Adam said.

The two went to the other side of the house and out the side door and into the yard that overlooked a small valley to the left.

"Everything going okay with Lily and your brothers?" Adam asked.

Dillon sighed. "Yeah. Really better than I'd imagined. To be honest, I gave this a snowball's chance in hell of working, and if I'm being even more honest, there was a small part of me that didn't want it to work out because I wanted her to myself. But it's good. Bizarre good, but I can honestly say that I'm happy with the arrangement."

"As long as you and your brothers...and Lily...are happy, son."

Dillon fidgeted uncomfortably. "It's not that. God, I sound like a first class wuss. I can't believe I'm having this conversation with my dad, for God's sake."

Adam chuckled. "I can't wait to hear this."

"Back when you and the other dads met Mom. I know

you've all said she was it. You knew she was the one. You never looked back, blah blah."

"Well I wouldn't call it blah blah," Adam said dryly.

"But when did you know you loved her? Was it instantaneous? When did you tell her?"

Pain creased his dad's face, and Dillon regretted bringing it up.

"No, I didn't tell her right away," Adam said quietly. "I waited until it was almost too late. I loved her. I knew I loved her but a part of me thought if I said it too soon that it somehow devalued it. Like it needed time to mean more."

"Yeah, that's the way I feel," Dillon said. "I feel a little stupid thinking it, much less saying it. I've never believed it, falling in love so fast and hard. I know you and the other dads have talked about it, but to be honest, I always thought it was a bunch of mushy horseshit."

Adam shook his head. "I swear son, I don't know whose kid you are, but I'd lay odds you must be mine. Well, except for the tattoos and that goddamn earring. Still baffles me where the hell you came from. I used to swear your mother found you somewhere. But you think like me and you're as thick headed and as stubborn as me.

"Let me give you a little piece of advice, and you can do with it what you will. Don't wait until you feel like the time is more legitimate. I held back because I worried it would cheapen the moment if I said it too soon. And maybe I had convinced myself that it wasn't really love yet. All I know is that I almost lost your mother without ever telling her how much I loved her. I still regret to this day that I was too damn stubborn to give her the words until it was almost too late."

"I feel a little ridiculous. I've never felt this way about a woman before. Not so hard and fast and deep. I feel like I'm in way over my head."

Adam smiled. "Yeah, I know that feeling. But Dillon, what are you waiting for, anyway? Approval? From whom? You've never given a rat's ass what anyone thinks in your life, including me and your mother and your other dads. You've always gone your own way, marched to the beat of your own drum and fuck anyone who tries to tell you different. I can't imagine you holding back because you're worried about timing or something equally absurd."

"Yeah, yeah, you're right," Dillon grumbled. "And yeah. I've never cared what anyone else thinks. Until now. I care what Lily thinks. I don't want to fuck this up, Dad."

Adam put his hand on Dillon's shoulder. "You won't, son. Lily seems like such a sweet girl. It's obvious she cares a lot about you and Seth and Michael. She has a heart of gold, but she's been beaten down by life. It's up to you to bring her back up and get her back on her feet. How better to do that than to offer her something she needs more than anything else in the world? Your love."

Dillon blew out his breath. "I really hate it when you're right. It's even worse when you make so goddamn much sense."

Adam chuckled. "It infuriates your mother too. Not that I get to be right too often around her, mind you."

"You and the dads taught me a lot growing up," Dillon said quietly. "If I can be half the man you and the dads are, I know we can make this work. I couldn't have asked for a better childhood. I don't know if I've told you lately, but I love you, Dad. I wouldn't change a thing about our family."

Adam swallowed, and his eyes glittered suspiciously as he hauled Dillon into a huge bear hug. He slapped Dillon on the back.

"We better stop this mushy shit before the others find us. You know they'd never let us live it down."

Dillon cracked a grin. "Thanks, Dad. For giving me perspective, I guess. And you're right. There's not a damn good reason in the world to wait when I know what's in my heart."

He started to turn to head back to find the others when his dad reached out to grab his arm.

"Dillon, I know me and Ryan and Ethan give you a hard time about what a little shit you were when you were young, but I want you to know something. I knew you were special from the day you were born. You scared the ever-loving crap out of us and gave your mother all kinds of trouble during the delivery. And from that day forward, you were never easy.

"But I could never be prouder of you. You grew up strong and independent with a firm set of values, and you are fiercely loyal. You have an unwavering sense of justice, and I've always known that when you love, you'd love with all your heart and give unreservedly of yourself. Of all my children, I've always known that you were the steadiest. I love you, son."

"Well goddamn, Dad. If you make me cry, I'm going to kick your ass."

Adam laughed and then shoved Dillon toward the door. "Let's go find your brothers and see when we can wrap this up for the day. I have a sudden urge to go find your mother and tell her how much I love her."

Chapter Twenty-Seven

"Knock, knock!"

Lily turned from the pile of art supplies she was organizing to see Holly standing in the doorway of Dillon's office. Even the cat picked her head up in greeting but then quickly curled into a tighter ball on the floor beside Lily before closing her eyes again.

"Hey!" Lily said with a broad smile.

"I hope I'm not interrupting," Holly said.

"No, of course not. Come on in. If you can find your way around the mess."

Holly picked her way around a few boxes and came to stand beside Lily. "With the guys all over at Michael's sorting out construction details, I thought you could use some help and some company."

It was all Lily could do not to squeeze the other woman to death. "Thank you. Just the company is nice."

"I see Dillon went a little overboard," Holly said with a laugh.

Lily gave a rueful nod. "Yeah, it's all great stuff, though. I've just been going through and drooling over it all. I didn't expect him to do this. He's crazy!"

Holly laughed. "You'll find that Dillon does nothing in half measures. Have you eaten? If you want to take a break, I noticed that Dillon left lunch in the fridge. Even I can handle warming something up in the oven."

Lily checked the clock on Dillon's desk, and her eyes widened. It was already past two. "Yeah, I could eat. I've been lost in my own little world here."

"Come on then. We'll tackle the oven together, and I promise not to burn Dillon's kitchen down."

Lily laughed and followed Holly out of the office and into the kitchen.

"Sit, sit," Holly urged. "I want to be able to say I was able to prepare my daughter-in-law at least one meal. It'll give me bragging rights the next time my husbands make a smartass crack about my cooking."

The casual way she said daughter-in-law jolted Lily. She froze in the process of getting onto the barstool and stared at the other woman, but Holly continued on as if what she'd said was the most natural thing in the world.

Holly turned at that moment and a frown creased her brow. "What's wrong?"

Lily eased onto the barstool and looked down at her hands for a moment.

Holly turned the oven on and stuck the casserole dish inside and then walked over to stand across the bar from Lily.

"Lily, what is it?"

"You said daughter-in-law," she croaked.

Holly's face softened and then she smiled gently as she leaned on the countertop.

"I know I'm getting way ahead of myself, but I know my boys. I know their fathers. When they love, they love passionately. With their whole heart. Up to now, no one has captured that heart. Until you."

Lily swallowed as her chest tightened and emotion crowded in so full and heavy. She didn't even know what to say.

Holly reached across the bar and laid her hands over Lily's. "I'm going to ask you something that's none of my business, and feel free to say so. I know how my boys feel about you. But how do you feel about them?"

Lily glanced up to see worry and concern in Holly's eyes. But also understanding. It was that understanding that prompted Lily to be completely honest even as the idea of saying aloud all that was in her heart terrified her.

"I love them," she whispered. "Is that stupid? I mean, three men?"

"No, honey," Holly said gently. "It's not stupid, but then look who you're talking to."

Lily laughed as she realized just how dumb of a question it truly had been.

"Oh God, Holly. I'm so terrified. I feel like I'm on the edge of a cliff with one foot in the air about to tip right over the edge."

Holly walked around the bar and slid onto the barstool next to Lily. She wrapped her arm around Lily's shoulders and squeezed.

"I might be the only woman in the world who knows exactly how you're feeling."

"My heart tells me I love them, but my mind asks how it's possible to love three very different people at the same time."

"The heart has an endless capacity for love," Holly said. "As a woman you love your family, your children—especially your children—your friends, and you love your husband or lover. Who's to say you can't love three men with all your heart and soul? I mean, really, who makes the rules?"

"Seth told me he loved me," Lily blurted.

Holly smiled. "I'm not surprised that he'd be the first. He might be the oldest, but he's so unlike my Adam in that regard. Adam... He's hard sometimes, and he doesn't easily share what's in his heart. Seth is more open and honest. Dillon?" She sighed as she mentioned her youngest. "That boy is completely unpredictable. And Michael is so intense and focused. He tends to be more analytical."

Lily nodded. "I still feel like I'm getting to know all of them and their personalities. That's why I ask myself how I can know I love them."

"I'm going to tell you something right now. If you wait to completely know someone, you'll wait forever. Sometimes you have to lead with your heart. Even after so many years, my husbands still do things that surprise me. I didn't know them any longer than you've known my boys, but I took a chance. I took the leap and I've never regretted it. Not once. Life is about taking chances. Sometimes they bite you on the ass, but sometimes you find pure perfection."

"This is going to sound stupid," Lily said in a low voice.

Holly chuckled. "I think we've already established that nothing about how you feel or react to this situation is stupid. Normal, yes. Stupid, no."

"I didn't tell him I loved him."

Holly paused, waiting for Lily to continue. When Lily remained silent, Holly rubbed her hand up and down Lily's arm.

"Did you not say it back because you were unsure?"

"This is where the stupid part comes in," Lily muttered. "I didn't tell him for two reasons. Well, maybe three. One, I didn't want him to think I was just saying it because he said it. Two, I was so surprised. I wasn't expecting the words and I was overwhelmed. And three...I felt guilty."

"Guilty?"

"I didn't want to tell him first. I mean before telling Dillon and Michael. I didn't want them to feel like my feelings were stronger for Seth. It all sounds so ridiculous but I love them all or at least I feel about them in a way I've never felt about anyone else. And it's different but the same. I don't have a favorite. Will they believe that? That I love them differently but the same?" She shook her head. "Did any of that even make sense?"

Holly hugged Lily to her. "You could be me thirty-plus years ago, honey. And you know, it was actually harder for me to square my feelings with myself than it was with each of my husbands individually. There's a lot of trust that has to go into a relationship like this. You have to trust that they're all going to make a firm commitment to you and that they're going to love you with every part of themselves. But in turn, they have to trust that you're going to love them with everything you have, individually and together. Does that make sense? There's only so much you can do. The rest is up to them. You love them. They have to accept that love and trust in it."

Lily smiled. "It makes perfect sense. Thank you. I've been so worried, not over the relationship itself. They make it seem so...normal. But I've worried about handling it the right way. What if I make a mistake? It seems so important to get it all right in the beginning."

"Oh, you'll make mistakes," Holly said cheerfully. "And

believe me, so will they. It's very much a discovery process that you tackle along the way. But the most important thing is that you're committed to making it work. As long as each of you has resolved within yourself that this is what you want and that you'll do whatever it takes to make it work, the rest will take care of itself."

"You should probably check the oven," Lily said as she sniffed the air.

"Oh shoot! Trust me to get sidetracked. I tell you this is why I stay out of the kitchen."

Holly hurried around to the oven and took out the casserole. She placed it on a large potholder on the counter and leaned over to inspect it.

"I think it's perfect! You're my witness, Lily. I not only did not burn down the kitchen, but the casserole is done to perfection."

Lily laughed, and in that moment the sun seemed to shine a little brighter through the kitchen window. It was okay. She was happy. She could make this work. Her future had taken an abrupt right turn from its path of just a few weeks ago. And the only obstacles to overcome were those that were self-imposed.

Chapter Twenty-Eight

Michael wiped an arm over his sweaty brow and put down the hammer he'd been wielding. A check of his watch told him that it was late. He and his brothers and dads had spent the entire week tearing out and rebuilding.

He had shoved all his appointments to the mornings so he could have the afternoons to work with his family on the new clinic, and as a result he was tired and to the point he needed a break.

They needed another week at least to finish the front, which would become the new reception area. They had one exam room completed and the rest could be built on a more relaxed schedule since Michael could use one temporarily.

He had barely seen Lily for days—a situation he planned to remedy in short order.

"You knocking off?" Ethan asked.

"Yeah, I think we should all call it a day," Michael said. "I'm ready to go home, see Lily and maybe have dinner together."

"Not a bad idea," Ryan piped in. "Things have gotten so desperate that Holly and Callie have taken over the kitchen."

Ethan shuddered and everyone laughed.

"No reason to kill ourselves," Adam said by way of agreement. "Michael still has the clinic he's working out of now."

Michael nodded. "Lily's home alone right now. Dillon's working the pub to give Callie a night off and Seth has been tied up in meetings with his deputies all day."

"Then I'd say you better get your ass home and take care of

your woman," Ethan teased.

They spent the next fifteen minutes putting away equipment, and then Michael said goodbye to his dads and got into his Jeep. He drummed his fingers impatiently on the steering wheel as he drove through town past the pub to the turn-off leading up to Dillon's house. His house. He was going to have to get used to the fact that Dillon's house was now their house. All of theirs.

Dusk was settling over the house when he pulled up to park. Seth wasn't home yet, and he was glad though he probably shouldn't be.

But he wasn't going to waste time feeling guilty that he'd have a few moments alone with Lily. Dillon and Seth both had had their moments while Michael was going between his practice and the construction on his new clinic.

When he entered the house, the first thing that registered was that it smelled absolutely amazing. His stomach growled. It had been hours since he'd last eaten, and he was positively salivating over the spicy aroma in the air.

He followed the smell to the kitchen where he found Lily humming as she tended a skillet on the stove. The cat was on the counter licking her paw and watching Lily with interest. Every once in a while, Lily paused and reached over to scratch the cat's ears.

Smiling, he crept up behind her and then slid his arms around her waist, his lips going to her neck.

"Mmmm, hello," she said as she twisted in his arms.

She offered her mouth, and he didn't resist being pulled down into a sweet kiss.

"I'm not sure what's better, the smell or the taste of you," he murmured.

She smiled. "You're home early. I wasn't sure when to expect you and Seth so I started, but it can be held for whenever."

"What you making?"

"Chicken and sausage gumbo. You like?"

He sighed. "I love. It smells fantastic and I'm starving."

She touched his cheek and smoothed her palm over the

roughness of his evening shadow. "Go shower and relax. I'll serve it up as soon as you're done."

He kissed her again and held on to her for a long moment, simply savoring the delight of coming home to his woman in the kitchen cooking for him. It probably made him a throwback Neanderthal from the Stone Age but hell, what man wouldn't be completely and utterly satisfied?

"Give me fifteen minutes and I'll be back," he said as he pulled away.

He hurried through his shower, amazed at how invigorated he felt just knowing he was going to spend the evening with Lily. The ease with which they'd all embraced their new living arrangement still surprised him.

It was as if Lily had always been a part of them. Or that maybe they'd been waiting for her all along.

He shook his head over that tidbit. Who was he to argue with fate?

He went back into the kitchen where Lily had set two places at the bar. She was just dishing up the delicious-smelling gumbo over bowls of rice when he slid onto his stool. She shooed the cat off the counter and then put the bowls on the bar.

"So how is the construction going?" she asked when she sat down beside him.

He waited to answer her, savoring that first spoonful of the spicy warm broth. "Damn, this is good."

She smiled. "Thank you. I'm glad you like it."

"To answer your question, it's going well. Faster than I imagined. The dads have been great. They've devoted almost all of their time to the project, and Seth and Dillon have been pitching in when they can. I wouldn't even be past the planning stages if it weren't for them."

"Nice to have so many males who are good with their hands," she said with a mischievous smile.

He laughed at the naughty innuendo. "Lucky for you, that is indeed the case."

"I've missed you," she said simply.

He put his spoon down and pulled her toward him, kissing

her, their tongues warm from the gumbo. "I've missed you too. It's why I'm home now. I couldn't wait to see you any longer."

Her smile was shy but her eyes lit up in pleasure. His stomach turned over with giddy satisfaction that he'd given her such joy.

"You must be sore," she said in a casual voice as they resumed eating. "I thought maybe after supper we could go into the living room and I could give you a massage."

If someone struck a match under his ass it would have nothing on the heat that scorched over his body as he imagined her hands on his skin.

"Why, Lily, are you trying to seduce me?"

Her eyes widened innocently. "Where on earth would you get that idea? I'm just trying to be a good girl and offer my man some comfort after a hard day at work."

He grinned at the cheeky tone of her voice. She'd relaxed so much in the time she'd been with him and his brothers. She'd lost the guarded, troubled look in her eyes, and the shadows had been chased away by new light. She teased them and got back at them every time they gave her shit. She gave as good as she got.

It was an amazing thing to watch. She'd blossomed in front of their very eyes.

He hurried through his meal, which was a crime, really, given how fantastic it tasted, but he'd lost any and all interest in eating the minute she talked massage.

She, on the other hand, took her time, and he knew she was deliberately teasing him.

"Just so you know, I don't get mad, I get even," he said as he got up to take his bowl to the sink.

She laughed but didn't look overly worried.

He stood to the side, waiting until she finished. As soon as she pushed her spoon away, he collected the bowl and added it to his own in the sink.

"I should probably do the dishes," she said, casting a dubious glance at the sink. "I'd hate for them to be left for Dillon to do when he gets in."

"Fuck Dillon," Michael said. "You have more important

things to take care of. Namely me."

Her eyes danced as she pretended to consider the matter, and then with an exaggerated sigh, she said, "Okay, okay. Go into the living room and get comfortable."

He started shedding his clothing as soon as he got past the doorway. By the time he made it to the couch, he was naked. Behind him, Lily burst out laughing.

"Just what kind of massage do you think this is?"

"I want your hands everywhere," he growled.

She sauntered over, a sassy smile curving her lips. Then she licked them and his cock surged upward.

"Where oh where should I start?"

"I have a good idea," he said hopefully.

"Turn over and stretch out," she said.

"You want me to turn over with a hard-on from hell?"

She pressed her lips together and her eyes twinkled. "Well, yes. Surely you can tuck it somewhere."

"I'll tell you where I can tuck it," he said darkly.

She rubbed her hands together. "Back first. Unless of course you'd rather not get the massage."

Reaching down to guard the sensitive parts, he rolled and gingerly eased his body down, stretching full length on the wide couch.

Lily moved softly up behind him and put a knee down between his legs. "Has anyone ever told you what a nice ass you have?"

He grunted in reply.

Then she placed both palms in the center of his back, and he groaned in sheer pleasure. Feather light, her hands smoothed over his back up to his shoulders and spread out, kneading the tired, tense muscles.

Her warmth bled into his skin as she continued to roll and massage every part of his back. He held his breath when her fingers glanced over his ass then stopped and cupped the cheeks.

His cock was going to become a permanent part of his stomach as hard as he was. It was growing increasingly uncomfortable. His balls ached, and his cock twitched against the confines of being trapped between the couch and his belly.

Then she leaned down and kissed the small of his back. Just one, gentle, sweet kiss. He closed his eyes and gave himself over to her tender regard.

For half an hour she rubbed and molded, touched and comforted until he was a boneless, spineless lump on the couch.

Then, finally, she rose and whispered for him to turn over.

Carefully he propped himself up and turned on his side and then again to his back.

"Whoa," she said as she stared down at his turgid erection.

"Yeah," he muttered. "I get that way around you."

She smiled and got back onto the couch, this time straddling his knees so that his legs remained together. The position pushed his cock up even further, and she stared down at it like she was set to devour it. God, he hoped like hell that was exactly what she planned to do.

Slowly and very deliberately, she lowered her mouth until the head was a mere inch from her lips. She blew over it, sending chill bumps over places he didn't think chill bumps were possible.

Then her tongue flicked out, lightly licking the tip. His cock bobbed in response and strained upward, so hard that he was to the point of agony.

"No directions for me?" she purred. "I thought you liked control."

"Oh hell no," he groaned. "You're doing just fine without my interference. It's my policy never to get involved in a lengthy discussion when I'm in a vulnerable position."

She chuckled lightly and licked over the tip again, this time tracing around the flared head.

"Jesus, Lily. You're killing me here."

She pursed her lips around the crown and very carefully began sucking his length into her mouth, inch by excruciating inch.

He arched up, trying to get more of it into her mouth, but she held him off by grasping the base with her hand and squeezing.

She continued her downward assault, laving her tongue over the thick vein on the underside of his cock. When she reached halfway, she slid back up again, taking him to the very tip. Before he fell away from her mouth, she went down again, this time sucking him so deep that he bumped against the back of her throat.

She swallowed, milking him, working her throat around the head until his hands curled into the couch, desperate and frantic.

"This might be a record," he gritted out. "I'm about two seconds from coming already."

She smiled around his length but paused, remaining still, him lodged deep. She fondled his balls, cupping and rolling them in her palm as she slid back up, leaving a warm, wet trail.

"You have the most amazing mouth," he said in a strained voice. "So fucking hot and wet and tight."

Her hand slipped from his balls to curl around the base of his cock again. She grasped him, worked him up and down with her hand while she held the tip in her mouth. And then she went for it, pulling him hard and deep, moving her hand in rhythm with her mouth.

Fast. Hard. Deep. Over and over until he shouted her name. His release boiled deep in his balls and shot up his cock like a volcano erupting. His cry was savage and guttural as she took everything he gave her and clamped down greedily for more.

He spilled into her throat, spurting more with each thrust. She swallowed and kept sliding her hot mouth tight over his pulsing cock until his orgasm eased.

He slumped into the couch, so sated and loose that he couldn't move if he wanted to. Lily carefully cleaned the remainder of his release from his cock and then gently let go of his lessening erection.

"Come here," he said huskily, reaching for her.

He pulled her up his body until she was lying flush against him, their faces close together. He brushed the curls from her forehead and stroked her hair, marveling at this one perfect moment where everything in the world seemed right.

Emotion throbbed in his chest, tightening it, overwhelming

him. He tried to find the words to express all she meant to him but could get nothing past uncooperative lips.

Finally he managed to get out the one thing he knew above all else. Three little words that he'd never spoken to another woman.

"I love you," he whispered.

Her eyes went soft and glowed in the dim light. There was such a loving set to her expression that his heart did flips.

"I love you too," she returned softly.

He wrapped his arms around her and crushed her to his chest, shaking with the magnitude of the moment. He pressed his lips firm to her temple and simply remained there, too shaken, too scattered to do anything more than hold her.

Chapter Twenty-Nine

Emboldened by her declaration the night before, Lily was a woman on a mission the next day. She woke with a smile and deep-seated contentment, the kind people waited a lifetime for.

She danced through her morning routine, showering and dressing. She made it out just in time to see Michael off with a lusty kiss and a murmured *I love you.*

Then she hugged herself and almost gave into the temptation to let out a giddy squeal.

It occurred to her as she was eating a quick breakfast that while she had a killer plan in place, she had no way to pull it off. She frowned. Okay, she wouldn't let something as simple as transportation sway her from her task.

When in doubt, call for back-up.

She picked up the phone and dialed Holly's number. She was a little discomfited when a male answered the phone. She didn't immediately know which Colter it was and she hesitated, her tongue suddenly uncooperative.

"Hello?"

"Uh hi," she said in a low voice. "This is Lily."

"Lily, how are you?"

It was then she realized it was Adam's quiet voice over the line.

"I'm good," she managed to stammer out. "I was hoping to speak to Holly. Is she there?"

"I'll get her for you. Give me just a minute," he said kindly.

Lily waited a few moments and then Holly's cheerful voice bled through the receiver. "Hi, Lily!"

"Hi, Holly. I wondered if you'd mind being my partner in crime today."

"Now that sounds intriguing. I'm in. Whatever it is, I'm in."

Lily chuckled. "I need a ride to Seth's office and then I need a ride by the pub. I won't be long in either place."

"I can be over in half an hour."

"Thank you. I appreciate this."

"Anytime, Lily. I'm glad to do it."

Lily finished arranging her hair and even applied light make-up that Callie had picked out. She finished with lip gloss and checked her appearance in the mirror.

She stared for a long moment, transfixed by the change in her. Gone was the sad, homeless, ragtag woman of a few weeks ago. In her place stood a vibrant young woman with love and happiness in her eyes. Hope.

She smiled at herself and then hurried off to find her shoes and her light jacket. Though spring seemed to have finally arrived for good, the mornings and evenings were still chilly.

When Holly drove up to the house, Lily met her on the front steps.

"You look positively radiant today," Holly observed as the two women climbed into the Rover.

"I'm on a mission," Lily said. "I got to spend a little while with Michael last night, but Dillon and Seth are both working right now, and I can't wait a minute longer. I have to tell them. So I'm going to where they are."

Holly gave a delighted laugh. "Oh how wonderful! I wish I could see the looks on their faces. This will be absolutely priceless. Want to do lunch after you flabbergast your men?"

Lily looked over and smiled at Holly. "I'd like that. I'd like it a lot."

Holly beamed back at her. "Great. And if you don't mind, I'll call Callie to meet us. It's good for her to get out. She spends too much time holed up in the house when she isn't working."

"It's really nice to have good friends," Lily said softly.

Holly reached over and squeezed her hand.

They drove first to the sheriff's department on Main Street. There were a few other parked cars in front and Lily nearly lost her nerve. What if Seth was busy or involved in a meeting? Suddenly what she planned didn't seem that appropriate.

"Go on," Holly urged. "Seth will be glad to see you."

With a nervous gulp, Lily got out of the Rover and walked toward the door. She hadn't actually seen the inside of the department yet and wasn't sure what to expect.

Inside there was a reception desk and a small sitting area with two people sitting while one stood talking to the woman manning the desk. Lily stood awkwardly to the side as she waited for the man to finish his business.

When he finally moved away, the receptionist turned a friendly smile in Lily's direction as Lily stepped forward.

"What can I help you with?"

"I'd like to see Sheriff Colter," she said in a low voice.

"I believe he's on a telephone call right now. Perhaps there's something I can help you with?"

"If you'll tell him that Lily is here, he'll see me," she quietly persisted.

The woman shot her an inquisitive look. "If you'll have a seat, I'll let him know you're here."

No sooner had Lily taken a seat than the door to one of the back offices burst open, and Seth loomed in the doorway looking so deliciously gorgeous in his uniform that Lily nearly had to wipe the drool from her chin.

"Lily? Is everything okay?"

She was on her feet and hurried behind the reception counter toward him. He backed into his office and once she was inside, he closed the door behind them.

Before he could say another word, she launched herself into his arms and planted a toe-curling kiss on him. He stumbled back but caught her against him to steady them both.

He reared back and stared at her through glazed eyes, confusion and a spark of lust in their depths.

"Whoa, what's this about?"

She kissed him again and curled her arms around his neck to squeeze him against her as tightly as she could.

He hugged her back, and she absorbed his steady strength. She closed her eyes for a long moment, simply savoring the connection. The sense of rightness. That this was where she belonged.

"Lily, honey, what's wrong?" he asked softly.

She pulled away and gifted him with a brilliant smile, allowing all of her joy—and love—to flow from the depths of her soul.

"I love you," she said fiercely. "I just wanted to tell you."

Then she pulled from his arms and smiled shyly again. "That's all I wanted. Your mom is waiting for me. I'll see you this evening."

She turned and walked out of his office, leaving him with a baffled, goofy expression, but when she looked back one more time, he wore a grin the size of the Colorado mountains.

Lily hurried from the office, sure her blush would give away the purpose of her visit. She slid into the Rover with Holly. As Holly backed from the parking space, she glanced over at Lily.

"Well?"

Lily grinned, and she found she couldn't stop smiling as they headed toward the pub.

"Let's just say I gave your son something to think about."

Holly laughed and shook her head. "Poor boy. He's probably going to be useless for the rest of the day."

"One down, one to go."

Holly drove the two blocks to the pub but had to park across the street. The lunch crowd was already starting to gather.

"I hope he's not too busy," Lily murmured.

"Oh, he'll probably be in his office. He tends to take care of the business stuff in the afternoon and then he fills in behind the bar when Callie isn't working. Of course if they get too busy for lunch, he'll pitch in, but I think it's early enough that you can catch him in the office."

"Okay then," she said after a deep breath. "Here I go."

Lily navigated her way through the people going into the pub and glanced around the crowded interior. Three waitresses bustled around the tables, dropping off drink orders and trays of food. Only two people sat at the actual bar, and an older man was wiping down the counter as they sipped at beers and ate nachos.

She squared her shoulders and marched in the direction of the office as if she had every right to be there. The older man quirked an eyebrow at her but didn't say anything as she passed.

She put her hand on the doorknob to just go in but then had second thoughts. Maybe Dillon wasn't alone. That could be embarrassing if she just barged in.

So she took a step back and knocked.

"It's open," she heard Dillon call.

She sucked in a deep breath and opened the door to see Dillon at his desk, head down as he examined a stack of receipts.

He looked up and did a double take. Then he shot out of his seat. "Lily! What on earth are you doing here? Is everything okay?"

Taking her courage into both hands, she launched herself across the distance and all but tackled Dillon. He caught her in midair, and she wrapped her legs around his waist as she curled her arms around his neck.

Her mouth found his, hot and hungry. She devoured him. There was no other word for it. He staggered back and sank onto the small loveseat against the wall, her still wrapped around him.

She framed his face in her hands and kissed him wildly, then peppered a line over his jaw and down to his neck. She nipped and then sank her teeth into the firm column of flesh just below his ear.

"Holy hell," he muttered.

"I love you," she said fiercely.

He went completely and utterly still, his muscles tense. Only a slight twitch at his jaw as he stared intensely back at her betrayed any movement.

She touched his face, brushing over it with tender strokes.

"I love you," she said again. "I couldn't wait another minute to let you know."

He opened his mouth to speak but let it hang open. And then he crushed her to him, holding on to her so tight that she could barely breathe.

"God, I love you too," he breathed against her hair. "So damn much. I've struggled so hard over the last few days, wanting and needing to tell you. Wanting the perfect moment. Not wanting to overwhelm you or give you words you weren't ready to hear."

His entire body shook against her, and he alternated between squeezing the breath from her and stroking over her back with urgent hands.

Then he released her. "Come here," he growled as he dragged her into a toe-curling, heart-melting kiss.

He tucked his arms underneath her ass and lifted, standing effortlessly with her still in his arms. He carried her over to his desk and then reached with one arm to sweep all the contents to the floor.

They landed with a crash, and he set her down, his mouth fused hotly to hers.

He tore at her clothing and she tore at his. She still wasn't sure who got naked first. He took only long enough to pull on a condom and then he spread her legs and dragged her to the edge of the desk, his palms cradling her ass.

He was inside her before she could process that they were naked, in his office, about to have wild and crazy sex.

She gasped when he reached full depth.

"Lean back," he rasped. "Lean back and brace yourself with your hands."

She reclined, reaching behind her until her palms slid across the polished surface of the desk. He looped her legs over his forearms and drove into her again.

The desk creaked and groaned but he didn't let up. Over and over he plunged, driving her up so fast and hard that she was precariously close to release after only a minute.

He leaned forward, holding himself deep, and his mouth found her nipples, tugging at them with his teeth. He nipped and then soothed the taut bud with his tongue. He pressed tender kisses and then nipped sharply again until she was a writhing mass of crazy.

His fingers dug into her ass, holding her to him. Then he

leaned back, sliding completely out. He opened her wider with his hands and hammered forward again, rocking until she lost her grip.

Her back hit the desk, and he went with her, never leaving her, his hips pumping urgently as he buried himself in her over and over until she was dizzy and riding an intense sexual high like she'd never experienced.

She was drunk on passion. Her orgasm was razor sharp, building and then exploding over her like a flash flood. Fast. Intense.

She started to scream his name but he slipped a hand over her mouth, holding in the hoarse shout of exquisite pleasure.

She didn't even know if he'd finished yet. Her body quaked and quivered around his cock. She let out little whimpers as each stroke sent excruciating shock waves through her ravaged body.

He leaned down, brushing his lips across hers. "Shhh, baby. It's okay. I've got you. I love you."

He was still inside her but she could feel the pulse of his cock as he came down from his own orgasm. She lay sprawled over his desk, boneless, helpless to move. She didn't even know her name at this point.

"Oh God, you killed me," he groaned.

"Huh uh. That's my line," she slurred out.

He picked himself up off her and carefully withdrew from her quivering body. Then he reached for her and helped her up.

She picked up her clothing but couldn't seem to get her hands to work right. Dillon gently took her jeans and shirt from her and dressed her with slow, tender hands. When he was done, he pulled her into his arms and pressed his lips to her forehead.

"I've wanted to tell you," he whispered. "I'm sorry it had to be when you came to me first. It should have been me. I needed to have told you before now. I was too caught up in it being the perfect time, the perfect moment."

She smiled up at him. "It's perfect now."

He caught her hand and raised it to his mouth, kissing each of her fingertips before nuzzling his mouth into her palm.

"You're perfect. I love you."

"I love you too," she whispered.

And then she looked at the clock. "Oh hell, I've got to go. Your mom is waiting for me in the car."

His look of horror was comical. "You came in here and we fucked like crazy people while my mom was waiting in the car?"

"Well, in my defense, I only planned to tell you I loved you."

He closed his eyes. "Oh God. This is awkward."

Lily laughed. "It hasn't been that long. I think we set a record for quickie sex."

His eyes darkened. "I plan to remedy that later."

"And I very much look forward to it."

She leaned up on tiptoe. "I'll see you later. I just hope to hell I can walk now."

His laughter followed her out the door.

Chapter Thirty

Lily peeked at the chicken in the oven and rubbed her hands together in delight. Tonight's meal was going to cap off an utterly perfect day. She hummed and smiled her way around the kitchen as she gave an absent stir to the potatoes and then checked on the vegetables.

It was so nice to have people to cook for again. She loved cooking. Loved being in the kitchen. It was second only to her love of drawing, and here...here she could indulge in both without judgment.

A few minutes later, she deemed the chicken perfect and took it out of the oven to rest on the stovetop while she finished the potatoes and turned the veggies down to simmer.

She looked at the clock and said a silent *yes*! The guys were due home any minute and she had everything ready.

She rushed to get the plates set out and the silverware neatly in place. Then she filled glasses with ice and put the tea pitcher within reaching distance.

After all the other food was set out, she transferred the chicken from the roaster to a platter and carried it to the table to carve.

Before she set knife to meat, she heard the door open and the murmur of male voices.

Her guys. Just the sound of them sent a thrill up her spine. She let her hands fall to the table and looked up in anticipation, waiting for them to round the corner into the kitchen.

Michael was first in, followed by Seth and then Dillon.

"Need help with that?" Michael said as he went around her

and came in close to nibble at her ear.

"It smells wonderful," Dillon said with a moan.

"Roasted chicken with apricot honey glaze along with garlic potatoes and vegetables," Lily announced.

Seth put his hand to his stomach and staggered back.

Lily smiled and handed over the carving knife to Michael.

"Have a seat, you guys. As soon as Michael carves it up, we're ready to eat."

"You're already hopelessly spoiling us," Dillon said.

"No more than you've spoiled me."

She went around to take a seat next to Dillon. She made the mistake of looking over at him and saw the fire in his eyes. She flushed and even felt heat surge over her scalp.

He chuckled low and then reached down between them to give her hand a squeeze.

Seth settled in on the other side of her and slid his hand over her knee and up her thigh. He stared intently at her as his hand caressed her leg and then his grip tightened, silently conveying the emotion she saw in his eyes.

She tilted toward him, inhaling his scent. "I do, you know."

Seth's lips found hers, a gentle smooch. "I love you too," he whispered. "And you're welcome to come maul me in my office anytime you want."

She laughed but couldn't keep the heat from her cheeks as she remembered a much more explicit mauling that had taken place in Dillon's office at the pub.

"Why do I get the impression there's something I'm missing here?" Michael asked with a raised eyebrow as he portioned out slices of chicken onto each plate.

"I visited Seth and Dillon at work today," she said with an innocent grin. "But don't be grumbly. You got your special attention last night before they came home."

Dillon's eyebrows shot up. "Oh? Do tell."

"A massage," Michael said smugly. "Then she might have had her wicked way with me."

"And you think you're the one missing out?" Seth asked.

"Oh hush," Lily scolded. "You can have a massage anytime you want one."

217

"I just want her to come into the office every day for lunch," Dillon smirked.

Both brothers turned to stare at Dillon and Lily smacked him hard on the arm.

They all laughed together, and the sweetness of the moment surged like honey through Lily's blood. They ate, joked. Laughter filled the air. Joy. And contentment.

She sighed as she looked between them all. Perfection.

When they finished eating, Dillon got up and collected all the plates. He dumped them into the dishwasher without so much as a rinse. Lily shook her head.

"What?" he asked.

"You don't stick plates with food on it in the dishwasher," she said in exasperation.

"Why the hell not? It's a dishwasher. It washes dishes. If I was going to hand wash them, I wouldn't need the dishwasher."

Michael and Seth both laughed but nodded their agreement.

"Besides, now I'm all done and we can move on to more important things," Dillon said with a wicked grin.

She raised one eyebrow. "Such as?"

"Such as you, naked, in the living room."

"Oh hell yes," Michael muttered.

"That gets my vote," Seth volunteered.

"Is that all you guys ever think about?" she asked in mock surprise.

"Yes!" came the answer from all three.

She laughed and turned, her fingers already at the waist of her jeans. She hurried into the living room, followed closely by the others.

When she reached the center, she stopped and turned to see them all standing still just inside the doorway, their eyes riveted to her.

"What?" she asked.

"We're waiting," Michael said.

Her fingers shaking—not from nervousness—she slowly undressed, taking her time with each piece as she pulled the clothing from her body.

She kicked away her shoes and jeans and stood before them, clad only in her bra and panties. Their gazes burned over her, touching fire to her nerve endings. Her nipples hardened, pushing against the delicate lace of her bra.

She reached behind her to slowly unhook the bra and then let the straps fall down her shoulders. Prolonging their anticipation, she took her time, shielding the cups with her arms before finally allowing the rest of the bra to fall away, bearing her breasts to their avid gazes.

"I'm not doing a solo strip tease," she said huskily. "And you can't make love to me fully clothed."

Her words pushed them into motion. They spread out, undressing with speed that amused her. Jeans and shirts and a uniform were tossed in all directions, and then three naked and very aroused men stalked toward her.

"Oh hell," she murmured as she backed away.

Michael circled behind her, trapping her between him and Dillon and Seth. He pressed into her back, his erection sliding up and down the seam of her ass before coming to rest in the small of her back.

He reached around to cup her breasts, plumping them outward, offering them up like twin prizes.

"Bend over," he commanded. "Right there over the arm of the couch."

Excitement fluttered deep in her chest, and her pussy clenched tight with need.

He went with her, pressing into her, forcing her to bend until her hands came down to brace against the cushions. All the while Seth and Dillon stood, watching, their eyes glittering with arousal.

There was only a brief moment of hesitation. She heard the crinkle of a condom wrapper and then his hand brushed over her ass. A moment later, he found her heat, fitting the broad head of his cock to her pussy.

He pushed into her, full and aching, stretching her to accommodate his width. He pushed again, tilting her ass a little higher and then thrust down, deep, so very deep that she gasped at the incredible stretching sensation.

"Get me some KY," Michael told one of his brothers, his voice tight and hoarse as he uttered the command.

The soft sound of footsteps told her that one of them was doing as he'd asked. Her mind was alive with the possibilities, with curiosity. Anticipation licked over her skin, leaving her tingly and alive and restless.

With his palms, he spread her ass, opening her further to his invasion. Then he brushed his thumb over her anal opening, stopping to tease and circle the tight entrance.

"I have a definite fantasy about being deep inside your ass," he rasped out. "You tight around my cock, trying to push me out. Tell me, Lily, do you want that? Do you want me in the deepest, darkest parts of your body? Do you want that kind of ownership where you're helpless beneath me, mine to do with as I like?"

"Son of a bitch," Dillon muttered from the side.

"Yes," she whispered. "I'm yours, Michael. I trust you. God, I want you."

The couch dipped in front of her. She raised her head enough to see that Dillon was there, just inches from her, his cock straining upward as he stroked his hand tight over his erection.

"Lift up," Dillon commanded. "I want your mouth around my dick while he fucks your ass."

She closed her eyes, trembling with the force of the images bombarding her senses.

But she did as he said, pushing herself upward as he moved so that his cock was just below her mouth.

Seth returned, and she heard the squeezing sound of the lubricant and then felt the cool, slick rub over the seam of her ass. Michael gently inserted one finger, smoothing more of the gel inside her opening.

He went back and forth, easing his way in, adding more.

Seth paused beside her to run his hand up the curve of her spine and then to her nape where he gently massaged just as Dillon guided her head down over his cock.

Seth stepped back, and Dillon and Michael took over.

Dillon grasped the base of his cock and guided himself

deeper, his hand replacing Seth's at her nape as he pushed gently.

Michael withdrew from her pussy and then fitted his cock to her ass, giving an experimental push.

She gasped and her body instinctively tightened, rejecting his invasion.

Michael groaned but held her firm, preventing her from pulling away. He pushed, persisting in his advance. She stretched to the point of pain and for a moment, Dillon eased from her mouth, allowing her to breathe easier as Michael forged relentlessly forward.

"Almost there," Michael ground out. "Don't move, baby. Let me do the work. It won't be so uncomfortable when I get inside you."

She closed her eyes, awash in the conflicting sensations. Discomfort. A little pain. Burning. And edgy, dark excitement that flushed through her body. She trembled, her arms shaking as she tried to brace herself.

"Lay your head on my lap," Dillon said softly. "Relax. I've got you. Put your arms down and let us take care of you."

She leaned down, pressing her cheek to his firm thigh, and curled her arms beneath her.

Michael continued to inch forward, and she was stretched so tight around him, she wasn't sure how he'd accomplish his goal. She was about to tell him no, that she couldn't take anymore, when he powered through and her body caved in around him.

She cried out, part in shock and part in relief as the burning lessened. Dillon stroked her cheek, petting and offering her reassurance and comfort.

"You're so fucking tight," Michael groaned. "God, Lily, you can't imagine how good you feel."

He pushed in further until she felt his balls come to rest against her pussy. Then Dillon lifted her head and fitted his cock to her mouth once more.

"I've got you," Dillon said again. "I've got you. Just relax."

He slipped inside her mouth, both hands supporting her head as he thrust upward, lodging himself as deeply as Michael was.

Then Michael withdrew, and she rippled over his cock, her anus tugging at him. The two men began a gentle rhythm, thrusting, withdrawing. Michael gripped her behind, spreading her, clutching and opening her wider as he pushed back inside her.

Gradually, as her body became more accustomed to the dual invasion, she twisted restlessly, fidgeting as edgy arousal sizzled over her, awakening her to new pleasures.

As if sensing her readiness, Dillon and Michael began moving harder, their thrusts deeper and more forceful. Dillon's hand tangled in her hair, gripping the tresses as his other hand circled her neck, holding her in place as he fucked her mouth.

Michael's fingers dug into her ass, and he began pumping hard and deep against her body. Then he withdrew, holding himself just inside her body before powering forward in one forceful lunge that had her crying out around Dillon's erection.

She needed release. She needed to come. Her body was tight and straining, her muscles so clenched and needy that she was to the point of pain.

A harsh cry tore from Michael's throat, and he began fucking her with ruthless, deep strokes. Harder. Faster. His hips slapping against her ass over and over. He trembled against her and then strained forward, holding himself as his orgasm blew through his body.

For a long moment he rested against her as Dillon continued his deliberate fucking of her mouth. Then Michael carefully withdrew, leaving her aching and wanting.

She nearly screamed in relief when Seth moved behind her and tucked his cock to her pussy. She arched her ass higher, wanting and needing his possession. He slid inside and immediately began pumping his hips against her as if he was already close to his breaking point.

Hoisting herself upward, she reached down, sliding her fingers over her mound to her clit. As soon as she touched herself, she felt the explosive orgasm burst over her.

If Dillon wasn't holding so tight to her head, she would have torn herself away and screamed her climax. It rolled over her and through her with excruciating force. She flew in about forty directions and lost awareness of everything but her endless release.

She slumped into Dillon, but he held her, his fingers gently stroking over her cheek as his thrusts gentled. She became aware of the two men still driving into her, Seth more urgently than Dillon.

With a guttural shout, Seth came, his fingers dug into her hips as he held her against his throbbing, pulsing cock.

Below her, Dillon stiffened and began thrusting upward, holding her firmly. Warm semen spilled into her mouth, spurting with each push.

She swallowed rapidly, taking everything he had to give, wanting more as his erection slid over her lips.

Then to her surprise, Michael was back, this time pushing into her swollen pussy, his erection not as rigid as last time, but still hard and forceful. How could he recover so quickly?

She moaned as Dillon's cock slipped from her mouth and once again he cradled her head on his lap, soothing and caressing her face with gentle hands as he waited for Michael to finish.

Michael didn't last nearly as long this time. He pumped against her without the patience he'd exhibited when he'd fucked her ass. After several more thrusts, he forced himself deep and held on to her as his body convulsed and his hips spasmed.

He leaned down and pressed his lips to the center of her back before carefully withdrawing.

Dillon immediately pulled her from the arm of the couch and into his arms, cradling her against his chest. She sucked in air, trying to catch her breath after such a volatile ride. She huddled against Dillon as he pressed kisses to the top of her head and smoothed his hands up and down her body in gentle strokes.

After a moment, the dreamy euphoria started to fade and she gained more awareness of her surroundings. The reassuring thud of Dillon's heartbeat against her ear comforted her. Made her feel safe and secure.

Then she moved, pushing her legs up so that she was snuggled a little closer to Dillon, and she felt warm stickiness between her legs.

Panic raced through her chest, and her pulse ratcheted up, kicking and pounding at her chest. She twisted free of Dillon and reached down, sliding her hand between her legs. Then she brought her hand up to see semen glistening from her fingers.

"Oh God," she whispered. "No. No, no, no!"

Chapter Thirty-One

Lily scrambled to her feet, still holding the hand in front of her, unable to look away.

"Lily, honey, what's wrong?" Seth demanded as he stepped to her.

Dillon bolted from the couch, reaching for his pants.

Her hand shook as she stared dumbly at the moisture, slick on her fingers.

"Did you use a condom?" she demanded in a nearly shrill voice. She turned to Michael. "Did you?"

Oh God, she was going to be ill. Her entire body shook now, and Dillon wrapped his arms around her, trying to pull her close, but she twisted away, her gazed fixed on Seth and Michael.

"Yeah, I did," Seth said. "Of course, I did. I wouldn't do that to you, Lily. You said you wanted them."

"I did too," Michael said in a strained voice.

"Then what is this?" she asked, thrusting her hand forward.

Seth swore. "One of them must have broken." He hurried toward the trash can just a few feet away and stared down. Then he gingerly pulled one out and stared back at Lily with regret and apology in his eyes.

"It broke, honey," he said in a low voice. "One of them broke. I'm sorry."

She bolted for the bathroom, went inside and locked the door. She turned on the shower, knowing in her heart it didn't matter. There was nothing she could do now. But still, she climbed into the shower and scrubbed until she was nearly raw, wiping away as much of the semen as she could.

How could she be sure the birth control was already effective? It was why she'd insisted they wear condoms. She couldn't—wouldn't—take the chance. What if it didn't work?

Oh God, she couldn't be pregnant. Surely fate wouldn't be that cruel.

As the water poured over her, she sank to her knees, her tears mixing with the heat and steam. She weakly gathered the washcloth in her hand and scrubbed again in a futile effort to remove the semen deposited into her body.

She bowed her head, her shoulders shaking as long-held grief and guilt boiled to the surface, exploding outward.

"Lily. Lily!"

"Dear God."

"Get her out of the shower."

"Lily, honey, you have to stop. You're rubbing yourself raw."

Strong hands gripped her shoulders and another hand gripped her wrist, pulling upward and forcing her to drop the soaked washcloth.

They carried her from the shower. Someone turned off the water, and she was enveloped by warm towels.

She didn't know who had her, who dried her or who spoke to her. She was lost. Adrift in mind-shattering pain and grief that had been too long locked under a shield of numbness.

They dried her body and her hair. One even dressed her in a loose fitting T-shirt. All the while they spoke in low urgent tones, asking—pleading with her to tell them what was wrong.

"I just want to be alone," she finally managed in a voice ravaged by tears. "Please," she whispered. "Just leave me alone for a little while."

They weren't happy. She sensed their frustration and their helplessness, but at the moment, she couldn't think about comforting them when she herself was inconsolable.

One by one they disappeared, and she wandered into the bedroom, closing the door behind her. She curled onto the bed, her heart so heavy and broken that she closed her eyes and prayed for oblivion.

"Son of a bitch. Son of a bitch," Seth swore as he paced back and forth in the living room. He balled his fist and rammed it into the wall in helpless fury.

"What the fuck just happened here?" Michael demanded.

Dillon swore and rubbed his hand over his hair then over his face as he blew out his breath. "This is bad. This is really bad. She was so adamant that we wear condoms. She said she didn't want to get pregnant. I accepted that. But this goes much deeper."

"She's never once hinted at her past," Michael said. "We haven't pushed her—haven't wanted to. I think I was afraid to. And maybe I thought we could just move on and if we made her happy now it was enough. But goddamn it, we can't go on like this."

Seth shook his head. "I was content to be patient. I know she's had a lot of hurt in her life. I told her I'd wait until she trusted me enough to tell me what happened and why she was homeless."

"We can't go on like this. She can't go on like this," Michael said again. "We have to know what we're dealing with here. We can't go forward until we've addressed the past—whatever it is."

"Did you see her?" Seth asked hoarsely. "Did you *see* her? She'd checked out. She was here but wasn't. She was caught in some horrible nightmare that only she knows about. And goddamn it, I can't help her if I don't know how."

"Give her time. Just a little. We'll do as she begged. For now," Dillon said grimly. "But tomorrow this stops. If I have to sit on her, we're going to find out what's hurting her so much."

Lily stared out the window from her position on the bed. Dawn was slowly creeping over the horizon. She hadn't slept. Hadn't been able to do anything more than lie there and exist in another time and another place. Her sins lay at her feet. Unavoidable.

She stirred and her full bladder protested. She considered lying there longer, but her need became more persistent until finally she got up and shuffled into the bathroom.

When she was done, she walked back into the bedroom and dismissed the bed, suddenly hating it and the comfort it offered. Quietly, she walked toward the living room, stopping a moment when she saw the three men sprawled at intervals on the couch and in the chairs.

The ache inside her heart intensified, and she crept by on soundless feet, still clad in only the T-shirt they'd put on her the night before.

At the back door, she pushed at the sliding glass door and shivered as the cool morning breeze blew over her skin. She stepped outside, her feet bare, and looked around with disinterest.

Her focus sharpened as she saw the wooden bench perched under an aspen tree several feet away from the deck she stood on. She walked mechanically, stopping in front to stare at the faded wood.

She turned again and eased down, her hands sliding across the rough surface before curling around the edges so tight her knuckles went white.

How long she sat there, she wasn't sure. She focused on the distant mountaintop and the rugged terrain surrounding her, trying to absorb the peace that seemed so prevalent no matter which direction she looked.

Then she looked heavenward as tears she didn't think she had to shed stung and crowded the corners of her eyes. "Please," she whispered. "I can't go through that again. If You're listening, please. I'm so sorry. I don't deserve forgiveness, but please give me Your mercy."

The sun gleamed, a bright orb that hung over the horizon, creeping higher with each passing second. The rays bathed her in warmth and yet nothing could fill the empty, aching void inside her.

"Lily, my God, what the hell are you doing out here?"

She turned to see Dillon hurrying out, Seth and Michael hot on his heels.

"You're going to freeze to death," Michael bit out. "You

aren't dressed, for God's sake."

Seth knelt in front her and took her cold hands in his. "Honey, you have to come inside. Please. We need to talk about this. We can't help you if we don't know what's going on."

He went blurry in front of her as tears streaked silently down her face. He rubbed them gently away, his eyes so filled with worry that she flinched.

Without another word, without asking or demanding, he simply scooped her into his arms and carried her back toward the house. He took her into the living room, placed her on the sofa and immediately enveloped her in the warmth of a blanket.

Dillon and Michael stood a mere foot away, concern etched into their brows.

She hugged her legs to her chest and rocked back and forth, praying for the strength to tell them what she'd hidden so deep inside her heart for so long.

They deserved to know. She should have told them long before now. They might not want her after they knew the truth. She'd been too involved in the fantasy—in the utter joy and contentment she'd found in their relationship.

But it couldn't last. The past always caught up no matter how hard or fast you ran.

Michael slid onto the couch beside her. Dillon took the other side and Seth hunkered down in front of her, his gaze imploring her to talk to them.

"I was married before," she began in a faltering voice.

She saw the surprise in their expressions, but they remained quiet, waiting for her to continue.

"I was an art student, not far from graduation. I was different. Did my own thing. Loved painting and drawing. Didn't pay a lot of attention to the world around me. I met Charles in my senior year. He seemed wildly attracted to me. Loved my quirks and my idiosyncrasies."

She took in a deep breath. "Before I knew it, I found myself pregnant. I was young and irresponsible. I was scared to death to tell Charles. He was older. Had an established, well-paying job as a financial planner. I needn't have worried. He was thrilled. He wanted to marry me, and I thought it was the right thing to do. I was half in love with him and warmed to the thought of us being a family.

"He insisted I quit school. He didn't approve of my career choice or my desire to paint and said there was no need since he could provide for me and the baby. He wanted a housewife. The perfect wife and mother to keep up his home, cook his meals and be a companion to dinners and parties.

"I loved to cook and was too young and infatuated to balk at putting aside my art. The few times I dabbled at home, he was dismissive of my efforts and frowned upon it taking time from my real duties."

"He sounds like a first-rate jackass," Dillon growled.

She smiled faintly. "I had a good pregnancy until the end. I was diagnosed with preeclampsia and had to be on bed rest the last few weeks before I delivered. I was tired and worn out and worried sick that something would happen to my baby. Charles was working long hours and so I was alone a lot in the house.

"I went into labor and delivered a perfectly healthy baby girl. Rose," she said softly. "I named her Rose because she was like a perfect bloom in the spring when the petals are so vibrant and start to unfurl.

"I had a long delivery and was exhausted. They sent me home after two days but I never seemed to catch up. It was a whole new world to me. Suddenly I didn't just have the house and the cooking. I had this new baby who was dependent on me twenty-four, seven. I breastfed her and sometimes she ate around the clock, it seemed.

"I remember thinking if I could just have one night's rest. Or even just a nap. Just a few hours where I could sleep that I'd be okay. That I could make it. Charles was working even longer hours. He was never at home. One night he came in at ten and I begged him to take the baby just for a few hours so I could sleep. He told me that he had an early meeting the next morning and that since he worked and I didn't, the baby was my responsibility."

"Jesus Christ," Seth muttered.

"I existed that way for eight weeks. Eight of the longest weeks of my life. I drifted from feeding to feeding, diaper change to diaper change. She didn't sleep at night and she was fussy during the day. There were days I cried while trying to quiet her because I was so desperate and I didn't know what to do. What kind of mother can't even comfort her own child? I didn't realize at the time that she was feeding off my stress and anxiety."

Dillon's hand slipped to her nape and massaged, offering her silent comfort.

"There was one night in particular that I didn't sleep the entire night. She cried and fussed, and I rocked and soothed. Charles went to the downstairs guestroom so he wouldn't be disturbed.

"The next day I was desperate for a nap. I was so happy when after I nursed her, I managed to get her to sleep in her crib. I remember staring down at her and thinking, *Thank you, God.*

"And then I laid down on the loveseat in her nursery. I just wanted thirty minutes. Maybe an hour if she slept that long."

Tears streamed down her cheeks, and her throat swelled so much she could barely manage to get the words out. "I was just so tired. I needed just a few minutes. I couldn't do it any longer. *Just a few minutes.*

"I woke up when Charles came in. He'd worried because he didn't hear either of us. I was horrified at how long I'd slept and that Rose was still asleep in her crib. I remember scrambling off the couch feeling guilty because I hadn't cooked. I hadn't cleaned. I went over to check on Rose and she was completely still."

"Oh God," Michael breathed. "Oh God, Lily."

"She was dead," Lily choked out. "She'd been dead for at least an hour they later said. While I slept on the couch, my baby died. *I killed her.* Oh my God, I killed her because I wasn't awake. I didn't hear her. I wasn't there when she needed me."

She dropped her face to her knees as sobs racked her body. They poured from her chest, tearing at her raw throat.

"He blamed me. He yelled at me. I stood there by the crib while he dialed 911, and he screamed at me the entire time that I'd let her die. How dare I go to sleep? How could I do this to our child?

"And I just stared at her, so numb, so disconnected. I couldn't believe it. I touched her and she was cold. Her skin was already stiff. But still, I tried. I took her out and I performed CPR. I wouldn't stop. I couldn't accept that she was gone.

"The paramedics got there and I could tell by their faces that they knew, but I'd started CPR and they had to continue and I rode in that ambulance, knowing the whole time that she couldn't be saved.

"Charles was so angry. He couldn't forgive me for what I'd done. I couldn't forgive myself. I went through the motions of her funeral. I dressed her myself. I couldn't bear the thought of someone else touching her. I put her favorite blanket with her and her little stuffed bear that I'd brought home from the hospital.

"I remember watching, so detached as they lowered her tiny casket into the grave. Charles was so furious. He couldn't even look at me. When we drove home, he tossed divorce papers at me and told me to sign. He wouldn't stay married to a woman who took so little care of her child.

"I signed them and I walked out. I kept walking. I didn't know where. It didn't matter. Everything that mattered to me in my life was gone."

"Sweet Mother of God," Seth swore.

"That son of a bitch," Dillon bit out. "That goddamn worthless son of a bitch."

She jumped at the vehemence in his voice and huddled further into the blankets.

Michael was tightlipped. There was so much fury in his eyes that Lily had to look away. Anger vibrated from them in waves.

"Lily," Seth began. He had to break off and look away for a moment while he visibly collected himself. "Lily, honey, it wasn't your fault. God almighty, *it wasn't your fault.*"

"I was responsible for her," Lily whispered. "If I hadn't gone to sleep. If I had been watching her. Crib death, they called it. But if I'd been there, I might have prevented it. I slept while my daughter died."

The last ended in a keening wail as grief swelled up in her throat and burst outward in an agonizing wave. Tears poured over her cheeks.

Seth yanked her into his arms and rocked her back and forth, holding her so tightly that she couldn't breathe around her sobs and his grasp.

"It wasn't your fault, baby. It wasn't your fault."

He rocked her until her sobs were spent. She lay limply against him, all her strength gone. Slowly and carefully he leaned her back against the couch and Dillon wrapped his arm around her.

Dillon nudged her chin until she was forced to look at him. There was terrible grief in his eyes—and anger. "Lily, listen to me and listen good. That son of bitch ex-husband of yours is a worthless piece of shit. He should have helped you. He should have been taking care of his daughter just as much if not more than you in those early days when you were so exhausted and beaten down. There is no excuse for him to have abdicated his responsibility. I don't give a goddamn if he was president of the fucking world. His first and *only* responsibility was to you and to his child. Full stop. No excuses.

"And furthermore that the son of a bitch actually had the balls to blame you—to *blame* you—for Rose's death just proves what a worthless piece of crap he is. Baby, you were at your breaking point. You took a nap. I don't know of a mom alive who hasn't slept while their baby naps. I can remember my mother laying down when Callie went down for her naps. She didn't stand guard over Callie's crib watching her every breath. You can't do that. You aren't a machine. You should have had help. Your husband damn well should have supported you. He's a fucking coward and it was his guilt that made him lash out at you. He blamed you because he knew what a fuck-up he was."

"I just wanted to rest. Just for a little while. Oh God, Dillon, I couldn't take it anymore. I was so tired. Why did she have to die? *Why?*"

Tears seeped into Dillon's shirt as he hugged her to him.

"I don't know, baby. I wish I had the answers. What I do know is that it wasn't your fault. You weren't to blame. Sometimes babies die and there's not a damn thing you can do about it. Even if you had been standing by her crib, she would have died. Crib death is a silent killer. There's no explanation. It just happens."

She closed her eyes against his chest, wanting his comfort even though she felt unworthy of it.

"So you were on the streets? All that time?" Michael asked, his tone tight with anger. "The son of a bitch never looked for you? Never made sure you were provided for?"

"I just wanted to be away from the pain," she said in a quiet voice. "I'm the coward. It was the only way I could turn it off. I didn't want to go back. I didn't want to live. So I existed. Day to day. On the streets where nothing matters. No one cares who you are. They don't care what your sins are or what your past is. You're just another nameless, faceless person that nobody ever sees."

"Oh God no, baby," Michael whispered as he pulled her from Dillon's embrace into his own. "You're not a coward. You're one of the bravest goddamn people I know. How you survived is a miracle, but I'm so damn grateful because it brought you to me—to us. And we're not letting go of you, Lily. I don't know what the hell you're thinking right now, but we're not letting you go. We're going to be right here. With you. Always. We'll work through this. You'll always have us to take care of you. You'll always have us to depend on."

"Always," Seth quietly confirmed.

She stirred and raised her head, taking in each of their expressions. Their eyes burned with purpose and intensity.

"You want me?" she asked in a creaky, incredulous voice. "After what I've told you, you want me?"

"Damn right we want you," Dillon bit out. "We're not your pansy-ass ex-husband, Lily. We don't throw out weak accusations and hide behind guilt. Living with us may not always be easy, but I'll be goddamned if we don't give it everything we have. We'll love you unconditionally, and you'll always, *always* have our full support."

"Even if I don't want more children?" she asked quietly.

Michael squeezed her tighter to him and brushed his mouth across her forehead. "Honey, I can only imagine the horrific grief you feel at your loss. I can't even wrap my brain around it. I won't say I understand it because I've never experienced anything of that magnitude. But even if we never have children, we're still going to love you and want you with us. In time, and when some of the rawness is gone, you may decide that children are something you want. And we'll support you one hundred percent. We can change diapers, burp and feed babies with the best of them. Every single one of us had a hand in raising Callie."

"It will be different this time, Lily," Seth said. "You never ever have to fear that you'll be alone with a baby to take care of. If we decide in the future that children are something we want, then we'll tackle it as a unit. Family. You'll not only have us, but you'll have Mom and Callie and the dads. You have a big family who loves you now. We support you unconditionally. That's what family is about."

"Oh God," she whispered. "I've been so afraid. I've shut it all out because I didn't want you to know. I knew you had to eventually, but every day I told myself I just wanted one more day. And then it turned into one more day and another and another. I kept telling myself later. I'd tell you later, but I didn't want to ruin something so perfect and the first real joy I've felt since the birth of Rose."

Michael kissed her again and Dillon rubbed his hand over her back.

"Now about the condom," Seth hesitantly began. "Honey, you have to know we're so damn sorry. We'd never do anything to hurt you or that went against your wishes. But I need you to know something okay? Look at me."

Her gaze drifted to Seth, to the fierceness on his face.

"I need you to hear this. If it ends up that you got pregnant, that your birth control wasn't effective yet, we are going to be there for you every single step of the way. We'll handle this together, and I guarantee you that there'll be no shortage of people to watch over our child every minute of the day so that you can rest and recover. I swear it, Lily. On my life."

Dillon and Michael both nodded and some of the awful tension eased just a tiny bit in her chest.

"Okay," she whispered. "I believe you."

Chapter Thirty-Two

"She's been this way for a goddamn week," Dillon swore.

The three brothers were gathered in the kitchen while Lily had secluded herself in Dillon's office painting. She'd spent most of her days there, coming out at dinner, even smiling and making casual conversation. But there were shadows under her eyes, and pain still lurked in their depths.

"I want to marry her," Michael said bluntly. "As soon as possible. I think we should ask her now."

Seth raised an eyebrow. "You really think now is good timing?"

"It's what we all want," Michael said. "And the thing is, I want to do it now, before she knows if she's pregnant or not. If it turns out that she's carrying our child, I don't want her to ever think that we married her for any other reason than we love her and want to spend the rest of our lives with her."

"He raises a good point," Dillon said. "I'd rather do it now, before we know one way or another. That way we can face the outcome together."

Seth grimaced. "I hope she's not pregnant. She has a lot of healing to do before we can even think about children. I have no doubt that we'd support her every step of the way, but I want her to have our child because that's what she wants more than anything. Not because a goddamn condom broke."

"I agree," Michael said quietly.

"It would seem we have a ring to buy, and we need to figure out the best way to pop the question," Dillon said. "I have to admit, I never expected the day I asked a woman to marry me to be a group effort."

Seth snorted. "I hear that. But I don't regret it, and maybe you two need to hear this because this is going to take a hell of a lot of patience and sacrifice on all our parts. I love Lily and I know you two do as well. I'm okay with that. I never thought I would be. I'll be honest. But she makes it all okay. I want her and I want her to be happy. I think the three of us can do that."

"Well damn," Dillon said. "Big brother's getting all mushy. You're going to have me tearing up in a minute. I think I feel one getting ready to fall."

Seth rolled his eyes. "You're such an asshole."

Michael laughed. "Just like old times. Dillon and Michael against Seth. It's a wonder you survived to adulthood."

"I can still kick the crap out of you two shitheads," Seth threatened. "And now you don't have Mom to hide behind like a bunch of damn girls."

Dillon flipped up his middle finger.

"Okay, you two, enough. We have a ring to buy and a proposal to work on. I want this to be perfect for her. Her first husband was a complete fuckwad," Michael said.

"One of us needs to go to Denver to get the ring, and it'll look damn suspicious if we all go, not to mention I don't want to leave Lily alone right now."

Dillon nodded his agreement to Seth's statement.

"Dillon has the best taste when it comes to jewelry," Michael said slyly. "He wears all those really cute earrings. I think he should be the one to go pick it out."

Dillon shot him a quelling look and Michael just laughed.

Seth smiled and turned to Dillon. "Looks like you're nominated. Get your ass on the road early in the morning so you can be back. Michael and I will work out the rest."

Lily marked through yet another drawing, frustrated by her inability to get to paper the image in her head. It had to be perfect—it *would* be perfect before it was over.

For the past few days she'd worked with single-minded focus, drawing and redrawing and then tossing when the image didn't meet her expectations.

She sighed and leaned back in her seat, stretching her tired back muscles. It probably looked to the guys like she was avoiding them. Like she'd sought solitude to wallow in her grief. But the truth was, she was pissed off.

Not just pissed off, but furious.

She'd done a lot of thinking. She'd done nothing else as she'd immersed herself in her art. And the more she thought, the more she realized that she would have to do something if she was ever going to move forward.

A light knock at the door startled her, and she swiveled in her seat to see all three men standing in the doorway. She quickly pulled down a blank piece of paper over her drawing and focused her attention on them.

"We have a surprise for you," Michael said. "Can you spare us a few hours? We have something planned."

Intrigued and eager to get out of the house, she nodded and stood, rubbing the kinks out of her neck.

"You'll need to change into jeans and bring along your light jacket," Seth said.

She nodded slowly. "Okay. Give me five minutes and I'll meet you out front."

She hurried into the bedroom where all her clothes were put away in the closet and pulled out one of her new pairs of jeans. She shimmied them on and then chose one of the nicer shirts Callie had picked out.

Her curls were more unruly than normal because she hadn't taken as much care in the past days, but after a look in the mirror, she deemed them acceptable and went in search of her boots.

When she went out the front door, all three brothers were standing around the Jeep waiting for her. Michael slid into the driver's seat while Dillon held the front passenger door open for Lily.

She smiled as she settled into her seat and Michael turned, his gaze roaming over her face.

"That's the first smile I've seen from you in days. I've missed it, Lily. I've missed you."

She reached over to touch his arm. "I'm sorry. I know I've been difficult. You all have been so patient with me."

He shook his head. "That's not what I'm saying, baby. I just like to see you happy and smiling. That's all."

She gifted him with another smile.

As they turned around to head down the drive, she asked, "Where are we going?"

"That would ruin the surprise," Dillon said.

Some of the heaviness weighing down on her lifted. She'd done a lot of thinking and a lot of soul searching since telling the guys the truth about her past. She knew what she had to do. Now she just had to find the courage to do it.

They drove a familiar path out of town and started up the mountain and around the switchbacks that led to their parents' house.

She smiled a bit broader when the Colters' cabin came into view. How quickly she considered them family. Her family. She already loved them. They'd accepted her and shown her nothing but love and unconditional support.

The guys got out and Dillon opened her door, holding out his hand to help her out.

"You're being awfully gallant today," she said as she stepped down.

He grinned. "I hope I'm gallant every day."

"Aren't we going in?" she asked when they bypassed the front porch and headed toward the barn.

Seth put his arm around her and propelled her forward. "Nope."

"Oh."

She followed behind Michael and Dillon, Seth's arm wrapped around her. They were all being so solicitous with her. And careful, as if she were incredibly fragile and they feared breaking her.

And in a way, she supposed their fear was justified. Her meltdown had been monumental. But freeing in a way she'd never imagined.

When they reached the barn, Seth stood with Lily while Dillon and Michael went in. A few moments later, they returned, each leading two mounts.

She glanced suspiciously up at Seth. There was no way they'd saddled the horses that quickly. Which meant that they'd been readied before they'd arrived.

Dillon stopped in front of Lily and handed Seth the reins to the horse Lily had ridden the time she'd gone with Callie. Then Dillon lifted her into the saddle and Seth handed up the reins.

She waited while the men mounted, and then Michael started toward the trail that led to Callie's Meadow. Dillon motioned for her to follow Michael, and he and Seth fell in behind.

They took a leisurely pace and Lily was enchanted with the changes that had taken place just since she and Callie had last taken the same path.

Spring had fully sprung. The fields were a lush cover of blooms in an array of colors that were so brilliant, she itched to put them to canvas. She stared at the beauty of the meadow, trying to commit every detail to memory. She'd need to update her drawing for Callie. The meadow was alive with new growth, bursting with vibrancy that enchanted her.

The stream that dissected the meadow gurgled and was fast running from the melting snow from nearby peaks. The sound mixed with the chirps of birds and the sounds of insects, the life and breath of the landscape.

Michael rode to the stream and dismounted, allowing his horse to nose into the stream to drink. Seth slid from his horse and then reached up for Lily.

They left the horses by the water and walked up a small incline that was particularly ablaze with wildflowers. She hadn't noticed until now that Michael carried a basket in one hand and had a blanket roll under his other arm.

It was a perfect day for a picnic, and she was delighted that they'd thought to surprise her with such a sweet gesture. After being cooped up in her makeshift studio for the week, alone with her thoughts and her drawing, being outside, surrounded by the beauty of spring, was a balm to her tattered soul.

Michael handed the basket to Dillon and then unfurled the blanket. The breeze caught it and it billowed out. Michael flapped it twice, arranging it just so before pulling it to the ground. Dillon set the basket on one corner to hold it down while Michael stepped on the other.

Then he turned back to Lily and motioned her forward.

Seth escorted her onto the blanket and sank down on the edge. Then he reached up to pull her down beside him. Dillon settled on her other side while Michael sat across from her.

"Are you hungry?" Michael asked.

"Starving."

Michael smiled. "Dillon has fried chicken. I made potato salad, and Seth made brownies. Dillon also dug into his highly prized collection of wines and brought along a bottle that he's been saving for just the right occasion."

She nearly moaned. "It all sounds fantastic."

Michael pulled out hard plastic plates and napkins and passed them around. Then he took out the container that held the chicken and placed it in the middle, followed by the bowl containing the potato salad.

He handed the wine over to Dillon to open and then Michael distributed glass wine flutes.

It was amazing. They'd thought of everything.

"White or dark?" Michael asked her.

She grinned. "Both. I want a thigh and a wing."

He plopped two pieces of chicken on her plate and then dished up a healthy helping of potato salad and handed it to her.

She wasted no time digging in and was soon enjoying the delicious, perfectly seasoned chicken. It was so good that she licked her fingers after every bite.

They ate in companionable silence. Lily stared up at the sky, mesmerized by the brilliant blue unmarred by a single cloud.

"It reminds me of your eyes," Seth murmured.

Startled, she turned to look at him. "What does?"

"The sky. Today it reminds me of your eyes. Beautiful and so vibrant."

"I never know quite what to say when you say such wonderful things," she said in a low voice.

He smiled. "Keeping a woman speechless isn't the worst

thing in the world."

"Ooohhh, you just had to go and ruin it," she said as she made a stabbing motion at him with her fork.

Michael chuckled. "Guess he gets the couch tonight."

Lily sipped at the wine, savoring the taste on her tongue. She took the last bite of her potato salad and put the plate away with a groan.

"Surely you're not full already? We still have brownies to eat," Dillon said.

"I'd have to be dead to turn down chocolate," she said.

Michael took a metal canister and opened it. Immediately the rich scent of chocolate wafted on the breeze, teasing her nostrils with the delicious smell.

"Oh my God," she murmured. "Gimme."

Seth laughed. "Give the woman her chocolate. She sounds slightly demonic."

She took the hunk of brownie from Michael and sank her teeth into it. "Oh sweet mother, this is heaven," she groaned.

Seth leaned in to nuzzle her neck. "It's not as sweet as you."

"Okay, you're forgiven for the speechless woman crack," she said magnanimously.

His expression turned serious. "There's something we want to talk to you about."

Her stomach did a complete flip and she glanced warily at Dillon and Michael.

"You're scaring her, dumbass. Quit being so serious," Dillon said.

"We have something to ask you," Michael corrected.

Michael reached into the picnic basket and pulled out a tiny box. He actually looked nervous and even a little pale as he scooted toward her and held out the box on his palm.

She reached for it, her fingers shaking.

"Open it," Seth urged.

She took off the top and found a velvet jeweler case inside. She turned the box upside down to shake out the smaller one, and it landed in her palm with a plop.

Her stomach was a big, tight ball of nerves as she fumbled

with the lid. When she finally got it open, diamonds flashed in the sun, stunning her with their dazzling brilliance.

She stared in absolute befuddlement at the gorgeous princess-cut diamond ring. In the middle of the arrangement were four square-cut diamonds put together as if they were one large single diamond. And then on both sides of the centerpiece were four smaller cut diamonds, again arranged together as if they were larger stones. Then smaller diamonds were embedded in the band all the way down the sides.

It was the most gorgeous ring she'd ever seen, and it was exactly something she would have chosen for herself. Simple, yet so elegant.

She didn't know what to say. She was completely and utterly overwhelmed and speechless.

Seth took the ring from its perch and gently slid it on the ring finger of her left hand.

"Will you marry us, Lily?" Dillon asked, his voice a velvet brush over her skin.

"Will you stay with us and love us as much as we love you?" Michael asked.

"In sickness and in health," Seth whispered next to her. "Until death do us part?"

It was on her lips to say yes. Yes, yes, a thousand times yes. There was no doubt in her mind or heart that they were what she wanted. That she loved them with every part of her soul and that her heart belonged only to them.

But she also knew that she owed it to them to come to them whole. Healed. Free of her past. She owed it to *herself*.

So she bit her lip because she couldn't say yes. Not yet. Oh, she would. There was no doubt. But first…first she had to do the most difficult thing she might ever face in her life. She had to face down her past. And then she had to forgive herself.

"I love you," she said fiercely. "I don't want you to ever doubt that."

She looked each of them in the eye as she spoke the words.

"You have no idea how much I want this."

She slid off the ring and carefully returned it to the safety of the velvet jeweler's box.

Before they could protest, she turned back to them, not wanting them to believe even for a moment that she was rejecting them or their love.

"Give me just a few days," she said. "Just give me that and then ask me again. There's something I must do. For us. And for me. Ask me then and I'll put that ring on, and I'll never take it off. Until then, hold it for me. And don't give up on me."

"Oh honey, that's never going to happen," Seth said as he hugged her to him.

She'd expected an argument or maybe anger. Insecurity or that they'd think she was rejecting their proposal. But they all looked at her with love and understanding in their eyes. No judgment. No anger. Nothing but love. Pure, unconditional love.

The sun slid over her skin, warming her through. She turned her face up, a sheen of tears making the sky a little shinier. She'd spent a lot of time railing against God. Asking why. Asking for a miracle. All this time she'd thought He'd turned a deaf ear to her. That He'd forgotten her or that she was unworthy of His grace or mercy.

She knew now that she was wrong.

He'd sent her the biggest miracle of all. Three wonderful, loving, patient men with an endless capacity for loyalty and love.

For the first time since Rose's death, she realized that she'd survive. And not only could she survive, but she could be happy again.

Chapter Thirty-Three

Lily carefully folded the drawing so that the image wasn't in any way compromised and then she tucked it into her pocket. It was perfect. Just as she'd envisioned it.

She took a deep breath and squared her shoulders. This was it. She was going to do it.

She scribbled a note for the guys and left it on the bar where they'd see it. Then she took the keys to Seth's truck that he'd left for her in case she needed a vehicle since he now drove an SUV that was his official duty vehicle when he was on the clock.

She didn't call Holly before she headed toward the Colter home. She hadn't wanted to explain over the phone. It was simply too complicated. She just hoped that Holly and Callie were home, because while much of what she was doing had to be done by herself, she needed the kind of support that the Colter women provided.

She pulled into the drive and saw the array of vehicles driven by Holly, Callie and Holly's husbands. If the cars were any indicators, they were all at home.

Gathering her courage, she got out and went to knock on the door.

Adam answered, and while there was surprise in his eyes, his smile was warm and welcoming. He held out his arms and gathered her into a quick hug, shocking the daylights out of Lily.

"How are you, honey?" he asked gently.

It dawned on her that Seth, Dillon and Michael had

probably told their family what had happened. It didn't anger her. The Colters were tight-knit and it seemed the most natural thing in the world that they would have spoken to their parents about her situation.

She smiled up at him. "I'm good. Are Holly and Callie here? I'd like to talk to them if possible."

"Of course. Why don't you come in. Would you like something to drink? I have tea and lemonade."

"I'm good, but thank you," she said shyly.

As they entered the living room, Ryan looked up from where he sat on the couch reading a book. He stood when he saw Lily, concern etched on his brow.

"Is everything okay, Lily?"

"Oh, I'm fine," she said hastily. "I just came to talk to Holly and Callie."

"I'll get them," Adam volunteered. "Last I saw them, they were holed up in Callie's room internet shopping. God help us."

Lily stifled her laughter as Adam left the room but then she stood awkwardly, bearing Ryan's scrutiny as she waited.

"Have a seat," he offered. "How are you doing? Are you enjoying your art?"

Lily's tension eased and she smiled, unaware of the way her entire face lit up and she glowed. But Ryan saw. He knew how incredibly talented the young woman was. He also knew that she'd endured a lot of hurt in her young life. She reminded him so much of Holly when she'd first come to him and his brothers. A wounded bird in need of a place to heal so she could spread her wings again.

He hoped like hell that his sons would prove to be exactly what Lily needed. He knew for certain that she was precisely what *they* needed.

Adam returned a moment later with both Holly and Callie hot on his heels. Ryan also wondered if Lily wouldn't be key in soothing some of the hurt he saw in his own daughter's eyes. Lily... She was special, and he'd known from the day he met her that she was going to make a huge difference in his family.

She was already entrenched in so many ways. Holly loved her, and Lily had won Callie's heart the day she'd given her the beautiful drawing of Callie's Meadow.

"Lily!" Holly exclaimed.

Holly was more obvious than Adam and he himself had been. She wrapped her arms around Lily and hugged her fiercely, rocking her back and forth just like she was a child in need of comfort.

"Oh honey, I've been so worried about you. What a terrible time you've had. But you're home now. You have a family who loves you."

Lily gave Holly a watery smile that tugged at Ryan's heart. He looked over at Adam, and Adam nodded his head in the direction of the door.

Ryan stood and on his way by, he gave Lily a hug of his own. She'd always seemed a little more uneasy around him than the others, but then he'd always been told he wasn't an easy guy to relax around. But he wanted Lily to feel loved and welcomed. Part of their family.

She seemed surprised by the gesture and then she hugged him back, briefly resting her head against his chest.

"I'm glad you're here," he said simply.

"Thank you," she whispered.

He pulled away. "We'll leave you ladies to it. Adam and I will be out in the barn if you need us."

As soon as the men had left, Holly all but dragged Lily to the couch and sat her down between her and Callie.

"How are you, really?"

"I'm good," Lily said. "I came by because..." She sighed. "It's complicated. I need your help."

"Name it," Callie said. "Whatever it is, we'll help you in any way we can."

Lily reached over to squeeze the other girl's hand. "I'm so grateful to have you as a friend."

Callie smiled. "The feeling is entirely mutual. Now tell us. What do you need?"

"I need you to go to Denver with me," she blurted.

Holly's eyes widened in surprise.

"There are two things I want...need...to do. The first one might sound silly."

As she spoke, she drew out the paper she'd put in her pocket and carefully unfolded it. The two other women leaned over to look.

"It's beautiful," Callie murmured. "It's them isn't it? Seth, Michael and Dillon."

"How did you know?" Lily asked in awe.

Callie smiled and pointed first to the circular band, threaded with four colors. A vibrant blue, green, brown and burnt orange. "This is the four of you. Unity. Never ending. This symbol is for Michael, the healer," she said, pointing to the intricate caduceus that Lily had drawn into the band. Then she pointed to the shield that was equidistant from the other two symbols embedded in the colorful band. "And this is Seth, the protector."

Holly pointed to the sword, the last symbol in the band. "This must be Dillon, the fighter."

"Fierce," Lily murmured. "He's fierce and loyal."

"And then there's you," Callie said quietly as she traced the lines of the delicate lily coiling from the midst of the circle, blooming, the petals just unfurling.

Lily smiled. "Do you think it's stupid?"

"I think it's awesome," Callie said. "Absolutely amazing. What are you going to do with it?"

"I want to get a tattoo."

Holly's mouth dropped open, and Callie's lips split into a broad grin. "Oh my God, that's perfect! Absolutely perfect! Where? You have to tell me where."

Lily brushed her fingers over her hip. "Here. I want it to be private, but I want it to be something they see. And know that it's us. I'm a little scared and I have no idea where to go. That's why I was hoping you would go with me. Dillon said you went with him when he got his ink done in Denver."

Callie clapped her hands in delight. "I know the perfect place. The guy there is an amazing artist. I might even get a tat myself while we're there. I would have done it when Dillon got his, but he got all snarly with me about it."

"As he should have," Holly said.

Callie rolled her eyes.

"You don't approve?" Lily asked Holly. The last thing she wanted was to drag her future mother-in-law to a tattoo parlor if the idea horrified her.

"Oh it's not that. Callie was a lot younger then and had no business getting a tattoo. What she does when she's older is her business. And I'm going with you two. It sounds like a lot of fun."

Her eyes twinkled and Callie and Lily cracked up at the idea of Holly hanging out in a tattoo parlor.

"Oh God," Callie groaned. "We can *not* tell the dads what we're doing. They'd have ten kittens and they'd tie us to chairs for the rest of the day."

Holly put a hand over her mouth but she nodded her agreement.

"There's another thing," Lily said softly.

"Go on," Callie encouraged.

"We'd need to be there overnight. I want to get the tattoo first. But then...then I'm going to go see my ex-husband."

Callie sucked in her breath and Holly's smile dimmed. She reached over and took Lily's hand in hers, squeezing.

"Do you really think that's wise? He hurt you, honey. Don't give him another chance to hurt you again."

"That's just it," Lily breathed. "I let him do and say all those things. I never fought back because I didn't feel like I deserved better. I believed in my heart that everything he said was true and that he was justified. But he was wrong," she said fiercely. "He had no right. He was wrong, and I won't let him get away with it. I have to confront him. I have to lay my demons to rest if I want to go forward with a new life with Seth, Dillon and Michael. I want to look him in the eye and tell him what a bastard he was for telling me I killed our child."

Tears ran freely down her cheeks. She was angry. Furious, even. But just saying the words. Her child. It made grief soar through her all over again.

Callie hugged her from one side while Holly wrapped her arms around both girls and rocked back and forth.

"You get mad, honey. You get pissed off. You're exactly right. He was a cock-sucking bastard for what he did to you."

"Mom!" Callie blurted.

Lily shoulders shook with helpless laughter at the shock in Callie's voice over Holly's crude language.

"Well he is," Holly huffed. "What kind of asshole lays the blame at his wife's door when he wasn't man enough to step up and help ease her burden? I hope you don't blame yourself anymore, Lily."

Holly leaned away and brushed her fingers through the strands of Lily's hair. "You have to know it wasn't your fault. What happened was a terrible, horrific thing that no mother should ever have to endure. But it wasn't your fault. It was never your fault."

"I know that now," Lily said in a low voice. "For so long, I didn't feel like I deserved forgiveness. Now I realize that I first have to forgive myself. And I have to face down the man who betrayed me in a way no woman should ever be betrayed. I can't *not* confront him. I've been thinking about this all week. It's something I have to do for me. So I can be whole again."

She glanced between Callie and Holly. "The guys asked me to marry them."

Callie's entire face lit up. "And? You said yes, right?"

"I asked them to ask me again in a few days," Lily said quietly. "I need to do this first so that I can come to them free of my past. Without any baggage. So we can have a fresh start."

Holly stood. "Well then, what are we waiting for? Let's get this girl to Denver so she can get back and put my boys out of their misery."

Chapter Thirty-Four

"That wasn't as bad as I thought it would be," Lily said as she and Holly and Callie walked out of the tattoo parlor.

She rubbed at her hip, feeling the bandage through the denim of her jeans. "I was expecting a lot worse."

"You did great," Callie complimented. "I think it looks awesome, and I think my brothers will think it's damn sexy. They're cave-mannish that way. To them it'll be like they're branded on you. Their stamp of ownership, so to speak."

Lily laughed. "I'll let them think that, anyway."

"Now you're catching on," Holly said as they climbed into the Rover.

Callie leaned up from the back seat. "So, uhm, Mom, what did you tell the dads we were doing, anyway?"

Holly pulled into traffic and started back toward the hotel. "I simply told them that I was going to spend some quality time with my two daughters, and I might have gone a little overboard in the sense that I let them believe that you needed some mothering, Lily."

"You're so evil, Mom. I like it," Callie said in a gleeful voice.

"A girl can always use mothering," Lily said as she shot Holly a grateful look.

Holly reached over and squeezed her hand. "I know you do, honey. Now, what we need to do is get you back to the hotel so you can relax for a while. Then what do you say we order in room service. Get into our jammies and eat some yummy food while we figure out your plan of attack for the morning."

"Room service sounds divine," Callie said. "Jammies and

girl time only make it better. I want to check out your tat again when we get back to the hotel, Lily. The artist there does such good work. I'm seriously considering getting something done. I just haven't settled on just the right art yet. Maybe you could draw me something."

Lily smiled back at her. "I'd love to. Whenever you have an inkling of what you'd like, just let me know and we'll see what we can come up with."

They valet parked at the hotel and went immediately up to the suite that Holly had booked.

"You girls get into your PJ's and tell me what you want to eat. I'll order it up," Holly said.

"You pick for me," Lily said. "I'll eat anything."

"Same here, Mom. You know what I like. Just get a lot of it."

Holly smiled. "Okay, then. Hop to it. I'll get our order placed."

Callie followed Lily into the second bedroom of the suite they were sharing. "Can I see it again?"

"Sure," Lily said.

She unzipped her jeans, peeled them away from her skin and let them fall to the floor. Then she stretched out on her side on the bed and carefully pulled the bandage away on one side.

"It's amazing, Lily. Seriously. You have such talent. I know the guy inked you, but this is your design. It's so intricate. It must have taken you hours to get all the detail you put into it."

"Try days," Lily said ruefully. "It's all I've worked on for the last week. I drew and I pondered what I wanted to say to Charles."

Callie grimaced and then plopped onto the bed next to Lily. "I admire you for doing this. I wish...I wish I had the balls to stand up and say, 'Hey, fuck you, you were wrong'."

"Is that what happened to you?" Lily asked softly. She replaced the bandage that the artist had told her to leave on for a few hours.

Callie hesitated for a long moment. "Yeah, I guess you could say that. I...I fell hard for someone. I thought he fell just as hard. I was wrong. He took what he wanted and then he was gone without a word."

Lily eased up and then wrapped her arms around Callie. "I'm sorry. That must hurt so much."

Callie hugged her back. "I'll be okay. I ran home to lick my wounds, and to be honest, I haven't had the desire to leave again. Maybe that'll change or maybe I've changed. I've always been so restless. Ready to take on the world. See new places. Meet new people. Right now I like being surrounded by my family—people that I know love me and would never hurt me. That's comforting, you know?"

Lily squeezed. "Yeah, I do know. Boy, do I know. I've felt that way ever since I met your brothers and was welcomed into your family. I'll never be able to express to any of you just how much that meant to me."

Callie smiled. "It's going to be fun having a sister."

"Oh crap, you're going to make me cry," Lily said with a sniff.

"We can't have that. We have to keep you strong tonight so that tomorrow you can walk into your ex-husband's home and kick his sorry ass."

"My home," Lily said softly. "Or at least it used to be."

Callie gaped at her. "You mean that all that time you were homeless, that bastard was living in your house?"

"I couldn't go back there. Tomorrow will be the first time I've been back since Rose's funeral." Pain still thudded in her chest as she imagined going back. Now. After three years. It seemed a lifetime and just like yesterday all rolled into one.

"I'd like to go with you so I could kick him in the balls," Callie said with a ferocious scowl.

"Girls, the food's here," Holly called from the next room.

"Oh crap, we've been gabbing and still haven't changed," Callie said as she bolted up.

They hurried into their sleepwear and then went into the next room where Holly was arranging the plates on the small dinette.

"I have to say, Mom, you may not cook worth a darn, but you know good food," Callie said as she surveyed the array of entrees.

Lily's mouth watered as she looked from the filet mignon to the lobster tail to the grilled shrimp skewer and the jumbo fried shrimp on a separate plate. There were steamed vegetables, rice and bread rolls. And the *pièce de résistance*: cheesecake with caramel topping.

Lily flopped into the chair. "Oh God, I don't even know where to start. It all looks wonderful."

"Which is why you take some of everything," Holly said.

"A very sound idea," Callie said as she reached over to snag a shrimp.

The women piled food onto their plates and chatted while they ate. Lily was glad she'd asked them to come. Not that Seth, Dillon and Michael wouldn't have come in a heartbeat, but she wanted to surprise them with the tattoo. More importantly, she wanted to confront Charles on her own, and she was pretty certain the guys would never allow her to go near him. They'd want to be the ones to confront him, and it would probably be with their fists.

"Are you nervous about tomorrow?" Holly asked gently.

Lily stirred from her thoughts and looked down at her half-eaten food. It did probably seem like she was distracted and maybe worried about the upcoming visit to her past. But in an odd way she was at peace. She'd already done the hard part.

"I'm not nervous about confronting him. I'm more nervous about seeing the place where my daughter was born and spent the first weeks of her life," Lily said in a quiet voice. "It's important to me that I don't come across as a raving lunatic. I don't want Charles to think he has any power over me. I need to be calm and rational when I tell him how wrong he was. Breaking down hurts my credibility."

"You're going to do fine," Callie said firmly. "I don't doubt you for a moment. When I think of all that you've endured and the fact that you still have such a warm, loving and generous spirit… It just amazes me. Most people wouldn't even find the strength to go on. But you survived and you didn't lose yourself in the process. You've given so much to my brothers. To our family. To me," she added.

"You girls need to stop or we'll all be crying," Holly said.

Lily smiled. "I'm so glad I'll have you as family. When I

think back, I realize how meeting Seth was such a godsend. I truly believe that God sent him to me," she said softly. "Or maybe He sent me into that soup kitchen that day. It's not a place I went often, but that day I was lonely and hungry and for just a little while I wanted to be somewhere that filled both needs."

"And I happen to think that God sent you to us," Holly said as she squeezed Lily's hand. "You brought Seth home to us, and for that I'll always be grateful to you. You've united us again, Lily. My boys are happy."

"Mo-om, stop," Callie wailed. "For God's sake, you're the one who said we were going to make you cry. If we keep this up, we're going to be masses of hormonal, deranged women."

"According to your fathers, we already are," Holly said with a grin.

"So what's the plan tomorrow, Lily?" Callie asked. "Do you want us to take you to your old house?"

Lily slowly shook her head. "I'd prefer for you to stay here. I'll take a cab. I don't know how long I'll be. I need the time to think. You've done more than you'll ever know just by being here with me and offering your support."

"Okay then. We'll be waiting here in the lobby for you and if you need us for anything at all, you call and we'll be there."

"Thanks, Holly. I can do this, though."

Holly stood and kissed both Callie and Lily on the forehead and stroked a hand over their hair. "Don't stay up too late. Lily needs her rest. Tomorrow is going to be tough. We'll go celebrate after she comes back from telling her ex to kiss her ass."

Laughter rang out through the room, and Lily felt courage lift her in its firm embrace.

Chapter Thirty-Five

Lily stood on the sidewalk in front of the two-story house that had been her home for such a short period of time. She stared at it, gauging her emotions. Aside from nervous butterflies scuttling around her belly, she was numb. And maybe she had to be to get through what she was about to do.

It was a Saturday, but there was no guarantee that Charles would be home. He often worked weekends when they were married. Long nights. Seven-day weeks. He hadn't known the meaning of family time. And he certainly hadn't shared the responsibility of the child they'd made together.

For too long she'd willingly shouldered the blame for it all. But she wouldn't do it any longer.

With a deep breath, she walked up the stone path leading to the front door. She knocked before she gave herself time to back out, and she waited, each second an eternity.

When the door opened, she was surprised to see a woman standing there, a baby that could be no more than eight or nine months old on her hip.

"Can I help you?" she asked in a friendly voice.

For a moment Lily couldn't find her voice. She stared at the happy, gurgling baby who had his fingers wrapped around his mama's hair. The woman gently pried his hand away and then refocused her attention on Lily.

"Does Charles Weston still live here?"

"Yes, he does. I'm his wife, Catherine. Can I help you with something?"

It hurt her more than it should. She didn't want to react to the fact that Charles had obviously moved on and replaced not only her but Rose as well. But the pain was there, beating steady inside her chest.

"Can you tell him that Lily is here and would like to speak to him for a moment?" she asked in a soft voice.

Catherine's entire demeanor changed. Her eyes rounded in shock and her mouth opened in surprise. "Lily?" she whispered. "Are you Lily Weston?"

Slowly, Lily nodded.

Catherine stepped back and opened the door wider. "Please, come in. I'll tell Charles you're here."

Surprised by Catherine's invitation, Lily hesitantly stepped inside the house that used to be hers.

"If you'll follow me," Catherine said as she swapped the baby to her other hip.

Lily took the familiar path through the foyer and past the formal living room to the family room on the other side of the formal dining room. As they approached, Lily saw a toddler scamper across the room with a squeal, and then she saw Charles sweep the child up and toss her high over his head.

She closed her eyes. Oh God, she couldn't do this after all. Before the sob choking her could escape, she turned, ready to flee. Catherine's plea stopped her.

"Lily, please don't go. I know this must be hard, but please talk to Charles. Hear what he has to say. He's looked for you for so long."

Lily froze and carefully turned around until she faced Catherine again.

Catherine held out her hand. "Please, just come with me. Charles will be so glad to see you."

Feeling like she had been plunked down in some bizarre alternate reality, Lily took a step forward and then another until she stood in the doorway just behind Catherine.

"Charles," Catherine called softly. "There's someone here to see you."

As he looked up, the toddler still firm in his grasp, Catherine stepped aside so that he got a full view of Lily.

He paled and slowly let the child slide down his body until

she found her own footing. He let her go, and she ran pell-mell across the room to where Catherine stood, shouting "Mama" the entire way.

"Lily?" he croaked. "My God, is it you?"

"Charles," she said by way of acknowledgement.

"Dear God."

Catherine tugged at the toddler and then looked to Charles. "I'll leave you two to talk."

With that, she walked out of the family room, leaving Lily and Charles staring at each other across several feet of distance.

"I came because there's something I need to say," Lily said evenly. She was proud that she hadn't broken down even if her heart was breaking on the inside. How long had he waited to remarry and have other children? Had she and Rose meant so little? Had he grieved at all?

It hurt her to look at those children, images of Charles, when her own baby had been taken from her. A child she'd never get back. It wasn't fair. He'd gone on as if nothing had happened. As if he'd lost nothing. He'd gained a new family. New kids. While she'd spent the last three years living in the agony of the fiercest pain a mother can ever know.

She wanted to scream at him. She wanted to call him a bastard. She wanted to slap him as hard as she could across the face. But she did none of those things.

"Okay," he said. "I'm listening."

"You were wrong. It wasn't my fault what happened to Rose. You were wrong to say it. You were wrong to throw me out of our house when I was so destroyed by grief that I couldn't even function. You turned your back on me at a time I needed you the most. You turned your back on your daughter when you refused any responsibility in her care.

"I was your wife. That should have meant something. I needed you desperately. Needed your help. I was so close to utterly breaking. I couldn't hold it together for another minute. I went to sleep because I'd gone without for night after night."

Her voice trembled, and it took every ounce of control she could muster not to allow the tears knotting her throat free.

"And she died."

She sucked in breaths through her nose. Charles' eyes glistened with tears, and his own face was ravaged with grief, and oddly, regret.

"But it wasn't my fault," she said fiercely. "It wasn't anyone's fault. A terrible, terrible thing happened to us, and you should have been there when I needed you the most. You should have held me when I cried, not screamed at me that I'd killed our child.

"You were wrong."

She turned, having said what was in her heart. She had no desire to stay and look at him a moment longer. She wanted out of this house before she completely lost her composure.

"Lily, wait. Please don't go."

Tears were thick in his voice. She hesitated, drawn by the heaviness and despair that was so evident in his tone.

She turned, surprised to see that tears were flowing openly down his cheeks. He took a step forward and then another.

"Please, stay. For just a moment. I have something I want to say too."

She blinked in confusion. This she hadn't expected, and she wasn't sure how to handle it. He reached for her arm, his fingers curling gently as he guided her toward one of the couches.

"Sit here before you fall."

Had she been unable to cover up the fact that she was utterly shattered?

He took a seat in the chair catty-corner to the couch. He rubbed his hand over his face and through his hair, his eyes filled with raw, terrible pain.

"You have every right to hate me. Everything you said is true. Absolutely, one hundred percent true. I have no excuse. I didn't support you like I should have. I worked too long. I made my job a priority. I left you at a time you needed me the most.

"When Rose died, I knew. I *knew* I'd made terrible mistakes I could never take back. I knew how tired you were. I could see your exhaustion. I knew you were running on empty. I knew all of this and I did nothing to help.

"I was so angry. Furious. I lashed out at you. I said terrible things, because God, the alternative was admitting the truth. That *I* killed our daughter. Not you. *Me.* And I couldn't accept it. I denied it. I couldn't bear to face you. I couldn't look you in the eye, so I drove you away. I thought if I could just have you out of the picture that I could forget. That I could live in denial and pretend you and Rose never existed."

Lily stared at his grief-ravaged face in shock. She'd never imagined. Never once.

"I wronged you, Lily," he said raggedly. "After you walked out of the house after signing those papers, I kept expecting you to come back. Maybe a part of me wanted you to come back. But then months passed and I knew you were gone, that I'd driven you away.

"And then I began to worry. Guilt was eating me alive. Not only that I'd placed the blame for our daughter's death on your shoulders when it was my blame to bear, but also guilt over the fact that I'd sent you away with nothing. You didn't contest the divorce. You didn't show up at the court date. You never asked for anything. Not a dime."

"I wanted nothing," she said quietly.

"Where did you go?" he asked. "I looked. I wanted to at least provide for you. I thought you deserved a settlement, at least. You gave up everything for me and Rose. Your art. I thought you could at least finish school if you wanted. But you'd disappeared."

"I didn't have a place to go, Charles," she said honestly. Not to hurt him, but she wouldn't lie either.

"Then where were you?"

She lifted her shoulder in a shrug. "Where is any homeless person? Sometimes they're on one street. Others they're in an alley."

"Oh dear God." Charles buried his face in his hands and his shoulders shook as quiet sobs spilled out, muffled by his palms.

"I was fine," she said in low tones. "I survived. I didn't come here to give you a guilt trip, Charles. I came because I needed to tell you that you were wrong so that I could move on and forgive myself. For three years I've lived with the knowledge that I killed my child and that my husband thought the worst of me. It was only recently that I was shown just how wrong I was. And how wrong you were."

"Yes, I was wrong," he said. "Not a day has gone by that I don't think about you. The look on your face the day I told you to get out. I'll go to my grave with that sin on my conscience, Lily."

They sat in bewildered silence before Lily once again started to edge to her feet.

Charles held out his hand. "No, not yet, Lily. Tell me, please. Are you still living on the streets? You have to let me help you. It's what I owe you. You should have gotten half of everything in the divorce settlement."

Some of her anger eased, replaced by deep sadness. They'd both spent the last three years torturing themselves. Fraught with guilt and anger. And grief.

"I don't anymore," she said quietly. "I don't live here in Denver. I merely came because in order for me to move on and to have a life, I had to confront my past. If it helps you, I forgive you. But I've learned in recent weeks that seeking forgiveness from others is meaningless unless you can forgive yourself."

He stared bleakly at her, his eyes filled with so much regret that it hurt her to look at him. "I want you to be happy, Lily. You deserve better than I ever gave you. I like to think I'm a better man now. I don't work as much. I'm here for Catherine and the kids. But I'll never be able to change the past, and I can't bring our daughter back."

Tears crowded the corners of Lily's eyes. "No, there's nothing either of us can do to bring her back. Perhaps what is more important is that there was nothing that either of us could have done to save her."

"Are you happy now, Lily? Are you going to be all right? Can you move on?"

For the first time since she'd arrived, a glimmer of a smile tingled at her lips. "Yes, I'm happy. It's taken me three years, but I'm going to be okay. I have people who love me. Family."

"I'm glad," he said simply. "But promise me something. Promise me that if you ever need anything, anything at all, that you'll call me or come to me. There's nothing I won't do to help you. Ever."

Lily stood shakily to her feet. She stared at the man who'd once been her husband. It was odd, really. He felt like a stranger to her. Before she'd arrived, she'd worked all of the grief and guilt into rage and fury. But now it all settled down and all she felt was an abiding sadness for all the things that couldn't be changed.

"I appreciate the offer. I do. And I appreciate you telling me everything you told me today. My hope is that we can both let go now and be happy."

Charles nodded. "Take care, Lily."

She turned and started toward the door, Charles trailing behind her. When they arrived in the kitchen, Catherine looked up anxiously from where she was feeding the two children.

Lily paused for just a moment as she stared at the two darling babies. "You have beautiful children," she said huskily.

Catherine looked like she wanted to cry, but she gave a shaky smile and said, "Thank you." Then she looked to the toddler, the daughter. "Her middle name is Rose. Charles insisted."

For a moment Lily couldn't speak around the knot in her throat. "It's a beautiful name for a beautiful little girl," she finally managed to get out.

Then she turned and hurried for the front door, desperate for air and desperate to get back to the comfort of people who loved her.

As soon as she hit the sidewalk, the tears started streaming down her cheeks. She walked faster, not yet wanting to get a cab. She needed to breathe, needed to free herself from the ache that swelled in her chest.

She'd done it. She'd faced him down, only it hadn't given her quite the satisfaction that she'd imagined. He'd suffered too. Was still suffering. And she knew what that was like, the awful guilt, the knowledge that you'd made mistakes—irreparable ones.

But she'd said the words aloud. He was wrong. And it had vindicated her when he'd admitted that yes, he was wrong. But the victory was hollow because at the end of the day, two people had lost a precious child, and it had destroyed a piece of both of them in the process.

She gathered her arms and crossed them in front of her, tucking her hands into the bends of her elbows. And she walked further, just wanting to clear away the lingering anguish.

She was free now. She could embrace her life with the Colter brothers. She had faced her fears and come out whole. Or at least not as shattered as she'd been. Healing. She was healing. And it might not be tomorrow or the next day or even the next year, but one day, she'd be able to think about Rose without the searing agony and the unbearable weight of despair.

Maybe it was her subconscious at work, because she hadn't set out to walk to the graveyard where Rose was buried. She hadn't even known that she was going in that direction. But when she looked up, she saw the iron gates that guarded the children's cemetery.

She stopped several feet in front of the opening and simply stared at a place she hadn't seen since the awful day when they'd put her in the ground.

She closed her eyes and inhaled a deep breath. Courage. Once she would have said she had none, but lately, she'd found it with increasing frequency. Life was about finding courage to live each day and to face obstacles head-on.

She walked slowly and nearly on tiptoe down the winding pathway. She searched her memory for where exactly Rose had been buried. So much of that time was a blur. She closed her eyes again and this time went back in time to the day. Rose had been buried in the shelter of a huge cottonwood tree, the branches sprawling over many graves as if gathering the little angels in its arms.

She looked up and saw the tree a short distance away. She swallowed and walked at a more determined pace until she searched out the headstone with Rose's name.

"Rose Weston. Beloved daughter. You were mine, and now you're His. May He take you on the wings of angels back home where you belong."

She'd written the inscription herself and until now hadn't allowed herself to even think it much less recite it aloud.

She raised her face to the sun. "I love you, baby," she whispered. "I don't regret a single moment I had with you. You'll always be my angel girl."

Peace descended and the area went quiet. Warmth enveloped her and wrapped her in its steady embrace. The sun's rays streamed through the big tree branches that shielded the graves from the weather.

She looked down again and then knelt to touch the cool marble.

"Goodbye," she whispered. "I never said it before. I couldn't. But goodbye, my sweet baby girl."

She rose and turned swiftly away, walking at a brisk pace from the graveyard. She wiped at her eyes with the back of her sleeve and began to scour the street for a cab. Holly and Callie would worry. She'd been gone longer than she'd anticipated.

She only had to walk two blocks before she hailed a cab. She leaned against the seat, eyes closed as she made the journey back to the hotel.

She was exhausted. Mentally and physically wiped. But she was lighter than she'd ever been. She couldn't wait to get back home to her men. She had a marriage proposal to accept.

Chapter Thirty-Six

"Where the fuck is she?" Dillon asked as he paced back and forth in the living room. "I don't buy that garbage about her and Mom and Callie being on a goddamn shopping trip and having a lark of a time in Denver."

Michael nodded silently.

Even the cat seemed to miss Lily. She paced back and forth between the living room and the front door as if expecting Lily to burst through at any moment. Michael reached down and idly scratched her ears when she issued a plaintive meow.

"You were a goddamn cop up there, Seth. Can't you call some of your buddies and have them check in on the women?" Dillon asked.

Seth laughed. "Uh no. They'd kill us. Mom wouldn't speak to us for a year, and Callie would just kick our ass."

"Aren't you in the least worried?" Michael demanded.

Seth sighed. "Of course I am. But she asked for time. She asked for our trust. We have to be willing to give her both. She'll come back to us."

"I'm not worried about her coming back to us," Dillon growled. "I'm worried about what she's off doing alone because she thinks she needs to do it. Alone."

The sound of the front door opening penetrated the air. The men swung around, and there was Lily standing in the doorway, her gaze locked on them.

There was subtle wariness in her expression, but at the same time there was a stillness and quietness to her spirit that had been absent before.

Seth sucked in his breath. It was going to be okay. Relief crushed him. As much as he'd said to his brothers about having to give her space, he'd been as worried as they had been.

"Lily," Michael breathed a mere second before he strode across the room and swept her into his arms.

She reacted with just as much emotion and wrapped herself around Michael, holding tight to him. She closed her eyes and buried her face into his chest as Michael stroked his hand over her hair.

Dillon only gave Michael a moment before he tugged Lily from Michael's arms and into his own. He cradled Lily protectively in his beefy embrace, his expression tender.

"Where have you been, sweetness?"

Lily stirred and then turned her blue eyes on Seth. He itched to hold her, but he waited as she carefully extricated herself from Dillon's hold and then came to him in a rush.

He closed his eyes and inhaled the sweet scent he identified as uniquely Lily.

"Welcome home," he murmured.

She raised her head and smiled so brilliantly at him that he was dumbstruck.

"It's good to be home," she whispered.

"Where did you go?" Dillon repeated. "Are you all right?"

She turned to face the others, remaining cradled in Seth's arms. "I went to see Charles."

Seth stiffened while Dillon swore and Michael's face grew stormy.

She leaned back and smiled. "I have something to show you."

She was definitely keeping them off balance. Maybe it was intentional to get their focus off the fact that she'd visited her ex-husband alone and without them being there to protect and support her. Emotionally and physically, but emotionally most of all.

She broke away from Seth and stood in the middle of the room at equal distance from the three men. She smiled when the cat did a figure eight through her legs, rubbing and purring her welcome. Lily bent long enough to pet the cat's sleek body before rising again to focus on the matter at hand.

"There were two reasons I went to Denver. I spent all week trying to create on paper what was in my head."

Her fingers tucked into the waist of her jeans and slid around to unbutton the fly. Then she unzipped her pants and wiggled carefully until they slid over her hips, revealing a freshly inked tattoo.

She presented her hip in silence, her fingers brushing lightly over the design.

Dillon strode over and feathered his hand over the tat. Michael and Seth followed, straining to see over Dillon.

"Do you know what this is?" she asked huskily.

Michael traced the caduceus with his fingertip. "It's us," he said in wonder. "All of us. This is you, Seth," he said pointing to the shield. "And you, Dillon," as he traced the sword. "And Lily here, in the center."

"This is fierce," Dillon said, admiration thick in his voice. "Did you design it? Is this what you were working on that you wouldn't let us see?"

She flushed. "I wasn't trying to hide it from you. I mean I wasn't hiding my work because I was ashamed or didn't think you'd approve. I wanted to surprise you."

"It's amazing," Dillon said sincerely. "It's beautiful ink, Lily. Did Callie go with you?"

Lily nodded. "I didn't want to go by myself. I asked her and your mom to go with me."

Dillon nodded approvingly. "Callie would have taken you to a good place. I'd have been pissed if you'd wandered into the first shop you came across and trusted them to do the job."

She pulled her jeans back up and refastened them, and then stared at them, her eyes shiny and light. There was a freshness to her gaze, and it was then Seth realized the shadows were gone. The vague unhappiness. The hint of pain. She was vibrant.

"I went to see Charles because I wanted to confront him," she said. "After what happened last week, I spent days thinking about it and with each day I grew angrier and angrier. It ate at me until I knew that if I didn't confront my past, I could never move beyond it and it would always hold me. And then you asked me to marry you."

She smiled at each of them, her eyes soft with love. "I wanted to shout yes. I wanted to more than anything, but I also knew it wouldn't be fair to you or to me if I committed before I tackled the issue of my past."

"And now?" Michael asked.

"Ask me," she whispered. "Ask me again."

Seth took her hand and dug into his pocket. Dillon cupped the side of her cheek then looked over at Michael and then Seth.

"Marry us, Lily," Dillon asked in a husky voice.

Seth gently slid the ring over her finger, over her knuckle until it sparkled on her hand. She glanced down and then curled her fingers into a fist, sealing her hand closed.

"Yes."

Michael shoved by Dillon and scooped Lily into his arms. He gave a whoop and twirled round and round the living room until Lily threw back her head, her delighted laughter echoing through the room.

He kissed her, long and lingering and then lowered his hand to caress her jean-clad hip where the tattoo rested.

"That tattoo says it all, Lily. Us around you. You at the center. First. Always."

She smiled and kissed him again. "I love you."

"And I love you."

Lily turned and flung herself at Dillon, nearly toppling him as he caught her against his chest. She kissed him exuberantly, his mouth, his jaw, back to his mouth. He finally laughed and cried uncle.

"Have mercy," he begged.

"Not going to happen," she purred. "You're mine."

"Damn straight I am," Dillon agreed. "Completely and wholly yours. You can have me any time you want. All you have to do is crook that little finger that you have me wrapped around in my direction and I'm all over it."

Lily sighed and burrowed into Dillon's neck, nuzzling and making those sweet little sounds of contentment that made

Seth crazy.

And then she pulled away and turned her gaze on Seth. Seth's heart turned over as she came to him, her eyes warm and full of acceptance. He was taken back to the first day he met her, when he looked up and was staggered by the most intense blue eyes he'd ever seen.

Thank God he'd acted on the overwhelming reaction she'd elicited. Thank God he'd gone after her. He couldn't imagine his life without her now.

"You amaze me," he said sincerely. "Your strength astounds me. I love you, Lily."

She launched herself at him, and he caught her as he staggered back, her wrapped around him. She curled both arms around his neck and held on until all he could smell or process was her.

"I love you too, Seth. You're my personal angel. God sent you to me or me to you. Either way, I'll never believe that it was just a chance meeting in a soup kitchen."

His heart twisted and he squeezed her a little harder. "No, Lily. You're our angel. Always. Our gift."

She brushed her lips over his neck and trembled gently against him.

"I stopped believing in miracles and second chances. Until I met you guys," she said in a voice that throbbed with emotion. "You all are my miracle and second chance all rolled into one. I love you. I'm so grateful for you."

Seth eased her down until her feet hit the floor and then she turned and extended her hands to Dillon and Michael. "Did anyone cook yet? I'm starving."

The men chuckled and then Dillon drew her in close again. "Tell you what. You come keep me company in the kitchen and I'll whip up something yummy."

Seth watched as Dillon pulled Lily into the kitchen followed by Michael. He hung back, content to watch for just a moment and savor the rightness of it all.

Never in a million years would he have predicted this, but then a few weeks ago, his life had been in Denver. His job. Now his life was Lily and the town of Clyde. He was back in the fold of his family. Stronger and closer than ever.

No, like Lily, he didn't believe for a moment that their meeting had been chance. And he'd give thanks every day for the rest of his life that he didn't let her walk out of that soup kitchen and out of his life.

About the Author

To learn more about Maya Banks please visit www.mayabanks.com. Send an email to Maya at maya@mayabanks.com.